1 MONTH OF FREE READING

at

www.ForgottenBooks.com

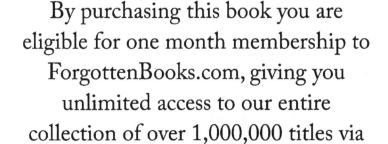

By purchasing this book you are eligible for one month membership to ForgottenBooks.com, giving you unlimited access to our entire collection of over 1,000,000 titles via our web site and mobile apps.

To claim your free month visit:

www.forgottenbooks.com/free459696

ISBN 978-0-483-52777-5
PIBN 10459696

ONLY AN ENSIGN.

A Tale of the Retreat from Cabul.

By JAMES GRANT,

AUTHOR OF "THE ROMANCE OF WAR," "FIRST LOVE AND LAST LOVE,"
"LADY WEDDERBURN'S WISH," ETC.

IN THREE VOLUMES.

VOL. III.

" Come what come may,
Time and the Hour runs through the roughest day."—*Macbeth.*

LONDON:

TINSLEY BROTHERS, 18, CATHERINE ST., STRAND.

1871.

LONDON:
BRADBURY, EVANS, AND CO., PRINTERS, WHITEFRIARS.

CONTENTS.

ONLY AN ENSIGN.

CHAPTER I.

PAR NOBILE FRATRUM !

" So, fellow, I am expected by you to swallow this 'tale of a tub,' which has been invented or revived solely for the purposes of monetary extortion!" exclaimed Downie Trevelyan, with the most intense and crushing hauteur, as he lay back in the same luxurious easy chair in which his uncle died, and played with his rich gold eye-glass and watered silk riband.

"It ain't a tale of a tub, my lord; but of the wreck of a *steamer*—the steamer *Admiral* of Montreal," replied Sharkley, meekly and sententiously.

Downie surveyed him through his double eye-glass, thinking that Sharkley was laughing covertly at him; but no such thought was hovering in the mind of that personage, who was not much of a laugher at any time, save when he had successfully outwitted or jockeyed any one. He seemed very ill at ease, and sat on the extreme edge of a handsome brass-nailed morocco chair, with his tall shiny hat placed upon his knees, and his long, bare, dirty-looking fingers played the while somewhat nervously on the crown thereof, as he glanced alternately and irresolutely from the speaker to the titular Lady Lamorna, who was also eyeing him, as a species of natural curiosity, through *her* glass, and whose absence he devoutly wished, but feared to hint that she might withdraw.

She was reclining languidly on a sofa, with her fan, her lace handkerchief, her agate scent-bottle, and her everlasting half-cut novel—she was never known to read one quite through—lying beside her; and she had only relinquished her chief employment of toying with Bijou, her waspish Maltese spaniel (which nestled in a little basket of mother-of-pearl, lined with white satin), when an aiguletted valet had ushered in "Mr. W. S. Sharkley, Solicitor."

"Leave us, Gartha, please," said her husband; "I must speak with this person alone."

Curiosity was never a prominent feature in the character of Downie's wife, who was too languid, lazy, or aristocratically indifferent to care about anything; so, with a proud sweep of her ample dress, she at once withdrew, followed by the gaze of the relieved Sharkley, who had a professional dislike for speaking before witnesses.

Mr. Sharkley's present surroundings were not calculated to add to his personal ease. The library at Rhoscadzhel—the same room in which poor Constance and Sybil had undergone, in presence of the pitying General Trecarrel, that humiliating interview, the bitterness of which the wife had never forgotten even to her dying hour, and in which Richard had, some time previously, found Downie by their dead uncle's side, with that suspicious-looking document in his hand, the history of which the former was too brotherly, too gentlemanly, and delicate ever to inquire about—the library, we say, was stately, spacious, and elegant enough, with its shelves of dark oak, filled by rare works in gay bindings, glittering in the sunlight; with the white marble busts of the great and learned of other days, looking stolidly down from the florid cornice that crowned the cases; with its massive and splendid furniture, gay with bright morocco and gilt nails; with the stained coats of arms, the koithgath and the seahorse of the Trevelyans, repeated again and again on the row of oriels that opened on one side, showing the far extent of field and chace, green upland and greener woodland, the present owner of which now sat eyeing him coldly, hostilely, and with that undoubted air and bearing which mark the high-bred and well-born gentleman—all combined to make the mean visitor feel very ill at ease.

He mentally contrasted these surroundings with those of his own dingy office, with its docquets of papers, dirty in aspect as in their contents; its old battered charter-boxes filled with the misfortunes of half the adjacent villages—a room, to many a hob-nailed client and grimy miner, more terrible than the torture chamber of the Spanish Inquisition—and the comparison roused envy and covetousness keenly in his heart, together with an emotion of malicious satisfaction, that he had it in his power perhaps to deprive of all this wealth, luxury, and rank, the cold, calm, and pale-faced personage who eyed him from time to time with his false and haughty smile—an expression that, ere long, passed away, and then his visage became rigid and stony as that of the Comandatore in Don Giovanni, for whatever he might feel, it was not a difficult thing for a man who possessed such habitual habits of self-command as Downie-Trevelyan, to appear at ease when he was far from being so. Yet Sharkley's mission tried him to the utmost, whatever real pride or temper he possessed.

"My lord," resumed the solicitor, while the revengeful emotion was in his heart—"if, indeed, you are entitled to be called 'my lord'——"

"Fellow, what *do* you mean by this studied insolence?" demanded Downie, putting his hand on a silver bell, which, however, he did not ring, an

indecision that caused a mocking smile to pass over
the face of Sharkley, while the iris of his eyes
dilated and shrunk as usual. "You are, I know,
Sharkley the—aw, well I must say it—the low
practitioner who got up by forgery and otherwise—don't look round, sir, we have no witnesses
—the case of the adventuress Devereaux against
me and my family. So what brings you here
now?"

"To tell you what I was beginning to state—
the story of the wreck, by which your brother
Richard, Lord Lamorna, perished at sea; and to
prove that the certificate of his marriage with Miss
Constance Devereaux, daughter of a merchant
trader in the city of Montreal, has been discovered
and safely preserved, and is here in Cornwall now,
together with his lordship's will."

Sharkley spoke with malicious bitterness, and
Downie paused for a moment ere he said,—

"You have seen them?"

"Yes."

"Well, when I see those documents I shall
believe in their existence—till then, you must hold
me excused; but even their existence does not
prove either their legality or authenticity. This
is merely some new scheme to extort money,"
added Downie, almost passionately; "but it shall
not succeed! That unhappy woman is dead—she

died of paralysis I have heard—the victim, I doubt not, of her own evil passions. Her son—"

"Your nephew, is with the army in India. Her daughter—"

"Has disappeared," said Downie, almost exult-ingly, "too probably taking a leaf out of her charm-ing mamma's book; and the army in Affghanistan has been destroyed—my son Audley's letters and the public papers assure me of that."

"Yet your lordship would like to see the documents ?"

"Or what may seem to be the documents—certainly; in whose hands are they—yours ?"

"No—in those of one who may be less your lordship's friend—Derrick Braddon."

"Braddon !" said Downie, growing if possible paler than usual; "Braddon, my brother's favourite servant, who was in all his secrets, and was with him in the Cornish regiment ? "

"The same, my lord."

"D—n—but this looks ill !" stammered Downie, thrown off his guard.

"For your lordship—very," said Sharkley with a covert smile.

Downie felt that he had forgot himself, so he said,

"Of course, this Braddon will show—perhaps deliver them to me."

"You are the last man on earth to whom he will *now* either show or deliver them. Be assured of that."

"For what reason, sir?"

"The account he received from his sister and old Mike Treherne of your treatment of—well, I suppose we must call her yet—Mrs. Devereaux."

Downie's steel-gray eyes stared coldly, glassily, and spitefully at Sharkley. He longed for the power to pulverise, to annihilate him by a glance. He loathed and hated, yet feared this low-bred legal reptile, for he felt that he, and all his family, were somehow in his power. Yet he could not quite abandon his first position of indignant denial and proud incredulity.

He spread a sheet of foolscap paper before him, and making a broad margin on the left side thereof, an old office habit that still adhered to him, like many more that were less harmless, he dipped a pen in the inkstand, as if to make memoranda, and balancing his gold glasses on the bridge of his sharp slender nose, said, while looking keenly over them,

"Attend to *me*, sir—please. When was this pretended discovery made?"

"Some nine months ago."

"Where—I say, where?"

"At Montreal, in the chapel where this Latour, of whom we have heard so much, was curate."

"A rascally scheme—a forgery in which you have a share."

"Take care, my lord—I'll file a bill against you."

"You forget, scoundrel, that we are without witnesses."

"Well—there are a pair of us," was the impudent rejoinder; "but what good might such a scheme ever do an old pensioner like Derrick Braddon?"

"I do not pretend to fathom—for who can?—the secret motives of people of that class," said Downie, haughtily.

"Ay—or for that of it, any class," added Sharkley, as he shrugged his high bony shoulders.

"Relate to me, succinctly and clearly, all that this man has told you," said Downie Trevelyan, dipping his pen again in the silver inkstand; and as Sharkley proceeded, he listened to the narrative of his brother's sufferings and terrible death with impatience, and without other interest than that it served to prove his non-existence by a competent witness, who, were it necessary, might bring others of the crew who were present on the wreck, and had escaped in a boat.

Ere the whole story was ended, Downie was ghastly pale, and tremulous with the mingled emo-

tions of rage and fear, doubt and mortification. He
felt certain that in all this there must lie something to be laid further open, or be, if possible,
crushed ; and on being reassured by Sharkley that
Derrick Braddon would " surrender the documents
only with his life——"

" We must not think of violence, Mr. Sharkley,"
said he, coldly and mildly.

" Well, it ain't much in my line, my lord—though
I have more than once got damages when a client
struck me."

" We must have recourse to stratagem or bribery.
For myself, I cannot, and shall not, come in personal
contact with any man who is so insolent as to mistrust me, nor is it beseeming I should do so. To
you I shall entrust the task of securing and placing
before me those alleged papers, for legal investiga-
tion, at your earliest convenience. For this, you
shall receive the sum of two thousand pounds ;
of this," he added, lowering his voice, " I shall
give you, in the first place, a cheque for five
hundred."

The eyes of Sharkley flashed, dilated, shrunk, and
dilated again, when he heard the sum mentioned ;
and rubbing his gorilla-like hands together, he said,
with a chuckle peculiarly his own,—

" Never fear for me, my lord ; I'll work a hole for
him—this Derrick Braddon. He spoke insultingly

of *the* profession last night—but I'll work a hole for him."

With an emotion of angry contempt, which he strove in vain to conceal, Downie gave him a cheque for the first instalment of his bribe, taking care that it was a *crossed* one, payable only at his own bankers, so that if there was any trickery in this matter, he might be able to recal or trace it.

Sharkley carefully placed it in the recesses of a greasy-looking black pocket-book, tied with red tape, and saying something, with a cringing smile, to the effect that he had "in his time, paid many a fee to counsel, but never before received one in return," bowed himself out, with slavish and reiterated promises of fealty, discretion, and fulfilment of the task in hand; but he quitted the stately porte-cochère, and long shady avenue of Rhoscadzhel, with very vague ideas, as yet, of how he was to win the additional fifteen hundred pounds.

So parted those brothers learned in the law.

CHAPTER II.

HIS odious visitor and tempter gone, Downie sat long, sunk in reverie. He lay back in the softly-cushioned chair, with his eyes vacantly and dreamily gazing through the lozenged panes, between the moulded mullions of the oriel windows, to where the sunlight fell in bright patches between the spreading oaks and elms, on the green sward of the chace, to where the brown deer nestled cosily among the tender ferns of spring, and to the distant isles of Scilly, afar in the deep blue sea; but he saw nothing of all these. His mind was completely inverted, and his thoughts were turned inward. "The wildest novel," says Ouida, "was never half so wild as the real state of many a human life, that to superficial eyes looks serene and placid and un-eventful enough; but life is just the same as in the ages of Œdipus' agony and the Orestes' crime."

Doubtless, the reader thought it very barbarous in the fierce Mohammedan Amen Oollah Khan to twist off his elder brother's head, and so secure his inherit-

ance ; but had the civilised Christian, Downie, been
in the Khan's place, he would have acted precisely
in the same way. The men's instincts were the
same ; the modes of achievement only different.

But a month before this, and Downie, at his club
in Pall Mall, had read with exultation, that, of all
General Elphinstone's army, his own son, Audley,
and Doctor Brydone, of the Shah's 6th Regiment,
had alone reached Jellalabad. Little cared he who
perished on that disastrous retreat, so that his son
was safe, for, selfish though he was, he loved well
and dearly that son, his successor—the holder of a
young life that was to stretch, perhaps, for half a
century beyond his own shorter span. Now it had
chanced that on the very morning of this remarkable visit, he had seen, with disgust, in the *Times*,
that, among those alleged to be safe in the hands of
an Afghan chief " was Ensign Denzil Devereaux,
of the Cornish Light Infantry, an officer, who, according to a letter received from Taj Mohammed
Khan the Wuzeer, had succeeded in saving a colour
of Her Majesty's 44th Regiment."

The daughter, whose artful plans upon his son's
affections he had, as he conceived, so cleverly
thwarted—the daughter Sybil gone no one knew
whither ; the son, a captive in a barbarous land
beyond the Indian frontier, and their mother dead,
the little family of Richard Trevelyan seemed on

the verge of being quietly blotted out altogether;
and *now* here was this ill-omened Derrick Braddon,
this Old Man of the Sea, come suddenly on the tapis,
with his confounded papers!

General Elphinstone had died in the hands of
the Afghans; so might Denzil; or he and the
other survivors or hostages might yet be slain or—
unless rescued by the troops from Candahar or
Jellalabad—be sold by Ackbar Khan (as Downie
had heard in his place in the House) to the chiefs in
Toorkistan, after which they would never be heard
of more. Oh, thought Downie, that I could but
correspond with this Shireen Khan of the Kuzzilbashes; doubtless such a worthy would "not be
above taking a retaining fee."

By the dreadful slaughter in the Khyber Pass,
and the capture of all the ladies and children, the
sympathies, indignation, and passions of the people
were keenly roused at home; thus if Denzil returned
at this crisis, with the slightest military *éclat*, it
would greatly favour any claims he might advance.

If the documents were genuine and could be
proved so in a court of Law—or Justice (these being
distinctly separate), were his title, his own honour
(as Downie thought it), the honour, wealth, and
position, privileges and prospects of his wife and
children, to be at the mercy of a mercenary wretch
like Schotten Sharkley; or of a broken-down,

wandering, and obscure Chelsea pensioner, who possessed the papers in question?

It was maddening even for one so cold in blood—so cautious and so slimy in his proceedings, as Mr. Downie Trevelyan. He had no great talents, but only instinct and cunning; barrister though he was, the cunning of the pettifogger. A legal education had developed all that were corrupt and vile in his nature. A country squire, Downie would have been a blackleg on the turf and a grinding landlord; a tradesman, he would have been far from being an honest one; a soldier, he might have been a poltroon and a malingerer; a legal man, he was—exactly what we find him, a master in subtlety, with a heart of stone. In the same luxurious chair in which he was now seated in fierce and bitter reverie, he had sat and regarded his brother's widow, in her pale and picturesque beauty, and watched the torture of her heart with something of the half amused expression of a cat when playing with the poor little mouse of which it intends to make a repast; and now he sat there shrinking from vague terrors of the future, and in abhorrence of suspense; but there was a species of dogged courage which he could summon to meet any legal emergency or danger, if he would but know its full extent. He was in the dark as yet, and his heart writhed within him at the prospect of coming peril, even as that of Constance had

been wrung by the emotions of sorrow and unmerited shame.

He knew himself to be degraded by acting the
part of a conspirator in all this ; yet how much was
at stake ! No family in ancient Cornwall was older
in history or tradition than his, and none was more
honoured: yet here by intrigue, fatality, and the
debasing influence of association was he, the twelfth
Lord Lamorna, the coadjutor of a man whose father
had been a poor rat-catcher, and, if report said true,
a felon. He felt as if on Damien's bed of steel, or
as if the velvet cushions of his chair had been
stuffed with long iron nails, and he repeated bitterly
aloud,—

"What! am I to be but a *locum tenens* after all—
and to whom? Denzil Devereaux—this *filius nullius*,
this son of an adventuress, or of nobody perhaps!"

The grave, grim, and somewhat grotesque por-
traits of Launcelot, Lord Lamorna, in Cavalier dress
—he who hid from Fairfax's troopers in the Tre-
woofe; of Lord Henry, with beard, ruff, and ribbed
armour, who was Governor of Rougemont in Devon,
and whose scruples did not find him favour with
the "Virgin" Queen; and even of his late uncle,
with his George IV. wig, false teeth, and brass-
buttoned blue swallow-tail, seemed to look coldly
and contemptuously down on him.

"Pshaw!" muttered Downie, "am I a fool or a

child to be swayed by such fancies?—I should think not; the days of superstition are gone!"

Yet he felt an influence, or something, he knew not what, and averted his stealthy eyes from the painted faces of the honester dead.

The irony of the malevolent and the vulgar; the gossip and surmises of the anonymous press; the "Honourable" cut from Audley's name in the Army List, the Peerage, and elsewhere, and from that of his daughter Gartha, who was just about to be brought out, and had begun to anticipate, with all a young beauty's pleasure, the glories of her first presentation at Court, were all before him now.

To have felt, enjoyed, and to lose all the sweets of rank, of wealth, of power, and patronage; the worship of the empty world, the slavish snobbery of trade, to have been congratulated by all the be-gowned and bewigged members of the Inns of Court, and by all his tenantry, for nothing—all this proved too much for Downie's brain, and certainly too much for his heart. It was intolerable.

He thought of his cold, unimpressionable, pale-faced, and aristocratic wife deprived of her place (not of rank, for she was a peer's daughter), through that "Canadian connection" of Richard's, as they were wont to term poor Constance—an issue to be tried at the bar, every legal celebrity of the day perhaps retained in the cause; money wasted, bets made, and speculation rife; himself eventually shut out from a sphere in which he had begun to figure, and to figure well! Would, he thought, that the sea had swallowed up Braddon, even as it had done his master! Would that some Afghan bullet might lay low this upstart lad, this Denzil Devereaux, and then his claims and papers might be laughed to scorn! Downie had never been without a secret dread of hearing more of Constance and her marriage, and that one day or other it might admit of legal proof, and now the dread was close and · palpable.

He cherished a dire vengeance against his dead brother, for what he deemed his duplicity in contracting such a marriage, unknown to all; and in his unjust ire forgot their late uncle's insane family pride, which was the real cause of all that had occurred.

Novelists, dramatists, and humourists, are usually severe upon the legal profession; yet in our narrative, Downie and his agent Sharkley are given but as types of a bad class of men. Far be it from us to think evil generally of that vast body from whose ranks have sprung so many brilliant orators, statesmen, and writers, especially in England; though Lord Brougham, in his Autobiography, designates the law as "the cursedest of all cursed professions," and even Sir Walter Scott, a member of the Scottish College of Justice, where the practice is loose, often barbarous and antiquated, wrote in his personal memoirs, that he liked it little at first, and it pleased God to make that little less upon further acquaintance; for the spirit and chicanery of the profession are liable to develop to the full that which the Irish, not inaptly, term "the black drop" which is in so many human hearts.

Downie Trèvelyan sat long buried in thoughts that galled and wrung his spirit of self-love, till the house-bell rang, sleek Mr. Jasper Funnel with his amplitude of paunch and white waistcoat came to announce that "luncheon was served," and Mr. Boxer, powdered and braided elaborately, came to ascertain at what time "her ladyship wished the carriage;" and even these trivial incidents, by their suggestiveness, were not without adding fuel to his evil instincts and passions.

Three entire days passed away—days of keen suspense and intense irritation to Downie, though far from being impulsive by nature, yet he heard nothing of his tool or agent, whom he began to doubt, fearing that he had pocketed the five hundred pounds, or obtained the documents thereby, and gone over with them to the enemy. But just as the third evening was closing in, and when, seated in the library alone, he was considering how he should find some means of communicating with Sharkley—write he would not, being much too cautious and legal to commit himself in that way, forgetting also that the other would be equally so— the door was thrown noiselessly open, and a servant as before announced "Mr. W. S. Sharkley, Solicitor," and the cadaverous and unwholesome-looking attorney, in his rusty black suit, sidled with a cringing air into the room, his pale visage and cat-like eyes wearing an unfathomable expression, in which one could neither read success nor defeat.

"Be seated, Mr. Sharkley," said his host, adding in a low voice, and with a piercing glance, when the door was completely closed, and striving to conceal his agitation, "You have the papers, I presume?"

"Your lordship shall hear," replied the other, who, prior to saying more, opened the door suddenly and sharply, to see that no "Jeames" had his curious ear at the keyhole, and then resumed his seat.

But before relating all that took place at this interview, we must go back a little in our story, to detail that which Mr. Sharkley would have termed his *modus operandi* in the matter.

CHAPTER III.

As Sharkley travelled back towards the little mining hamlet, where the Trevanion Arms stood conspicuously where two roads branched off, one towards Lanteglos, and the other towards the sea, he revolved in his cunning mind several projects for obtaining possession of the papers; but knowing that the old soldier mistrusted him, that he was quite aware of their value, and that he was as obstinate in his resolution to preserve them, as he was faithful and true to the son of Richard Trevelyan, there was an extreme difficulty in deciding on any one line or plan for proper or honest action, so knavery alone had scope.

Could he, out of the five hundred pounds received to account, but bribe Derrick Braddon to *lend* the papers ostensibly for a time, receiving in return a receipt in a feigned handwriting, with a forged or fancy signature, so totally unlike that used by the solicitor, that he might afterwards safely repudiate the document, and deny he had ever written it!

To attempt to possess them by main force never came within the scope of Sharkley's imagination, for the old soldier was strong and wiry as a young bull, and had been famous as a wrestler in his youth; and then force was illegal, whatever craft might be.

Ultimately he resolved to ignore the subject of the papers, and seem to forget all about them; to talk on other matters, military if possible (though such were not much in Sharkley's way), and thus endeavour to throw Braddon off his guard, and hence get them into his possession by a very simple process—one neither romantic nor melo-dramatic, but resorted to frequently enough by the lawless, in London and elsewhere—in fact by drugging his victim; and for this purpose, by affecting illness and deceiving a medical man, he provided himself with ample means by the way.

Quitting the railway he hastened on foot next day towards the picturesque little tavern, his only fear being that Derrick might have suddenly changed his mind, and being somewhat erratic now, have gone elsewhere.

As he walked onward, immersed in his own selfish thoughts, scheming out the investment of the two thousand pounds, perhaps of *more*, for why should he not wring or screw more out of his employer's purse ?—it was ample enough !—the beauty of the

spring evening and of the surrounding scenery had
no soothing effect on the heart of this human reptile.
The picturesque banks of the winding Camel, then
rolling brown in full flood from recent rains; Boscastle on its steep hill, overlooking deep and furzy
hollows, and its inlet or creek where the blue sea
lay sparkling in light under the storm-beaten head-
lands and desolate cliffs; away in the distance on
another hand, the craggy ridges of Bron Welli, and
the Row Tor all reddened by the setting sun, were
unnoticed by Sharkley, who ere long found himself
under the pretty porch and swinging sign-board of
the little inn (all smothered in its bright greenery,
budding flowers, and birds' nests), where the scene of
his nefarious operations lay.

A frocked wagoner, ruddy and jolly, whipping up
his sleek horses with one hand while wiping the
froth of the last tankard from his mouth with the
other, departed from the door with his team as
Sharkley entered and heard a voice that was familiar, singing vociferously upstairs.

"Who is the musical party?" asked he of the
round-headed, short-necked and barrel-shaped landlord, whose comely paunch was covered by a white
apron.

"Your friend the old pensioner, Mr. Sharkley,"
replied the other, "and main noisy he be."

"Friend?" said Sharkley nervously; "he ain't a

friend of mine—only a kind of client in a humble
way."

"I wouldn't have given such, house-room; but
trade is bad—the coaches are all off the road now,
and business be all taken by the rail to Launceston,
Bodmin, and elsewhere."

"Has he been drinking?"

"Yes."

"Pretty freely?" asked Sharpley hopefully.

"Well—yes; we're licensed to get drunk on the
premises."

"Come," thought the emissary, "this is en-
couraging! His intellect," he added aloud, "is
weak; after a time he grows furious and is apt to
accuse people of robbing him, especially of certain
papers of which he imagines himself the custodian;
it is quite a monomania."

"A what, sur?"

"A monomania."

"I hopes as he don't bite; but any way," said the
landlord, who had vague ideas of hydrophobia, "I had
better turn him out at once, as I want no bobberies
here."

"No—no; that would be precipitate. I shall try
to soothe him over; besides, I have express business
with him to-night."

"But if he won't be soothed?" asked Boniface,
anxiously.

"Then you have the police station at hand."

Meanwhile they could hear Derrick above them, drumming on the bare table with a pint-pot, and singing some barrack-room ditty of which the elegant refrain was always,—

> "Stick to the colour, boys, while there's a rag on it,
>   And tickle them behind with a touch of the bagonet:
>   So, love, farewell, for *all* for a-marching!"

As Sharkley entered, it was evident that the old soldier, whose voice rose at times into a shrill, discordant, and hideous falsetto, had been imbibing pretty freely; his weather-beaten face was flushed, his eyes watery, and his voice somewhat husky, but he was in excellent humour with himself and all the world. The visitor's sharp eyes took in the whole details of the little room occupied by his victim; a small window, which he knew to be twelve feet from a flower-bed outside; a bed in a corner; two Windsor chairs, a table and wash-stand, all of the most humble construction; these, with Derrick's tiny carpet-bag and walking staff, comprised its furniture.

"Come along, Master Sharkley—glad to see you —glad to see any one—it's dreary work drinking alone. This is my billet, and there is a shot in the locker yet—help yourself," he added, pushing a large three-handled tankard of ale across the table.

"Thank you, Braddon," replied the other, careful to omit the prefix of "Mr.," which Derrick always resented, "and you must share mine with me. Have you heard the news?"

"From where—India?"

"Yes."

"And what are they that I have not heard—tell me that, Mr. Sharkley—what are they that I have *not* heard?" said Braddon with the angry emphasis assumed at times unnecessarily by the inebriated.

"Is it that your young master is shut up among the Afghans, and likely, I fear, to remain so?"

"Her Majesty the Queen don't think so—no, sir —d—n me, whatever you, and such as you, may think," responded Derrick, becoming suddenly sulky and gloomy.

"Who *do* you mean, Braddon?" asked the other, drinking, and eying him keenly over his pewter-pot.

"Did you see to-day's Gazette?"

"The Bankruptcy list?"

"Bankrupts be—" roared Braddon, contemptuously, striking his clenched hand on the deal table; "no—the *War Office Gazette*."

Mr. W. S. Sharkley faintly and timidly indicated that as it was a part of the newspapers which possessed but small interest for him, he certainly had **not** seen it.

"Well, that is strange now," said Derrick; "it is almost the only bit of a paper I ever read."

"It ain't very lively, I should think."

"Ain't it—well, had you looked there to-day, you would have seen that young master Denzil—that is my Lord Lamorna as should be—has been gazetted to a Lieutenancy in the old Cornish—yes, in the-old-Cornish-Light-Infantry!" added Derrick, running five words into one.

"Indeed! but he may die in the hands of the enemy for all that—though I hope not."

"Give me your hand, Mr. Sharkley, for that wish," said Derrick, with tipsy solemnity; "moreover, he is to have the third class of the Dooranee Empire, whatever the dickens that may be. I've drawed my pension to-day, Mr. Sharkley, and I mean to spend every penny of it in wetting the young master's new commission, and the Dooranee Empire to boot. Try the beer again—it's homebrewed, and a first-rate quencher—here's-his-jolly good-health!"

"So say I—his jolly good health."

"With three times three!"

"Yes," added Sharkley, as he wrung the pensioner's proffered hand, "and three to that."

Derrick, who, though winding up the day on beer, had commenced it with brandy, was fast becoming more noisy and confused, to his wary visitor's intense satisfaction.

"Yes—yes—master Denzil will escape all and come home safe, please God," said Derrick, becoming sad and sentimental for a minute; "yet in my time I heard many a fellow—yes, many a fellow —before we went into action, or were just looking to our locks, and getting the cartridges loose, say to another, 'write for me,' to my father, or mother, or it might be 'poor Bess, or Nora,' meaning his wife, 'in case I get knocked on the head;' and I have seen them shot in their belts within ten minutes after. I often think—yes, by jingo I do —that a man sometimes knows when death is a-nigh him, for I have heard some say they were sure they'd be shot, and shot they were sure enough; while others—I for one—were always sure they'd escape. It's what we soldiers call a presentiment; but of course, you, as a lawyer, can know nothing about it. With sixty rounds of ammunition at his back, a poor fellow will have a better chance of seeing Heaven than if he died with a blue bagfull of writs and rubbish."

Then Derrick indulged in a tipsy fit of laughter, mingled with tears, as he said,

"You'd have died o' laughing, Mr. Sharkley, if

you'd seen the captain my master one day—but perhaps you don't care about stories?"

"By all means, Braddon," replied Sharkley, feeling in his vest pocket with a fore-finger and thumb for a phial which lurked there; "I dearly love to hear an old soldier's yarn."

"Well, it was when we were fighting against the rebels in Canada—the rebels under Papineau. We were only a handful, as the saying is—a handful of British troops, and they were thousands in number —discontented French, Irish Rapparees, and Yankee sympathisers, armed with everything they could lay hands on; but we licked them at St. Denis and St. Charles, on the Chamblay river—yes, and lastly at Napierville, under General Sir John Colborne; and pretty maddish we Cornish lads were at them, for they had just got one of our officers, a poor young fellow named Lieutenant George Weir, into their savage hands by treachery, after which they tied him to a cart-tail, and cut him into joints with his own sword. Well—where was I?—at Napierville. We were lying in a field in extended order to avoid the discharge of a field gun or two, that the devils had got into position against us, when a ball from one ploughed up the turf in a very open place, and Captain Trevelyan seated himself right in the furrow it had made, and proceeded to light a cigar, laughing as he did so.

"'Are you wise to sit there, right in the line of fire?' asked the colonel, looking down from his horse.

"'Yes,' says my master.

"'How so?'

"Master took the cigar between his fingers, and while watching the smoke curling upwards, said,

"'You see, colonel, that *another* cannon ball is extremely unlikely to pass in the same place; two never go after each other thus.'

"But he had barely spoken, ere the shako was torn off his head by a second shot from the field piece; so everybody laughed, while he scrambled out of the furrow, looking rather white and confused, though pretending to think it as good a joke as any one else—that was funny, wasn't it!"

So, while Derrick lay back and laughed heartily at his own reminiscence, Sharkley, quick as lightning, poured into his tankard a little phial-full of morphine, a colourless but powerful narcotic extracted from opium. He then took an opportunity of casting the phial into the fire unseen, and by the aid of the poker effectually concealed it.

"What a fine thing it would have been for Mr. Downie Trevelyan if that rebel shot had been a little lower down—eh, Derrick?" said he, chuckling.

" Not while the proud old lord lived, for he ever loved my master best."

" But he is in possession now—and that, you know, is nine points of the law."

" Yes—and he has a heart as hard as Cornish granite," said Braddon, grinding his set teeth; " aye, hard as the Logan Stone of Treryn Dinas! Here is confusion to him and all such!" he added, energetically, as he drained the drugged tankard to the dregs; " if such a fellow were in the army, he'd be better known to the Provost Marshal than to the Colonel or Adjutant, and would soon find himself at shot-drill, with B. C. branded on his side. But here's Mr. Denzil's jolly good-health-and-hooray-for-the-Dooranee-Empire!" he continued, and applied the empty tankard mechanically to his lips, while his eyes began to roll, as the four corners of the room seemed to be in pursuit of each other round him. " I dreamt I was on the wreck last night—ugh! and saw the black fins of the sea-lawyers, sticking up all about us."

" Sea-lawyers—what may they be ?"

" Sharks," replied Braddon, his eyes glaring with a curious expression, that hovered between fun and ferocity, at his companion, whose figure seemed suddenly to waver, and then to multiply.

" Ha, ha, very good; an old soldier must have his joke."

" So had my master, when he sat in the fur-ur-
urrow made by the shell. You see, we were engaged
with Canada rebels at Napierville — ville—yes
exactly, at Naperville, when a twelve-pound
shot——"

He was proceeding, with twitching mouth and
thickened utterance, to relate the whole anecdote
deliberately over again, when Sharkley, who saw
that he was becoming so fatuously tipsy that further
concealment was useless, rose impatiently, and
abruptly left the room, to give the landlord some
fresh hints for his future guidance.

" Halt! come back here—here, you sir—I say! "
exclaimed Braddon, in a low, fierce, and husky
voice, as this sudden and unexplained movement
seemed to rouse all his suspicions and quicken his
perceptive qualities ; but in attempting to leave his
chair he fell heavily on the floor.

He grew ghastly pale as he staggered into a
sitting posture. Tipsy and stupefied though he
was, some strange conviction of treachery came over
him ; he staggered, or dragged himself, partly on his
hands and knees, towards the bed, and drawing from
his breast-pocket the tin case, with the documents
so treasured, by a last effort of strength and of
judgment, thrust it between the mattress and
palliasse, and flung himself above it.

Then, as the powerful narcotic he had imbibed

overspread all his faculties, he sank into a deep and dreamless but snoring slumber, that in its heaviness almost boded death!

*   *   *   *   *

The noon of the next day was far advanced when poor old Derrick awoke to consciousness, but could, with extreme difficulty, remember where he was. A throat parched, as if fire was scorching it; an overpowering headache and throbbing of the temples; hot and tremulous hands, with an intense thirst, served to warn him that 'he must have been overnight, that which he had not been for many a year, very tipsy and "totally unfit for duty."

He staggered up in search of a water-jug, and then found that he had lain abed with his clothes on. A pleasant breeze came through the open window; the waves of the bright blue sea were rolling against Tintagel cliffs and up Boscastle creek; hundreds of birds were twittering in the warm spring sunshine about the clematis and briar that covered all the tavern walls, and the hum of the bee came softly and gratefully to his ear, as he strove to recall the events of the past night.

Sharkley!—it had been spent with Sharkley the solicitor, and where now was he?

The papers! He mechanically put his trembling hand to his coat pocket, and then, as a pang of fear shot through his heart, under the mattress.

They were not there; vacantly he groped and gasped, as recollections flashed upon him, and the chain of ideas became more distinct; madly he tossed up all the bedding and scattered it about. The case was gone, and with it the precious papers, too, were gone—GONE!

Sobered in an instant by this overwhelming catastrophe—most terribly sobered—a hoarse cry of mingled rage and despair escaped him. The landlord, who had been listening for an outbreak of some kind, now came promptly up.

"Beast, drunkard, fool that I have been!" exclaimed Derrick, in bitter accents of self-reprobation; "this is how I have kept my promise to a dying master—duped by the first scoundrel who came across me! I have been juggled—drugged, perhaps—then juggled, and robbed after!"

"Robbed of what?" asked the burly landlord, laughing.

"Papers—my master's papers," groaned Derrick.

"Bah—I thought as much; now look ye here, old fellow——"

"Robbed by a low lawyer," continued Derrick, hoarsely; "and no fiend begotten in hell can be lower in the scale of humanity or more dangerous to peaceful society. Oh, how often has poor master said so," he added, waxing magniloquent, and almost beside himself with grief and rage; "how often have I heard him say, ' I have had so much to do with lawyers, that I have lost all proper abhorrence for their master, the devil."

"Now, I ain't going to stand any o' this nonsense —just you clear out," said the landlord, peremptorily.

Then as his passionate Cornish temper got the better of his reason, Derrick on hearing this suddenly seized Jack Trevanion's successor by the throat, and dashing him on the floor, accused him of being art and part, or an aider and abettor of the robbery, in which, to say truth, he was not. His cries speedily brought the county constabulary, to whom, by Sharkley's advice, he had previously given a hint, and before the sun was well in the west, honest Derrick Braddon was raving almost with madness and despair under safe keeping in the nearest station house.

CHAPTER IV.

THE HOPE OF THE DEAD.

THE disappearance of the papers which had so terrible an effect upon the nervous system, and usually iron frame of Derrick Braddon, is accounted for by the circumstance that Sharkley on returning to see how matters were progressing in the room, lingered for a moment by the half-opened door, and saw his dupe pale, gasping, muttering, and though half-senseless, yet conscious enough to feel a necessity for providing against any trickery or future contingency, in the act of concealing the tin case among his bedding, from whence it was speedily drawn, after he had flung himself in sleepy torpor above it; and then stealing softly down stairs with the prize, Sharkley paid his bill and departed without loss of time and in high spirits, delighted with his own success.

Too wary to start westward in the direction of Rhoscadzhel, he made an ostentatious display of departing by a hired dog-cart for his own residence, at the village or small market town (which was

afflicted by his presence) in quite an opposite
direction. From thence, by a circuitous route,
he now revisited his employer, and hence the
delay which occasioned the latter so much torture
and anxiety.

"Two thousand—a beggarly sum!" thought
Sharkley, scornfully and covetously, as he walked
up the stately and over-arching avenue, and found
himself under the groined arches of the *porte-
cochère*, the pavement of which was of black and
white tesselated marble; "why should I not de-
mand double the sum, or more—yes, or more—he
is in my power, in my power, is he not?" he continued, with vicious joy, through his set teeth,
while his eyes filled with green light, and the
glow of avarice grew in his flinty heart, though
even the first sum mentioned was a princely one
to him.

Clutching the tin case with a vulture-like grasp,
he broadly and coarsely hinted his wish to Downie,
who sat in his library chair, pale, nervous, and
striving to conceal his emotion, while hearing a
narration of the late proceedings at the Trevanion
Arms; and hastily drawing a cheque book towards
him, he filled up another bank order, saying,—

"There, sir, this is a cheque for *two* thousand
pounds; surely two thousand five hundred are quite
enough for all you have done in procuring for my

inspection, documents which may prove but as so much waste paper after all."

"Their examination will prove that such is not the case," said Sharkley, as he gave one of his ugly smiles, scrutinised the document, and slowly and carefully consigned it to where its predecessor lay, in the greasy old pocket-book, wherein many a time and oft the hard-won earnings of the poor, the unfortunate and confiding, had been swallowed up. When Downie had heard briefly and rapidly a narration of the means by which the papers had been abstracted, he rather shrunk with disgust from a contemplation of them; they seemed so disreputable, so felonious and vile!

He had vaguely hoped that by the more constitutional and legal plans of bribery and corruption Mr. W. S. Sharkley might have received them from the custodier; but now they were in his hands and he was all impatience, tremulous with eagerness, and spectacles on nose, to peruse them, and test their value by that legal knowledge which he undoubtedly possessed.

His fingers, white and delicate, and on one of which sparkled the magnificent diamond ring which his late uncle had received when on his Russian embassy, literally trembled and shook, as if with ague, when he opened the old battered and well-

worn tin case. The first document drawn forth had
a somewhat unpromising appearance; it was sorely
soiled, frayed, and seemed to have been frequently
handled.

"What the deuce is this, Mr. Sharkley?" asked
Downie, with some contempt of tone.

"Can't say, my lord—never saw such a thing
before; it ain't a writ or a summons, surely!"

It was simply a soldier's "Parchment Certificate,"
and ran thus:—

Cornish Regiment of Light Infantry.

"These are to certify that Derrick Braddon,
Private, was born in the Parish of Gulval, Duchy
of Cornwall; was enlisted there for the said
corps, &c., was five years in the West Indies,
ten in North America, and six at Gibraltar;
was twice wounded in action with the Canadian
rebels, and has been granted a pension of one
shilling per diem. A well conducted soldier, of
unexceptionably good character." Then followed
the signature of his colonel and some other
formula.

"Pshaw!" said Downie, tossing it aside; but the
more wary Sharkley, to obliterate all links or proofs
of conspiracy, deposited it carefully in the fire,
when it shrivelled up and vanished; so the little

record of his twenty-one years' faithful service, of his two wounds, and his good character, attested by his colonel, whom he had ever looked up to as a demigod, and which Derrick had borne about with him as Gil Blas did his patent of nobility, was lost to him for ever.

But more than ever did Downie's hands tremble when he drew forth the other documents; when he saw their tenor, and by the mode in which they were framed, worded, stamped, and signed, he was compelled to recognise their undoubted authority! A sigh of mingled rage and relief escaped him; but, as yet, no thought of compunction. He glanced at the fire, at the papers, and at Sharkley, more than once in succession, and hesitated either to move or speak. He began to feel now that the lingering of his emissary in his presence, when no longer wanted, was intolerable; but he was too politic to destroy the papers before him, though no other witness was present.

Full of secret motives themselves, each of these men, by habit and profession, was ever liable to suspect secret motives in every one else; and each was now desirous to be out of the other's presence; Downie, of course, most of all. The lower in rank and more contemptible in character, perhaps was less so, having somewhat of the vulgar toady's desire to linger in the presence and atmosphere of one he deemed a greater, certainly more wealthy, and a titled man; till the latter said with a stiff bow full of significance,—

"I thank you, sir, and have paid you; these are the documents I wished to possess."

"I am glad your lordship is pleased with my humble services," replied Sharkley, but still tarrying irresolutely.

"Is there anything more you have to communicate to me?"

"No, my lord."

"Then I have the—I must wish you good evening."

Sharkley brushed his shiny hat with his dusty handkerchief, and the wish for a further gratuity was hovering on his lips.

"You have been well paid for your services, surely?"

"Quite, my lord—that is—but—"

"No one has seen those papers, I presume?" asked Downie.

"As I have Heaven to answer to, no eye has looked on them while in my hands—my own excepted."

"Good—I am busy—you may go," said Downie, haughtily, and as he had apparently quite recovered his composure, he rang the bell, and a servant appeared.

"Shew this—person out, please," said Downie.

And in a moment more Sharkley was gone. The door closed, and they little suspected they were never to meet again.

"Thank God, he is gone! Useful though the scoundrel has been, and but for his discovery of those papers we know not what may have happened, his presence was suffocating me!" thought Downie.

The perceptions of the latter were sufficiently keen to have his *amour propre* wounded by a peculiar sneering tone and more confident bearing in Sharkley; there had been a companionship in the task in hand, which lowered him to the level of the other, and the blunt rejoinder he had used so recently—"there are a *pair* of us," still rankled in his memory. Thus he had felt that he could not get rid of him too soon, or too politely to all appearance; and with a grimace of mingled satisfaction and contempt, he saw the solicitor's thin, ungainly figure lessening as he shambled down the long and beautiful avenue of elms and oaks, which ended at the grey stone pillars, that were surmounted each by a grotesque koithgath, *sejant*, with its four paws resting on a shield, charged with a Cavallo Marino, rising from the sea.

"And *now* for another and final perusal of these most accursed papers!" said Downie Trevelyan, huskily.

The first was the certificate of marriage, between Richard Pencarrow Trevelyan, Captain in the Cornish Light Infantry, and Constance Devereaux of Montreal, duly by *banns*, at the chapel of Père Latour. Then followed the date, and attestation, to the effect, "that the above named parties were this day married by me, as hereby certified, at Ste. Marie de Montreal.

> " C. LATOUR, *Catholic Curé,*
> " BAPTISTE OLIVIER, *Acolyte.*
> " DERRICK BRADDON, *Private Cornish Light Infantry.*

"JEHAN DURASSIER, *Sacristan.*"

About this document there could not be a shadow of a doubt—even the water-mark was anterior to the date, and the brow of Downie grew very dark as he read it; darker still grew that expression of malevolent wrath, and more swollen were the veins of his temples as he turned to the next document, which purported to be the "Last Will and Testament of Richard Pencarrow, Lord Lamorna," and which after the usual dry formula concerning his just debts, testamentary and funeral expenses, continued, " *I give, devise, and bequeath* unto Constance Devereaux, Lady Lamorna, my wife," the entire property, (then followed a careful enumeration thereof,) into which he had come by the death of his uncle Audley, Lord

Lamorna, for the term of her natural life; and after her death to their children Denzil and Sybil absolutely, in the several portions to follow. The reader Downie (to whom a handsome bequest was made), General Trecarrel, and the Rector of Porthellick were named as Executors, and then followed the duly witnessed signature of the Testator, written in a bold hand LAMORNA, and dated at Montreal, about nine months before.

"Hah!" exclaimed Downie, through his clenched teeth; "here is that in my hand, which, were Audley a wicked or undutiful son, might effect wonders at Rhoscadzhel, and furnish all England with food for gossip and surmise; but that shall never, never be; nor shall son nor daughter of that Canadian adventuress ever place their heads under this roof tree of ours!"

And as he spoke, he fiercely crumpled up the will and the certificate together.

Then he paused, spread them out upon his writing table, and smoothing them over, read them carefully over again. As he did so, the handsome face, the honest smile and manly figure of his brother Richard came upbraidingly to memory; there were thoughts of other and long-remembered days of happy boyhood, of their fishing, their bird-nesting expeditions, and of an old garret in which they were wont to play when the days were wet, or the snow

lay deep on the hills. How was it, that, till now
forgotten, the old garret roof, with its rafters big
and brown, and which seemed then such a fine old
place for sport, with the very sound of its echoes,
and of the rain without as it came pouring down to
gorge the stone gutters of the old house, came
back to memory now, with Richard's face and
voice, out of the mists of nearly half a century?
"It was one of those flashes of the soul that
for a moment unshroud to us the dark depths
of the past." Thus he really wavered in purpose, and actually thought of concealing the documents in his strong box, to the end that there
they might be found after his death, and after he
had enjoyed the title for what remained to him of
life.

Would not such duplicity be unfair to his own
sons, and to his daughter? was the next reflection.

And if fate permitted Denzil to escape the
perils of the Afghan war, was the son of that
mysterious little woman, or was her daughter
—the daughter of one whom he doubted not,
and wished not to doubt — had entrapped his
silly brother into a secret marriage, in a remote
and sequestered chapel, and whose memory he
actually loathed—ever to rule and reside in
Rhoscadzhel?

No—a thousand times no! Then muttering the lines from Shakespeare,—

> " Let not our babbling dreams affright our souls.
> Conscience is but a word that cowards use,
> Devised at first to keep the strong in awe :"

he drew near the resplendent grate of burnished steel, and resolutely casting in both documents, thrust them with the aid of the poker deep among the fuel, and they speedily perished. The deed was done, and could no more be recalled than the last year's melted snow!

He watched the last sparks die out in the tinder ashes of those papers, on the preservation and production of which so much depended, so much was won and lost ; and a sigh of relief was blended with his angry laugh.

He felt that then, indeed, the richly carpeted floor beneath his feet; the gilded roof above his head, the sweet, soft landscape—one unusually so for bold and rugged Cornwall—that stretched away in the soft, hazy, and yellow twilight, and all that he had been on the verge of losing, were again more surely his, and the heritage of his children, and of theirs in the time to come, and that none " of Banquo's line "—none of that strange woman's blood, could ever eject them now!

Even Derrick's old tin-case—lest, if found, it should lead to a trace or suspicion of where the papers had gone—he carefully, and with a legal caution worthy of his satellite the solicitor, beat out of all shape with his heel and threw into the fire, heaping the coals upon it.

This was perhaps needless in Downie Trevelyan, that smooth, smug, closely shaven, and white-shirted lawyer-lord, that man of legal facts and stern truths, so abstemious, temperate, and regular in his habits and attendance at church, and to all the outward tokens of worldly rectitude. Do what he might, none could, would, or dare believe evil of him !

Yet, after the excitement he had undergone, there were moments when he felt but partially satisfied with himself, till force of habit resumed its sway—moments when he remained sunk in thought, with his eyes fixed on that portion of the sea and sky where the sun had set, while the sombre twilight deepened around, and strange shadows were cast by the oriels across the library floor.

"For what have I done this thing?" thought he; "for my children of course, rather than for myself. I would that I had not been tempted, for nothing on earth remains for ever—nothing !" And as he muttered thus, his eyes rested on the distant Isles

of Scilly that loomed like dark purple spots in the
golden sea, which yet weltered in the ruddy glory
of the sun that had set, and he reflected, he knew
not why, for it was not Downie's wont, on the muta-
bility of all human things and wishes, of the change
that inexorable Time for ever brought about, and of
the futility of all that man might attempt to do in
the hope of perpetuity; for did not even the mighty
sea and firm land change places in the fulness of
years!

Where now was all the land tradition named as
Lyonesse of old—the vast tract which stretched
from the eastern shore of Mount's Bay, even to what
are now the Isles of Scilly, on which his dreamy
eyes were fixed—the land where once, in story and
in verse we are told,

> "That all day long the noise of battle rolled
> Among the mountains by the winter sea;
> Until king Arthur's Table, man by man,
> Had fall'n in Lyonesse about their lord."

There, where now he saw the sea rolling between
the rocky isles and the Land's End, were once green
waving woods and verdant meadows, lands that
were arable, mills whose busy wheels revolved in
streams now passed away, and one hundred-and-
forty parish churches, whose bells summoned the
people to prayer, but which are all now—if we are

to believe William of Worcester—submerged by
the encroaching sea; yet whether gradually, or
by one mighty throe of nature, on that day when
the first of the line of Trevelyan swam his wonderful horse from the north-western isle, back to
the rent and riven land, we know not, but so the
story runs.

From these day-dreams, such as he was seldom
used to indulge in, Downie's mind rapidly reverted
to practical considerations.

"Two thousand five hundred pounds in two
cheques!" he muttered; "will not my bankers,
and more than all, Gorbelly and Culverhole, my
solicitors, wonder what singular service a creature
such as this William Schotten Sharkley can
possibly have rendered me, to receive so large a
sum? If that drunken old soldier, Braddon, tells
this story of his last meeting with Sharkley, and
the subsequent loss of the papers, and permits
himself to make a noise about them, may there not
be many who, while remembering the former affair,
by putting this and that together, will patch up a
scandalous story after all? Bah—let them; there
lie the proofs!" he added, glancing with a fierce
and vindictive smile at the fragments of black
tinder which yet fluttered in the grate.

So perished, at his remorseless hands, all the
past hopes of the tender and affectionate dead, and

all the present hopes of the living—of Richard and his wife who were buried so far apart—of Denzil and his sister, who were separated by fate, by peril, and so many thousand miles of land and sea!

But our story may have a sequel for all that.

CHAPTER V.

RETRIBUTION.

GREATLY to the surprise of the granter, the two cheques for 500*l*. and 2000*l*. respectively, were never presented at his bankers, and Mr. Sharkley returned no more to his office ; that dingy chamber of torture, with its dusty dockets, ink-spotted table; and tin charter-boxes arranged in formal rows upon an iron frame, and its damp discoloured walls, ornamented by time-tables, bills of sale, and fly-blown prospectuses, knew him never again; and days, weeks, and months rolled on, but he was never seen by human eye after the time he issued from the lodge-gate of Rhoscadzhel, and the keeper, with a contemptuous bang, clanked it behind him.

When Derrick heard of his disappearance, he felt convinced more than ever that he had abstracted his papers ; but believed he had started with them to India, perhaps to make capital out of Denzil. Some who knew what the solicitor's legal course had been, thought of a dark and speedy end having befallen him; others surmised that the fear of certain trickeries, or " errors in practice," had caused him suddenly to depart for America; but all were wide of the truth.

Lord Lamorna knew not what to think, but maintained a dead and rigid silence as to his ever having had any meeting or transaction with the missing man in any way; and as many hated, and none regretted Mr. W. S. Sharkley, his existence was speedily forgotten in that district, and it was not until long after that a light was thrown on the mystery that enveloped his disappearance.

Much money, chiefly that of others, had passed through Sharkley's hands in his time, and much of it, as a matter of course, was never accounted for by him; but he had never before possessed so large a sum at once, and certainly seldom one so easily won, as that presented to him by the titular Lord Lamorna. All the exultation that avarice, covetousness, and successful roguery can inspire glowed in his arid heart, and he walked slowly onward, immersed in thoughts peculiarly his own, as to the mode in which he would invest it, and foresaw how it must and should double, treble, and quadruple itself ere long; how lands, and houses, messuages and tenements, mills and meadows, should all become his; and so he wove his golden visions, even as Alnaschar in the

Arabian fable wove his over the basket of frail and brittle glass; and as he proceeded, ever and anon he felt, with a grimace of satisfaction, for the pocket-book containing his beloved cheques.

Some miles of country lay between Rhoscadzhel and Penzance, where he meant to take the railway for his own place. As his penurious spirit had prevented him from hiring a vehicle, he pursued the way on foot; but he sometimes lost it, darkness having set in, and yet he saw nothing of the lights of the town. He had, in his mental abstraction, walked, or wandered on, he scarcely knew whither, and he only paused from time to time to uplift his clenched hands, to mutter and sigh in angry bitterness of spirit that he had not extracted *more* from Downie Trevelyan, when he had it in his power to put on the screw with vigour, and anon he would ponder as to whether he had not been too precipitate, and whether he had done a wise thing in selling to him the interests of young Denzil, as these might have proved pecuniarily more valuable; but then poor Denzil was so far away, and from all Sharkley could hear and read in the newspapers, he might never see England more. For the first time in his life, Mr. Sharkley found himself taking an interest in our Indian military affairs.

Some of the deep lanes bordered by those high stone walls peculiar to Cornwall, were left behind, and also many a pretty cottage, in the gardens of which, the fragrant myrtle, the gay fuchsia with its drooping petals, and the hydrangea, flourish all the year round; and now he was roused by the sound of the sea breaking at a distance round the promontory from which Penzance takes its name—the holy headland of the ancient Cornish men. From a slight eminence which he was traversing, he could see, but at a distance also, the lights of the town twinkling amid the moorland haze, and that at the harbour head, sending long rays of tremulous radiance far across Mount's Bay; then as the pathway dipped down into a furzy hollow, he lost sight of them. He was still within half a mile of the shore, but was traversing a bleak and uneven moorland, and on his right lay a scene of peculiar desolation, encumbered by masses of vast granite rock, here and there tipped by the cold green light of a pale crescent moon, that rose from the wild waste of the vast Atlantic.

Suddenly something like a black hole yawned before him; a gasping, half-stifled cry escaped him; he stumbled and fell—*where ?* "

Mechanically and involuntarily, acting more like a machine than a human being, he had in falling grasped something, he knew not what, and clutching at it madly, tenaciously, yea desperately, he clung thereto, swinging he knew not where or how, over space; but soon the conviction that forced itself upon him, was sufficient to make the hairs of his scalp bristle up, and a perspiration, cold as snow, to start from the pores of his skin.

Old mines may seem somehow to have a certain connection with the story or destiny of Sybil Devereaux, if not of her brother Denzil, and the betrayer of both their interests, who now found himself swinging by the branch of a frail gorse-bush, over the mouth of the ancient shaft of an abandoned one—a shaft, the depth of which he knew not, and dared not to contemplate! He only knew that in Cornwall they were usually the deepest in the known world.

If few persons who are uninitiated, descend the shaft of an ordinary coal-pit, amid all the careful appliances of engineering, without a keen sense of vague danger, what must have been the emotions of the wretch who, with arms perpendicularly above his head, and legs outspread, wildly and vainly seeking to catch some footing, swung pendent over the black profundity that vanished away into the bowels of the earth below, perhaps, for all he knew, nearly a *mile* in depth!

It was beneath him he knew; the quiet stars were above; no aid was near; there was no sound in the air, and none near him, save the dreadful beating of his heart, and a roaring, hissing sound in his ears.

In this awful situation, after his first exclamation of deadly and palsied fear, not a word, not a whisper —only sighs—escaped him. He had never prayed in his life, and knew not how to do so now. The blessed name of God had been often on his cruel lips, in many a matter-of-fact affidavit, and in many an affirmation, made falsely, but never in his heart; so now, he never thought of God or devil, of heaven nor hell, his only fear was death—extinction!

And there he swung, every respiration a gasping, sobbing sigh, every pulsation a sharp pang; he had not the power to groan; as yet his long, lean, bony hands were not weary; but the branch might rend, the gorse bush uproot, and *then*——

Nevertheless he made wild and desperate efforts to escape the dreadful peril, by writhing his body upward, as his head was only some four feet below the edge of the upper rim or course of crumbling brickwork, which lined the circular shaft, and often he felt his toes scratch the wall, and heard the fragments detached thereby pass whizzing downwards; but he never heard the ascending sound of the fall below—because below was far, far down indeed!

The silence was dreary—awful: he dared not look beneath, for nothing was to be seen there but the blackness of utter profundity; he could only gaze upward to where the placid stars that sparkled in the blue dome of heaven, seemed to be winking at him. He dared not cry, lest he should waste his breath and failing strength; and had he attempted to do so the sound would have died on his parched and quivering lips.

In every pulsation he lived his lifetime over again, and all the secret crimes of that lifetime were, perhaps, being atoned for now.

The widows who, without avail or winning pity, had wept, (in that inquisitorial camera de los tormentos, his " office,"), for the loss of the hard-won savings of dead husbands, their children's bread; wretches from under whose emaciated forms he had dragged the bare pallet, leaving them to die on a bed of cinders, and all in form and process of law; the strong and brave spirited men, who had lifted up their hard hands and hoarsely cursed him, ere they betook them to the parish union or worse; the starvelings who had perhaps gained their *suits*, but only in their last coats; the crimes that some had committed through the poverty and despair he had brought upon them; the unsuspecting, into whose private and monetary matters he had wormed himself by specious offers of gratuitous assistance and advice—a special legal snare—by the open and too often secret appropriation of valuable papers;

and by the thousand wiles and crooks of policy known only to that curse of society, the low legal practitioner, seemed all to rise before him like a black cloud now; and out of that cloud, the faces of his pale victims seemed to mock, jibe, and jabber at him.

And there, too, were the handwritings he had imitated, the signatures he had forged, the sham accounts he had fabricated against the wealthy or the needy, the ignorant and the wary alike; but Sharkley felt no real penitence, for he knew not that he had committed any sin. Had he not always kept the shady side of the law? and, if rescued, would he not return to his sharp practice thereof as usual? Yet he felt, as the moments sped on, a strange agony creeping into his soul:

> " So writhes the mind Remorse hath riven,
> Unfit for earth, undoomed for heaven,
> Darkness above, despair beneath,
> Around it flame, within it death !"

The bush bending under his weight, hung more perpendicularly now, and thus Sharkley's knees, for the first time, grazed till they were skinned and bloody against the rough brickwork. Was the root yielding? Oh no, no; forbid it fate! He must live—live—*live;* he was not fit to die—and thus, too! The cold, salt perspiration, wrung by agony, flowed from the roots of his hair, till it well nigh blinded him, and tears, for even a creature such as he can weep, began to mingle with them. They were perfectly genuine, however, as Master William S. Sharkley wept the probabilities of his own untimely demise.

He had once been on a coroner's inquest. It sat in the principal room of a village inn, upon some human bones—nearly an entire skeleton—found in an old, disused, and partially filled-up pit. He remembered their aspect, so like a few white, bleached winter branches, as they lay on a sheet on the dining-table. He could recal the surmises of the jurors. Did the person fall? Had he, or she—for even sex was doubtful then—been murdered? or had it been a case of suicide? None might say.

The poor bones of the dead alone could have told, and they were voiceless. All was mystery, and yet the story of some forgotten life, of some unknown crime, or hidden sorrow, lay there; the story that man could never, never know.

This episode had long since been forgotten by Sharkley; and now, in an instant, it flashed vividly before him, adding poignancy to the keen horrors of his situation. Was such a fate to be his?

He could distinctly see the upper ledge of bricks, as he looked upward from where, though he had not swung above three minutes, he seemed to have been for an eternity now; and though he knew not how to pray, he thought that he could spend the remainder of his life happily there, if but permitted to rest his toes upon that narrow ledge, as a place for footing, as now his arms seemed about to be rent from his shoulders. His eyes were closed for a time, and he scarcely dared to breathe—still less to think.

Sharkley was not a dreamer; he had too little imagination, and had only intense cunning and the instincts that accompany it; so he had never known what a nightmare is; yet the few minutes of his present existence seemed to be only such. He had still sense enough to perceive, that the wild and frenzied efforts he made at intervals to writhe his body up, were loosening the root of the gorse-bush, and he strove in the dusky light, but strove in vain, to see *how much* he had yet to depend upon; and then he hung quite still and pendant, with a glare in his starting eyeballs, and a sensation as if of palsy in his heart.

His arms were stiffening fast, his fingers were relaxing, and his spine felt as if a sharply pointed knife was traversing it; he knew that the end was nigh—most fearfully nigh—and his tongue clove to the roof of his mouth, though it was dry as a parched pea.

Oh for one grasp of a human hand; the sound of

any voice ; the sight of a human face ere he passed
away for ever !

There was a sudden sound of tearing as the gorse-
root parted from the soil; he felt himself slipping
through space, the cold air rushed whistling upward,
and he vanished, prayerless, breathless, and despairing, from the light of the blessed stars, and then the
black mouth of the shaft seemed vacant.

CHAPTER VI.

AT JELALABAD.

Downie Trevelyan's applications to the War Office, the Horse Guards, to the Military Secretary for the Home Department of the East India Company, and even questions asked in his place in the House of Lords, were unremitting for a time, on the affairs of Afghanistan, as he wished to elicit some information concerning the safety of his son, and the probable *non*-safety of Lieutenant Devereaux, more particularly; but he totally failed in extracting more than vague generalities, or that one was believed to be safe with Sir Robert Sale's garrison in Jelalabad; and that the other was supposed to be a prisoner of war with many others. How long he might remain so, if surviving, or how long he had remained so, if dead, no one could tell; but dark rumours had reached Peshawur, that the male hostages had been beheaded in the Char Chowk of Cabul, while the females had been sold to the Tartars.

On the assassination of the Shah Sujah, whose ally we had so foolishly become by the mistaken policy of the Earl of Auckland, the prince, his son, had gained possession of the Bala Hissar, the guns and garrison of which gave him for a time full sway over the city of Cabul, when he made the cunning, plotting, and ambitious Ackbar Khan his Vizier.

The latter, however, always on the watch, and by nature suspicious, intercepted a letter written by his young master to General Nott, who commanded our troops in Candahar. This contained some amicable proposals, quite at variance with the inborn hate and rancour which Ackbar bore the English; and hence a quarrel ensued at the new court.

The prince demanded that the hostages, male and female—the fair Saxon beauty of some of the latter was supposed to have some influence in the request—left by the deceased General Elphinstone, should be delivered up to *him*, without question or delay.

Ackbar sternly refused to comply, and it was on this that the young Shah wrote to General Nott, urging him to march at once on Cabul to release the captives; and, moreover, to free the city from the interference and overweening tyranny of Sirdir, who thereupon resolved to take strong measures, and, with the aid of Amen Oollah Khan, Zohrab Zubberdust, and some others, made his new Sovereign captive. The latter escaped by making a hole in the roof of his prison; a purse of mohurs, a sharp sword, and a fleet horse, enabled him to reach in safety the cantonments of the British General, to whom he gave a sad detail of the miseries to which the prisoners, especially the delicate ladies, were subjected.

This movement was nearly the means of causing the destruction of all who were left at Ackbar's mercy. All communication between them and the troops in Jelalabad was cut off more strictly and hopelessly than ever; and Ackbar Khan swore by the Black Stone of Mecca, and by many a solemn and fearful oath, that "the moment he should hear of the approach of British troops again towards Cabul, the hostages should, each and all, man, woman, and child alike, be sold as slaves to the Usbec Tartars! "And remember," he added, with clenched teeth and flashing eyes, to Zohrab the Overbearing, and others who heard him; "that my word is precious to me, even as the *Mohur Soli-mani*—the seal of Solomon Jared was to him!"

This was the signet of the fifth monarch of the world after Adam; and the holder thereof had, for the time, the entire command of the elements, of all demons, and all created things.

"Now," he exclaimed, with fierce vehemence, "I cannot violate my oath, for as the sixteenth chapter of the Koran says, '*I have made God a witness over me!*'"

Hence, perhaps, the rumour that came to Pesha-wur, and thus any attempt to save or succour them, would, it seemed, but accelerate their ruin, for if once removed to Khoordistan, they should never, never be heard of more, nor could they be traced among the nomadic tribes who dwell in that vast region of Western Asia, known as the "country of the Khoords."

The last that, as yet, was known of them, was that they were all in charge of an old Khan, named Saleh Mohammed, and shut up in a fortress three miles from Cabul. There they were kept in hor-rible suspense as to their future fate; and to them now were added nine of our officers who had fallen into Ackbar's hands, when, in the month of August, he recaptured the city of Ghuznee.

How many Christian companions in misfortune were with the Ladies Sale and Macnaghten, the garrisons in Jelalabad and Candahar knew not; neither did they know who, out of the original number taken in the passes, were surviving now those sufferings of mind and body which they all had to undergo. Among them was one poor lady, the widow of an officer, who had the care of eight young children, to add to her mental misery.

The steady and unexpected refusal of Sir Robert Sale to evacuate Jelalabad, completely baulked all the plans of Ackbar Khan, who supplemented his threatening messages by investing the city in person at the head of two thousand five hundred horse and six thousand five hundred juzailchees; but fortunately Sir Robert had collected provisions for three months, and made a vigorous defence, though the lives or liberties of the hostages, among whom were his own wife and daughter, were held in the balance, and he trusted only to his artillery, the bayonets and the stout hearts of his little garrison, who, in addition to the assaults and missiles of the Afghans, had to contend with earthquakes; for in one month more than a hundred of those throes of nature shook the city, crumbling beneath their feet the old walls they were defending.

In daily expectation of being relieved, Sale's stout English heart never failed him, for he had learned through our faithful friend, Taj Mohammed, the ex-vizier, that Colonel Wild, with a force, was marching to his aid from one quarter, while General Pollock was crossing the Punjaub from another. Yet a long time, he knew, must elapse before the latter could traverse six hundred miles; and ere long came the tidings that Wild had totally failed, either by force of arms or dint of bribery, to achieve a march through the now doubly terrible Khyber Pass.

General Nott, however, held out in Candahar, and, on receiving some supplies and reinforcements, he was ready to co-operate with Sale and Pollock in a joint advance upon Cabul, to rescue the hostages at all hazards, or, if *too late* for that, to avenge their fate and the fate of our slaughtered army by a terrible retribution.

A severe defeat sustained by Ackbar Khan, when Sale, on the 7th of August, made a resolute sortie and cut his army to pieces, taking two standards, four of our guns lost at Cabul, all his stores and tents, relieved Jelalabad of his presence; and in this state were matters while Waller and Audley Trevelyan were serving there, doing any duty on which they might be ordered, foraging, trenching, and skirmishing, for they were unattached to any regiment; and the former was still ignorant as to the fate of his *fiancée*, the bright-faced and auburn-haired Mabel Trecarrel, and equally so as to that of her sister and his friend Denzil. He had long since reckoned the two latter as with the dead, and mourned for them as such; for he knew nothing of their being retained as special "loot" by Shereen Khan, who now kept himself aloof from Ackbar, of whom he had conceived a truly Oriental jealousy and mistrust.

Though so near them, Waller knew no more concerning the number, treatment, or the safety of the hostages held for the evacuation of the city he had assisted to defend, than those to whom Downie Trevelyan was applying in London—perhaps less.

To the original number of captives were now

added thirty more, from the following circumstance, which in some of its details is curiously illustrative of the cunning and avaricious nature of the Afghan mountaineers. A pretended friendly *cossid*, or messenger, arrived at Jelalabad, bearer of a letter from Captain Souter, of Her Majesty's 44th Regiment, dated from a village near the hill of Gundamuck, detailing the last stand made there by the few unhappy survivors of Elphinstone's army, and adding that he and Major Griffiths, of the 37th Regiment, were the prisoners of a chief who, on a sufficient ransom being paid—a thousand rupees for each—would send them to Jelalabad with their heads on their shoulders. The brave fellows of the 13th Light Infantry instantly subscribed a thousand rupees at the drum-head; a thousand more were collected with difficulty by their now-impoverished officers; and then came a proposal to ransom twenty-eight privates of the 13th and 44th Regiments, who were in the hands of the same chief, for a *lac* of rupees. By incredible efforts, and by encroachment on the military chest, this sum was sent with certain messengers, who, by a previously concerted scheme, were waylaid and robbed of it by men sent by Ackbar Khan, who, seizing the thirty Europeans, added them to the other hostages whose lives or liberties were to pay for the surrender of Jelalabad!

The poor soldiers had given all they possessed in the world, save their kits and ammunition, to save their comrades from perilous bondage, and had given it in vain. They had but the consolation of having done for the best.

Amid even the exciting bustle of military duty, the reflections of Waller were sometimes intolerable. He could never for a moment forget. Though he was not, as a matter-of-fact young English officer, prone to flights of romantic fancy, imagination *would* force upon him with poignant horror all that Mabel might be forced to endure at the hands of those on whose mercy she and her companions were cast by a fate that none could have foreseen, especially during the pleasant days of the year that was passed at Cabul, when the race-course, the band-stand, picnics, hunting-parties, morning drives, and rides to see Sinclair's boat upon the lake, tiffin parties at noon, others for whist or music in the evening, made up the round of European social life there, ere Mohammed Ackbar Khan came to the surface again with his deep-laid plots for aggrandisement and revenge.

Mabel Trecarrel, his affianced wife, so gently soft and lady-like—her image was ever before him, her voice ever in his ear, and the varying expressions of her clear grey eyes, with all her winning ways, came keenly and vividly to memory, more especially in the lonely watches of the night, when muffled in his poshteen, with only a Chinsurrah cheroot to soothe his nerves and keep him warm, he trod from post to post visiting his sentinels, or listened for the sounds that might precede an Afghan assault, or perhaps an earthquake; for the troops had both to encounter, though often nothing came but the melancholy howl of the jackal on the night wind, as it sighed over the vast plain around the city of Jelalabad—the Zarang of the historians of Alexander.

He had frequent thoughts of returning to Cabul in disguise as an Afghan. He had already been pretty successful in his Protean attempts to conceal his identity; but Sir Robert Sale would by no means accord him permission to risk his life again in a manner so perilous; so, as partial inactivity was maddening to him, after Ackbar Khan's defeat had left all the avenues from the city open, he volunteered, if furnished with a suitable escort, to ride to Candahar, and urge on General Nott the policy of instantly advancing. Sir Robert Sale agreed to this, and furnished him with a despatch and a guard of twenty Native Cavalry; so Bob Waller departed, actually in high spirits, thankful that even in this small way he was doing something that might ultimately lead to the recapture of Cabul, and, more than all, the rescue of her he loved.

At a quick pace he crossed the arid desert that surrounds the city, and ascended into the well-wooded and magnificent mountain ranges that rise all around it, but more especially to the westward, whither his route lay, and his spirits rose as his party spurred onward. "What pleasure there is in a gallop!" says Paul Ferroll; "the object is before one, at which to arrive quickly; the still air becomes a wind marking the swiftness of one's pace—the fleet horse is his own master, yet one's slave; the bodily employment leaves care, thought, and time behind. One feels the pleasure of danger, because there might be danger, and yet there may be none."

So thought Waller, as he careered at the head of his party, with a cigar between his teeth, the which to keep alight while riding at full speed, he had previously dipped in saltpetre, a camp-fashion peculiar to India.

Candahar is distant from Jelalabad two hundred and seventy British miles, and, considering the state of the whole country, the undertaking, at the head of twenty horse, was a brave and arduous one; but Waller confidently set out on his expedition, after having carefully inspected his escort of picked men, and personally examined their arms, ammunition, and saddlery, as he knew not whom they might meet, or have to encounter.

By a curious coincidence, on the very day he

bade adieu to his brother-officer, Audley Trevelyan,
and other friends, to urge and effect a junction of
the forces, a fresh and loud burst of indignation
against the now-desponding Indian Executive was
excited in the minds of Sale's troops by the arrival
of a messenger with a startling proposal from the
Governor-General, Auckland, to the effect that
Jelalabad was *not* a place to retain any longer;
that a retreat was to be made from there to Peshawur; that, in effect, the whole of Afghanistan was
to be—as Ackbar Khan wished it—abandoned by
our forces, and that the helpless women and children,
wounded and sick, at Cabul, were to be left at the
mercy of irresponsible barbarians until rescued by
quiet negotiations or a judicious distribution of
money; and thus to have peace at any price, leaving
our disgraces without remedy, our revenge unac-
complished, and our prestige destroyed—in that
quarter of the world at least!

Even the English women who were captives in
Afghanistan knew better than this; for, amid the
earnest prayers which they put up for their libera-
tion, they ever seemed to know that it was "not to
be obtained by negotiation and ransom, *but by hard
fighting*," and they had more trust in the bayonets
of Sale's Brigade than in all the diplomatists in
London or Calcutta.

Fortunately, ere all these disastrous arrangements could be made, a new Governor-General in the person of Lord Ellenborough arrived, and to him Sir Robert Sale despatched Audley Trevelyan with a letter descriptive of his plans, and giving details of his force; and on this mission, with a few attendants, our young staff officer and his companion departed by the way of Peshawur, the gate of Western India, on a long and arduous journey of nearly five hundred miles, by Rawul Pindee and Umritsur, to Simla, on the slopes of the Himalayas—a journey to be performed by horse and elephant, as the occasion might suit; for the railway to Lahore had not as yet sent up its whistle in the realms of Runjeet Sing.

Meanwhile Waller was proceeding in precisely an opposite direction. Compelled to avoid Ghuznee, which was now in the hands of the Afghans under Ameen Oollah Khan, he and his escort, the half-Rissallah of Native Horse, travelled among the mountains, unnoticed and uncared for by the nomadic dwellers in black tents, whose temporary settlements dotted the green slopes. His sowars all wore turbans in lieu of light-cavalry helmets; and as he too had one, with it, his poshteen, and now weather-beaten visage, he passed as a native chief of some kind; and the route they traversed was sometimes as beautiful as picturesque villages, long shady lanes overarched by mulberry-trees, orchards of plums, apples, pomegranates, and those great cherries which were introduced by the Emperor Baber, could make it. And so on they rode, by Kurraba and Killaut, till they reached Candahar in safety; and thankful indeed was honest Bob Waller when from the hills, amid the plain, he beheld the city, with its fortress crowning a precipitous rock, its long low walls of sun-dried brick, and the gilded cupola that shrines the tomb of Ahmed Shah, once "the Pearl of his age," the object of many a Dooranee's prayer, and around which so many recluses spend the remainder of their lives in repeating the Koran over and over again without end.

There Waller was welcomed by the gallant General Nott, whom he found full of stern resolution and high in hope for the future, for he was on the very eve of marching with seven thousand well-tried and well-trained troops to the aid of his friend Sale; and on the 15th of August the movement was made, *en route* recapturing Ghuznee. It was stormed, and the Afghans again driven out at the point of the bayonet. The whole place was dismantled; and, among others, Waller had the pleasure of standing where no "unbeliever" ever stood before, in the tomb of the Sultan Mahmud, which is entirely of white marble and sculptured over with Arabic verses from the Koran. Around

it, beneath the mighty cupola stand thrones of
mother-of-pearl; and upon the slab that covers his
grave lies the mace he used in battle, with a head
of iron, so heavy that few men now-a-days can use it.
The gates of this tomb were miracles of carving
and beauty; they were of that hard yellow timber
known as sandal-wood, which grows on the coast of
Malabar and in the Indian Archipelago, and is
highly esteemed for its fragrant perfume and as a
material for cabinet work. Those gates had been
brought as trophies from the famous Hindoo
temple of Somnath in Goojerat, when sacked by
Mahmud in his last expedition during the tenth
century; and after hanging on his tomb for eight
hundred years, they were now torn down by order of
General Nott, and carried off by our victorious
troops, for restoration on their original site.

Prior to all this, General Pollock with his army
had reached Jelalabad, which he entered under a
joyful salute of sixteen pieces of cannon, and then
" forward!" was the word heard on all sides, " forward to Cabul!"

Then it was seen how the weather-beaten and
hollow faces of our jaded soldiers brightened with
joy and ardour, with a flush for vengeance too;
for certain tidings came that, prior to this long-
delayed * junction having been effected, the relent-

* It was with something of waggery, perhaps, that the band of

less Ackbar, true to his oath, had hurried off all his captives, male and female, in charge of Saleh Mohammed towards the confines of savage Toor-kistan—tidings heard by many a husband, father, and lover with despair and rage! . . . . .

the 13th Light Infantry, on this occasion, welcomed Pollock, by playing the old Scottish melody,

> " Oh, but you've been lang o' comin',
> Lang, lang, lang o' comin'."

CHAPTER VII.

THE SCHEME OF ZOHRAB.

TIME, to the young, seems but a slow and cold comforter (alas! how different it must appear to the old); so Denzil knew that, though sluggish, time must eventually bring about some change in the captivity he was enduring in the hands of Shireen Khan—a mode of life that, but for the sweet companionship of Rose, would have been simply so intolerable that he should certainly have attempted to escape even at the risk of death.

In perfect ignorance of all that was passing in the outer world of far-away Europe, of India, and even Afghanistan, they and the other hostages, from whom they were, happily for themselves, kept apart, knew nothing of all that was passing elsewhere, or of the plans that were forming and the hopes that grew for their rescue or release.

We say, happily they were sequestered from those who were in the hands of Ackbar Khan: thus they were not harassed by dreadful and incessant doubts

of their future fate, especially the vague and terrible
one of transmission to Toorkistan; for the old
Kuzzilbash lord treated them kindly, and, to the
best of his resources, hospitably, confidently believing that it was his personal interest to do so,
as the gaily embroidered regimental colour of the
44th, or East Essex, in which Denzil purposely
aired his figure occasionally in the garden of the
fort, still impressed him with the idea that he had
secured a great Feringhee Nawab whom the Queen
or Company might ransom, or who might prove a
powerful friend to him if reverses came upon Cabul,
and *not* a poor Ensign, or Lieutenant, as Denzil
was now; though he knew not that, consequent to
slaughter, death by disease, and so forth, he had
now been promoted in the corps.

Chess-playing was the great bond between old
Shireen and the bright laughing Rose, whom he
treated with infinitely more care and tenderness than
either of his own daughters; but to Denzil he would
frequently say in his hoarse, guttural, and most un-
musical language, between the whiffs of his silk-
bound and silver-cupped hubble-bubble—

"I am thy friend; yet remember that friendship with unbelievers is forbidden by the Koran,
especially with Jews or Christians; for saith the fifth
chapter, 'Are they not friends one with another?'
and they will corrupt us, their alms being like the

icy winds which blow on the fields of the perverse, and blast their corn in the ear."

Denzil could not repress an impatient grimace under a smile, for it was the Koran—always and ever the Koran—among these Afghans; every casual remark or idea suggested a quotation from or a reference to it, so that the Khanum could not dye her nails, adjust her veil, put pepper in the kabobs, or chillis among the pillau of rice, without a reference to something that was said or done on a similar occasion by the Holy Camel-driver of Mecca,—their whole conversation being interlarded with pious sayings, like that of the Scottish Covenanters or English Puritans of old.

Isolated as they were in that lonely Afghan fort, surrounded by towering green hills, the interest that Denzil and Rose had in each other grew daily and hourly deeper; so that at last she learned to love him—yes, actually to love him—as fondly as he had ever loved her, and to feel little emotions of pique and jealousy when he strove to address the daughters of the house and teach them a very strange kind of broken English.

Propinquity and a just appreciation of his sterling character achieved this for him, and he felt supremely happy in the conviction of this returned love, though the end of it yet was difficult to foresee.

But it was such a divine happiness to dream

softly on for the present, shut in there as they were alone for themselves apparently, and, as it seemed, "the world forgetting, by the world forgot." Denzil's doubts of her were gone now; yet Rose had the power to conceal for a long time the gradual change in her own sentiments and secret thoughts from him who had inspired them; for the coquette was loth to admit that she had succumbed at last.

Denzil had contrived, after innumerable essays, in the most remarkable species of polyglot language, to make old Shireen comprehend that they had not, as yet, been married before a Cadi (or Moollah, as the Christians are), and had to wait the permission of others. On this he stroked his vast beard in token of assent, and thrice muttered "Shabash!" with great solemnity, meaning, "Well-done—agreed."

Rose had lost much of her heedlessness of manner now; her latest flirtation, which had been with Audley Trevelyan, was utterly forgotten, as many others had been; and the quaint Afghan dress she was compelled by the exigencies of her scanty wardrobe to wear—to wit, a yellow chemise of silk embroidered with black, trousers of fine white muslin, which revealed through its thin texture the roundness of each tapered ankle, with her veil floating loose, in token of her being unmarried, did not afford her much room for coquetry, although it afforded scope for her old waggery, and her long unbound auburn tresses, that spread over her shoulders in brilliant ripples, she was wont to ridicule as a *coiffure à la sauvage*, though one with which Denzil's fingers—when unobserved by the Afghan household, he and she could ramble among the parterres, rosaries, and shrubberies of the Khan's garden—were never weary of toying.

"You will tire of this life, as I do, and more soon of waiting too," said she one day.

"I shall wait and be faithful to you, Rose, even as I was taught at school Jacob was to Rachel," he replied, fondly caressing her hands in his.

"Oh! that is much more solemn than Paul and Virginia," said she laughing; "but, for Heaven's sake, don't imitate our dingy friends here in pious quotations."

When Rose Trecarrel calmly learned to know herself, she found upon consideration, and came to the conclusion, that it was not mere admiration for Denzil's handsome person and earnest winning manner; it was not gratitude for his steady faith to herself, it was not the charm of propinquity, nor the emotion of self-flattery at his passion,— that it was not any of these singly, but all put together, that made her love him so dearly now, and wonder at her heedless blindness in the time that was past.

Save Zohrab Zubberdust, that handsome, reckless, and wandering Mohammedan soldier of fortune, no visitor at this time came to the fort; and he was openly permitted to see Rose with the other ladies of the family, and occasionally to converse and smoke a cherry-stick pipe with Denzil, who deemed it rash on the part of Shireen to permit them — Rose and himself — to be seen so freely by one who was a paid follower of Ackbar Khan; but the leader of five thousand mounted Kuzzilbash spearmen doubtless felt himself pretty independent in action now. Moreover, since Ackbar's signal defeat before the walls of Jelalabad, his influence had been lessening in Cabul and all the surrounding country; and Zohrab, like many other " khans," who had only their swords and pistols, and, like many other Afghan *snobs*, that title to maintain, was beginning to wax cool in his service, even as the funds ebbed in his treasury; for Ackbar now had but one hope of replenishing these—the ransom or sale of the captives left in his hands, and each head of these he reckoned at so many mohurs of gold.

It was from some casual remarks of Zohrab that Rose and Denzil first learned, with mingled emotions of satisfaction and fear, compassion and hope, that so many more hostages, male and female, were in the hands of Ackbar, and that their own hopes of rescue or ransom were thereby increased.

Rose, through the medium of the Khan and of
Denzil, overwhelmed Zubberdust with questions as
to *who* these prisoners were. Was her father among
them? No description he gave her answered to
that of the burly, bronzed, and grizzle-haired
" Sirdir Trecarrel; " but there was *one* " mem
sahib," whose appearance tallied so closely in
stature, face, eyes, and colour of hair with her own,
that knowing as she did all the ladies who had .
been in the cantonments, Rose could not doubt
but that she was Mabel—Mabel, her dear . and
only sister, who must have been within a few miles
of her all those weary, anxious months, and yet
neither could know of the other's existence ; for
Mabel, like all who were with Elphinstone's ill-
fated host, had now learned to number all who had
loved her with the dead.

Now it happened that Zohrab Zubberdust had
frequently seen Mabel Trecarrel among the hostages, and been struck by her beauty. Indeed,
Ackbar Khan, who cared not for such personal
attributes as she possessed, and was long since
past all soft emotions now, or, indeed, any save
those of ferocity, ambition, and avarice, had frequently indicated her to Ameen Oollah Khan and
others as the one upon whom he put most value,
and for whom he expected the largest sum from
a certain Toorkoman chief whom he named, and

who was in the habit of purchasing or exchanging horses for such pleasant commodities; for at that precise time, or in that year of Queen Victoria's reign, Mohammed Ackbar could scarcely realise as a probability the fact that the year 1871 would see a descendant of the Great Mogul — he who was lord of Persia, Transoxana, and Hindostan—one of the royal race of Delhi, sentenced in a Feringhee court of law, by a cadi in a tow wig, to four years' imprisonment with hard labour " for burying a slave-girl " in the city of Benares! So,

> " Manners with fortunes, humours turn with climes,
> Tenets with books, and principles with times ! "

Thus Zohrab, perceiving that the power and influence of Ackbar had been daily growing less in Cabul, especially since the flight of the young Shah to the British General, had begun to dream of possessing himself of this rare European beauty, and departing with her, his horse and lance, in search of "fresh fields and pastures new," and, if possible, of another paymaster; perchance to the court of the Emir of Bokhara, the Shah of Persia, or some one else, alike beyond the ken of Ackbar and the influence of the Feringhees and their queen. In this intention, Zohrab felt the less compunction, that Ackbar had of late permitted his pay to be in arrears several *tillas* of gold.

G 2

But how to get her quietly out of his power, still more how to get her out of the immediate care and wardship of such a wary old soldier and chief as Saleh Mohammed, to whom the especial keeping of the hostages had been confided by the Sirdir, were the two principal difficulties of Zohrab.

He hoped to achieve much through the real or supposed relationship to Rose, with whom he conversed freely, at times, on this and other subjects (Denzil acting as their interpreter), and from him she gradually learned much of which Shireen and his household had, perhaps, kept her in ignorance—the state of affairs before Jelalabad and in the Passes.

"Are not the poor dead creatures buried there?" Rose once asked, while many a face and voice came back to memory.

"Buried? a few—but not deep," replied Zohrab, evasively.

"How—what mean you?"

"Because, as I rode through the Pass but yesterday, my horse's hoofs turned up great pieces of human flesh, while the jackals and hyænas have been busy with the rest; they are dry bones now."

Rose tremulously clasped her white hands and shuddered.

"And those bones," was the sententious remark

of Shireen, who was listening, "not even the voice
of Ezekiel could, as we are told it once did, call
back to life, as it called the dead Israelites of
old."

"A fortunate thing for us, Khan," said the irreve-
rent Zohrab, laughingly.

"Why?"

"I mean, if the result was to be the same; for all
arose and lived for years after; and is it not written
that they moved among living men with a stench
and colour of corpses, and had to wear garments
blackened with pitch?"

"That weary Koran again!" murmured Rose;
while the Khan frowned, and, to change the subject,
said,

"Tell us, Zohrab, more about the Feringhee damsel
whom this lady deems must be her sister, and your
plans regarding her."

"I fear she could not be prevailed upon to trust
herself to me under any pretext, or to leave the
companionship of her friends in misfortune without
some assurance that she who is with you, Khan
Shireen, is indeed her sister in blood.'

"Most true," said Shireen, running his brown
fingers through his dense beard with an air of perplexity.

"Oh, that may be easily arranged," said Denzil,
full of hope at the prospect of seeing Mabel,

of the joy it would afford Rose, and the wish to
learn from her own lips all that had happened
to so many dear friends since that terrible day
when so many thousands perished, and so many
were separated never to meet more.   Thus, he
suggested that Rose should entrust Zohrab with a
note to be delivered, on the first convenient opportunity, to Mabel, or the lady who was supposed to
be she.   Zohrab did not care about her identity
the value of a cowrie-shell, provided his own plans
succeeded.

"And you shall bring her here without delay?"
said Shireen, while he knit his bushy and impending
eyebrows.

"Where else would she be safe, Khan?"

"Not with you, at all events," was the dubious
response.

Zohrab coloured perceptibly, and a covert gleam
flashed in his glossy black eyes, as he said,

"My head may answer for this project, Khan, if
I am taken."

"Taken—how? Do you mean to fly?" asked
Shireen, with another keen glance.

"Nay—nay; not if I can help it," stammered
Zohrab, who saw that the Khan's sunken eyes were
full of strange light.

"If it becomes known that she is here, the fact
will embroil me with Ackbar; but, bah! what

matter is it?" said Shireen, proudly. "The city is divided against him, and he knows I can bring five thousand red caps into the field; and she will be one more prisoner for Shireen of the Kuzzil-bashes!" he muttered under his beard. "Go then, Zohrab; go and prosper."

"May I not accompany him?" asked Denzil, eagerly, as for months he had never been beyond the wall and ditch of the fort, and he longed to make a reconnaissance with a future eye to escape.

"Nay," said Zohrab, "you know not what you propose, Sahib. Your presence would but en-cumber me, and add to the lady's peril: it is not to be thought of."

Rose added her entreaties that he would not think of it either; for she might lose her lover, and not regain her sister, so suddenly, so recently, heard of; and then an emphatic and brief command from the Khan ended the matter, so far as poor Denzil was concerned, and he felt himself compelled to succumb.

Writing materials, such as the Afghans use, the strong fibrous paper, a reed split for a pen, with deep black and perfumed Indian ink, were soon brought; and Rose, with a prayerful emotion in her fluttering heart, and a hand that more than once almost failed in its office, so great was her excite-ment, wrote a single line assuring Mabel that she,

herself, was safe, and to "confide in the bearer of
this, who would bring her to where she was residing;" and with this tiny missive—which he
placed to his lips and then to his forehead in token
of faith, while his black eyes flashed with an expression which Rose saw, but failed to analyse—safely
deposited in the folds of his turban, Zohrab took
his departure; and with a heartfelt invocation for
his success on her lips, Rose heard the sound of
the hoofs of his swift Tartar horse die away on
the road that led towards the dark rocky hills of
Siah Sung.

"Shabash! such children of burnt fathers those
Feringhees are!" said Zohrab, laughing as he galloped along. "Well, well, let me enjoy the world
ere I become the prey of the world!"

Zohrab had promised to return with the lady, or,
if without her, to bring some sure tidings, not later
than the evening of the second day; but the evening
sun of the third had reddened and died out on the
mountain peaks, the third, the fourth, the fifth, and
a whole week passed away, yet there came no word
or sign from Zohrab, and never more did he cross
the threshold of Shireen's dwelling!

Had he been discovered and slain by Saleh Mohammed, or what had happened?

Rose wept, for the tender hope, so suddenly lighted
in her impulsive heart, only to be as suddenly

extinguished; but as yet no suspicion of treachery on the part of Zohrab Zubberdust had entered the minds of her or Denzil, whatever Shireen Khan, as an Afghan naturally prone to suspicion, may have thought.

CHAPTER VIII.

MABEL DELUDED.

On receiving the note from Rose Trecarrel, the cunning Zohrab, full of his own nefarious plans, had ridden straight from the white-walled fort of Shireen Khan to that commanded by Saleh Mohammed, which is situated exactly three miles from Cabul, amid a well-cultivated country; and there, knowing well the time when, after hearing morning prayers read according to the service of the Church of England by one lady who had preserved her "Book of Common Prayer," the poor captives, with the children who were among them, were wont to take an airing in the garden, he chose the occasion; for, as he was aware, Saleh Mohammed, kneeling upon a piece of black xummul, under the shadow of a great cypress, would be also at *his* orisons, and telling over his string of ninety-nine sandal-wood beads, with his face bowed towards the *west*, as is the custom in India and Persia. The precept of the Koran is, that when men pray they shall turn towards the Kaaba, or holy house of Mecca; and, consequently, throughout the whole Moslem world, indicators are put up to enable the faithful to fulfil this stringent injunction. So selecting, we say, a time when the grim old commandant of the fort was deep in his orisons, with his head bowed, and his silver beard floating over the weapons with which his Cashmere girdle bristled—for the modern Afghan (like the Scottish Highlander of old) is never found unarmed, even by his own fireside—he made a sign to Mabel that he wished to speak with her; but he had to repeat this salaam more than once ere she understood him, as she was intently toying with and caressing a little boy, whose parents had perished in the late disasters, and who clung specially to her alone.

Mabel, pale and colourless now more than was her wont, though she never had possessed a complexion so brilliant as her sister Rose, bowed to Zohrab, whom she little more than knew by sight, and by the force of local custom was lowering her veil (for she, too, like all the rest, now wore the Afghan female dress) and turning away, when Zohrab placed a hand on his lips, and, making a motion indicative of entreaty, silence, and haste, held up the tiny note of Rose.

On this Mabel's pale cheek flushed; she hesitated, and many ideas shot swiftly through her mind, while she glanced hastily about her, to see who

observed them. Was this note some plot for her
release and the release of her friends—some political
or military stratagem? Had it tidings of her
father's burial—for she knew that he had fallen in
the Pass—of the army, of those who were in Jelalabad? Was it a love-letter? Zohrab Zubberdust
was certainly very handsome; her woman's eye ad-
mitted that. This idea occurred last of all; yet the
note might be from Waller—dear Bob Waller, with
his fair honest face and ample whiskers. All these
thoughts passed like lightning through her mind
as she took the missive, which was written on a
small piece of paper, folded triangularly and without
an address.

Then, as she opened it, a half-stifled cry of mingled
astonishment and rapture escaped her.

"Rose, it is from Rose; she yet lives! Oh, my God,
I thank Thee! I thank Thee!—she yet lives, but
where?" she exclaimed, in a voice rendered low by
excess of emotion, as she burst into tears, and read
again and again the few words her sister had written.

Zohrab was attentively observing her. He saw
how pure and beautiful she was; how unlike aught
that he had ever looked upon before—even the
fairest, softest, and most languishing maids of Iraun;
for Mabel was an English girl, above the middle
height, and fully rounded in all her proportions.
All that he had heard of houris, of those black-eyed

girls of paradise, the special care of the Angel
Zamiyad, seemed to be embodied in her who was
before him. Her quiet eyes seemed wondrously
soft, clear, and pleading in expression, to one accustomed ever to the black, beady orbs of the Orientals;
and as he gazed, he felt bewildered, bewitched by
the idea that in a little time, if he was wary, all this
fair beauty might be his—his as completely as his
horse and sabre!

"My sister! my dear, dear sister!" exclaimed
Mabel, impulsively, kissing the note and pressing
it to her breast. "Oh, I must tell of this. Lady
Sale, Lady Sale!" she exclaimed, looking around
her; but Zohrab laid a hand on her arm, and a
finger on his lip significantly.

"Lady Sahib," said he, in a low guttural voice,
" you will go with me ? "

"Yes, yes—oh yes; but how? to where?—and I
must confer with my friends and the Khan, Saleh
Mohammed."

"Nay; to do so would ruin all."

" With my friends, surely ? "

"Nay; that too would be unwise: to none."

"None ? "

"I repeat, none," said Zohrab, whose habit of
mind, like that of all Orientals, was inclined to suspicion, secresy, and mistrust.

" Why ? " asked Mabel.

"Does not your letter tell you?"

"No—but can I—ought I to—to——" she paused and glanced irresolutely towards the group of her companions in misfortune, who were generally clustered round the chief matrons of their party, Lady Sale and the widowed Lady Macnaghten; and the idea flashed upon her mind that she might be unwise to leave the shelter of their presence and society, and trust herself to this Afghan warrior. But, then, had not Rose bade her confide in him?

"Where is my sister, and with whom?" she asked.

"I can only tell you that she is in perfect safety," replied Zubberdust, unwilling in that locality to compromise himself by mentioning the name of Shireen Khan.

"I shall be silent, and go with you," said Mabel, making an effort to master her deep and varied emotions.

"When?"

"Now—this instant, if you choose."

"That is impossible. At dusk, when the sun is set, I shall be here again on this spot, and take you to her. Till then, be silent, and confide in *none*: to talk may ruin all!" said Zubberdust, whose active mind had already conceived a plan for outwitting Saleh Mohammed and his guard of Dooranees, who watched the walls of the fort from the four round towers which terminated each angle, and on each of which was mounted a nine-pounder gun taken from our old cantonments.

Too wary to remain needlessly in her company, with all her allurements, now that his pretended mission was partly performed, and thereby draw the eyes of the observant or suspicious upon them, and more particularly upon himself, he at once withdrew, leaving poor Mabel, who naturally was intensely anxious to question him further, overwhelmed by emotions which she longed eagerly to share by confidence with her friends; for news of any European, especially of one who belonged to the little circle of English society at Cabul, must prove dear and of deepest interest to them all. Yet had not this mysterious messenger impressed upon her, that if she was to see her sister, to rejoin her, and hear the story of her wonderful disappearance at the mouth of the Khyber Pass, if she would soothe, console, it might be protect her, she must be silent?

Slowly passed the day in the fort of Saleh Mohammed. The tall and leafy poplars, the slender white minars, the four towers of the fort, which was a perfect parallelogram, and the wooded and rocky hills that overlooked them all, cast their shadows across the plain (through which the Cabul winds towards the Indus) gradually in a circle, and then, when stretching far due westward, they gradually faded away; the snow-capped peaks of the Hindu-Kush, the mighty Indian Caucasus, rose cold and pale against the clear blue sky, where the stars were twinkling out in succession; and with a nervous anxiety, which she found it almost impossible to control, Mabel Trecarrel stole away, with mingled emotions, from the apartments assigned to the lady hostages—emotions of sorrow, half of shame for her silence concerning the project she had in hand, and her enforced reticence to those who loved her, and had ever been so kind to her amid their own heavy afflictions—compunction for the honest alarm her absence would certainly occasion them on the morrow; but hope and joy in the anticipated reunion with her sister soon swept all such minor thoughts away, and she longed and thirsted for the embrace and companionship of Rose, to whom, though the difference in their years was but small, she had ever been a species of mother and monitress—never so much as when in their happy English home in Cornwall, far away!

Since their strange separation on that fatal morning, when their poor father, in his despair and sorrow, galloped rearward to perish in the skirmish, how much must the pretty, the once-playful, and coquettish Rose have to tell; and how much had she, herself, to impart in return!

Her heart beat almost painfully, when, on approaching the appointed spot for the last time, she saw the figure of Zohrab Zubberdust standing quite motionless under the shadow of the great cypress, where in the morning Saleh Mohammed had knelt at prayer. He wore his steel cap (with its neck-flap of mail), on which the starlight glinted; he had a small round gilded shield slung on his back by a leather belt; his poshteen was buttoned up close to his throat, and he was, as usual, fully armed; but in one hand he carried a large, loose chogah, or man's cloak, of dull-coloured red cloth; and now Mabel felt that the decisive moment had, indeed, all but arrived: beyond that, her ideas were vague in the extreme, and her breathing became but a series of hurried and thick respirations.

"Is all safe? is all ready—prepared?" she asked, in a broken voice.

"Inshallah—all," replied the taciturn Mahommedan, who, like all of his race and religion, had few words to spare.

The idea of escaping by ladders of rope or wood had never seemed to him as possible. The walls of the fort were twenty-five feet high, and surrounded by a deep wet ditch, the water of which came by a a canal, through a rice-field, from the Cabul river. Its only gate was guarded by a party of Saleh Mohammed's men, under a Naick (or subaltern), with whom Zohrab was very intimate; and beyond or outside these barriers he had left his horse haltered (in sight of the sentinels), and so that it could not stir from the place, as the only portion of the gate which the Naick was permitted to open was the *kikree*, or wicket, through which but one at a time could pass.

Zohrab Zubberdust, scarcely daring to trust himself to look on Mabel's fair, anxious, and imploring face, lest it might bewilder him from his fixed purpose, took from his steel cap the white turban cloth he wore twisted round it, and, speedily forming it into a single turban with a falling end, placed it on her head. He enveloped her in the ample chogah, hiding half her face, gave her his sabre to place under her arm, and the simple disguise was complete; for, in the dusk now, none could perceive that she wore slippers in lieu of the brown leather jorabs or ankle-boots of the Afghans; and looking every inch a taller and perhaps a manlier Osmanlie than himself, Mabel walked leisurely by his side towards the gate, where, as watch-words, parole, and countersign were alike unknown to the guard, fortunately none were required of them; but her emotions almost stifled her, when she saw the black, keen, and glossy eyes of the Dooranees surveying her, as they leaned leisurely on their long juzails, which were furnished with socket bayonets nearly a yard in length.

She moved mechanically, like one in a dream, and

the circumstance of striking her head as she failed
to stoop low enough in passing through the wicket
added to her confusion; nor was she quite aware
that they had been permitted to pass free and un-
questioned, as two men, by the Naick, to whom
Zohrab made some jesting remark about the "awkwardness of his friend," until she saw behind her
the lofty white walls of the fort gleaming in the
pale starlight, their loopholes and outline reflected
downward in the slimy wet ditch where water-lilies
were floating in profusion.

Unhaltering his horse and mounting, her new companion desired her, with more impressiveness than
tenderness of tone—for the former was his habit,
and the moment was a perilous and exciting one—to
walk on by his side a little way, as if they were conversing, and thereby to lull any suspicion in the
minds of such Dooranees as might be observing
them; for they were still within an unpleasant distance of the long rifles of those who were posted on
the towers of the fort; and still more were they
within range of those ginjauls which are still used
in India, and are precisely similar to the swivel
wall-pieces invented long ago by Marshal Vauban,
and throw a pound ball to a vast distance.

On descending the other side of an intervening
eminence, that was covered by wild sugar-canes and
aromatic shrubs, the leaves of which were tossing

in the evening breeze, he curtly desired her to place her right foot upon his left within the stirrup-iron, and then, with the aid of his hand, he readily placed her on the holsters of his saddle before him. He now applied the spurs with vigour to his strong, active, and long-bodied Tartar horse, and, with a speed which its double burden certainly served to diminish, it began quickly to leave behind the dreaded fort of Mohammed Saleh.

As the latter began to sink and lessen in the distance, Mabel Trecarrel felt as if there was a strange and dreamy unreality about all this episode. Many an officer and Indian Sowar had ridden into the Khoord Cabul Pass with his wife or his children before him, even as she was now borne by Zohrab; she had heard and seen many wild and terrible things since her father, with other officers of the Company's service, had come, in an evil hour, "up country," to command Shah Sujah's Native Contingent; she had read and heard of many such adventures, escapes, flights, and abductions in romance and reality; but what might be her fate now, if this should prove to be the latter—an *abduction* of herself—some trick of which she had permitted herself to become the too-ready victim?

She was in a land where the people were prone to wild and predatory habits, and, moreover, were masters in trickery, cunning, and cruelty. Had she been deceived? she asked of herself, when she felt the strong, sinewy, and bony arm of Zohrab tightening round her waist, while his wiry little horse, with its fierce nose and muscular neck outstretched, and its dancing mane streaming behind like a tiny smoke-wreath, sped on and on, she knew not whither!

Had she been deceived, was the ever-recurring dread, when the handwriting was that of Rose, beyond all doubt? But written *when?* or had Rose been deluded? Was this horseman *the* person in whom she had been desired "to confide," or had he stolen the note from another?—perhaps, after killing him! Those Afghans were such subtle tricksters that she felt her mistrust equalled only by her loathing of them all.

Mabel asked herself all these tormenting questions when, perhaps, too late; and she knew that, whether armed or unarmed, Heaven had never intended her to be a heroine, or to play the part of one: she felt a conviction that she was merely "an every-day young lady," and that if "much more of this kind of thing went, she must die of fright."

Just as she came to this conclusion an involuntary cry escaped her. The boom of a cannon—one of Her Majesty's nine-pounders, of which the Khan had possessed himself—pealed out on the calm still atmosphere of the Indian evening, now deepening into

night. Another and another followed, waking the
echoes of the woods and hills; and, though distant
now, each red flash momentarily lit up the sky. They
came from the fort of Saleh Mohammed to alarm
the country; and still further to effect this and
announce the escape of a prisoner, a vast quantity
of those wonderful and beautiful crimson, blue,
green, and golden lights, in the manufacture of
which all Oriental pyrotechnists excel so particularly, were shot off·in every direction from the
walls, showering upward and downward like falling
stars, describing brilliant arcs through the cloudless
sky; and with an exclamation on his bearded mouth,
expressive of mockery and malison with fierce exultation mingled, Zohrab Zubberdust looked back for
a moment, while his black eyes flashed fire in the
reflected light.

"Hah!" he muttered, "dog of a Dooranee, may
the grave of the slave that bore thee be defiled!"

And while one hand tightened around his prize,
with the other he urged his horse to greater speed
than ever.

CHAPTER IX.

As they proceeded, past groves of drooping willows, past rows of leafy poplars, rice-fields where pools of water glittered in the starlight, and past where clumps of the flowering oleaster filled the air with delicious perfume, Mabel began to recognise the features of the landscape, and knew by the familiar locality that she was once more within a very short distance of Cabul. Again, in the light of the rising moon, as she sailed, white and silvery, above the black jagged crests of the Siah Sung, Mabel Trecarrel could recognise the burned and devastated cantonments, where in flame and ruin the fragile bungalows, the compounds of once-trim hedgerows, and all, had passed away,—the bare boundary walls and angular bastions alone remaining. She saw the site of her father's pretty villa, a place of so many pleasant and happy memories—the daily lounge of all the young officers of the garrison; and there, too, were the remains of the Residency, where Sir William Macnaghten, as

the Queen's representative, dispensed hospitality to
all. Yonder were the hills and village of Beymaru;
and further off a few red lights that twinkled high
in air announced the Bala Hissar, the present residence of Ackbar Khan; but to take her in *that*
direction formed then no part of the plans of Zohrab
Zubberdust.

He rode straight towards a lonely place which lay
between the Beymaru Hills and the Lake of Istaliff;
and as the locality grew more and more sequestered
he slackened the speed of his horse, now weary and
foam-flaked. After a time he drew up, and, request-
ing her to alight, lifted her to the ground, and politely
and gently urged her to rest herself for a little space.

"My sister?" said Mabel, tremulously.

"Is not here," replied he.

"But where, then?"

"Patience yet a while," said he with a smile,
which she could not perceive; while he, to be prepared for any emergency, proceeded at once to shift
his saddle, rub down his horse with a handful of
dry grass, give it a mouthful or two from a certain
kind of cake which he carried in his girdle; and
then he looked to his bridle, stirrup-leather, and
the charges of his pistols. Accustomed to arms and
strife of late, Mabel looked quietly on, taking all
the preparations for uncertain contingencies as
mere matters of course.

Breathless and weary with her strange mode of progression, she had seated herself on a stone close by; and while the careful rider was grooming his steed and making him drink a little of the shining waters of the long narrow lake, she looked anxiously around her, surmising when or in what manner of habitation she should find her sister. Not a house or homestead, not even the black tent of a mountain shepherd, was in sight. On all sides the lonely green and silent hills towered up in the quiet moonlight, and the still, calm lake reflected their undulating outlines downward in its starry depth.

The holly-oak, the wild almond, and the khinjuck tree, which distils myrrh, and in that warlike land of cuts and slashes is in great repute for healing sabre wounds, the homely dog-rose, the sweet-briar, the juniper bush, and the wild geranium, all grew among the clefts of the rocks in luxuriant masses; while sheets of wild tulips waved their gorgeous cups among the green sedges by the lake.

Not far from where she sat was a grove, which she remembered to have been the scene of a once-happy picnic party, of which Bob Waller was one. She recognised the place now. She knew it was a lonely solitude, that in summer was ever full of the perfume of dewy branches, fresh leaves, and opening flowers; but the immediate spot where they had halted had been anciently used as a burying-ground.

A portion of an old temple, covered by luxuriant creepers, lay there, and two magnificent cypresses still towered skyward amid the half-flattened mounds and sinking grave-stones of the long-forgotten dead. The remains of a little musjid, or place for prayer, long since ruined by some savage and idolatrous Khonds, who came down from the hills, lay there among the débris, which included a shattered well, built by some pious Moslem of old. The water from it gurgled past her feet towards the lake, and she remembered how Waller had placed the bottles of champagne and red Cabul wine in the runnel to cool them.

And now, as if contrasting the joyous past with the bitter present, a shudder came over Mabel. She held out her pale hand, which looked like ivory in the moonlight, and said to Zohrab, as he approached her—

"It is a gloomy place, this. Is my sister far from here?"

"About five coss," said he, confidently; and he spoke the truth, and charmed by seeing her outstretched hand, an action which betokened reliance or trust—he flattered himself, perhaps, regard—he took a seat by her side, and then Mabel began to view him with positive distrust and uneasiness. She said—

"Five coss—ten miles yet! Let us go at once, then!"

" Stay," said he, " let us rest a little. You are—nay, must be weary ;" and arresting her attempt to rise with a hand upon her arm, he drew nearer her ; and sooth to say, though he was confident in bearing, bravely embroidered in apparel, and had a handsome exterior, Zohrab Zubberdust was but an indifferent love-maker, and knew not how to go about it, with a "Feringhee mem sahib " least of all. He was puzzled, and made a pause, during which Mabel's large, clear, grey eyes regarded him curiously, warily, and half sternly.

As the mistress of her father's late extensive household, with its great retinue of native servants (each of whom had half a dozen others to perform his or her work), and, as such, coming hourly in contact with the dealers and others in the bazaars and elsewhere, Mabel Trecarrel had, of necessity, picked up a knowledge of the Hindostanee and the Afghan, far beyond her heedless sister Rose, who, as these were neither the languages of flirtation or the flowers, scarcely made any attempt to do so; hence Mabel could converse with Zohrab with considerable fluency.

Her beauty was as soft and as bright as that of Rose, but it was less girlish and of a much higher and more statuesque character; so " Zohrab the Overbearing " now felt himself rather at a loss to account for the emotion of awe—we have no other name for it—with which she inspired him. The point, the time, and the place when he should have her all to himself had arrived, true to all his calculations and beyond his hopes; and yet his tongue and spirit failed him, as if a spell were upon him.

In his lawless roving life, now serving the Khan of Khiva, on the eastern shores of the Caspian Sea, now the Emir of Bhokara, far away beyond the waters of the Oxus, and lastly Ackbar Khan, he had, in predatory war, carried off many a girl with all her wealth of bracelets and bangles, the spoil of his spear and sabre, trussing her up behind him like the fodder or oats for his Tartar nag; but never had he felt before as he did now, for, unlike the maids of the desert, the Feringhee failed to accept the situation. He felt perplexed— secretly enraged, and yet he murmured half to him- self and half to her, as his dark face and darker gleaming eyes drew nearer hers—

" The whiteness of her bosom surpasses the egg of the ostrich or the leaf of the lily, and her breath is sweét as the roses of Irem—yea, as those of Zulistan! Listen to me," he added abruptly, in a louder and sharper tone, and in his figurative language; "fair daughter of love, give ear. You have won my heart, my love, my soul, subduing me—even Zohrab! Learn in turn to be subdued, submissive, and obedient. Happy is he who shall call you wife; and that happy man—is Zohrab!"

The intense bewilderment of poor Mabel increased to extreme fear at those words, so absurdly inflated, yet so blunt in import, and she shrunk back, but could not turn from the dark, glittering eyes that gleamed with a serpent-like fascination into hers.

So she *had* been deluded after all, and her worst anticipations were about to be realised at last! Zohrab grasped her left hand with his right, and planting his left cheek on the other hand, with an elbow on his knee, began to take courage, and, surveying her steadily, to speak more distinctly and with an admiring smile; for the silence of the night was around them, and no sound came on the wind that moaned past the grove or the great cypresses close by; so from the silence, perhaps, he gathered confidence, if, indeed, he really required it.

"Allah has been good to us," said he, "exceedingly good, in creating such beautiful beings as women to please us. You are more beautiful than any I have seen—too much so to be left to gladden a Kaffir's heart; so you shall remain with me, and be the light of my eyes."

"Wretch!—fool that I have been! Rose, Rose!" gasped Mabel, scarcely knowing what she said.

" I love you," he resumed softly, while his hot'
clasp tightened on her hand, and his lips approached
her ear; "you hear—and understand me?"

" *You* love me!" exclaimed Mabel rashly, with
proud scorn in her tone, despite the deadly fear
that gathered in her heart, and while her eyes
flashed with an expression to which the Oriental
was quite unaccustomed in a captive woman.

"Yes, I love you—I, Zohrab," was the somewhat egotistical response.

" You know not what love is; but, even if you
did, you shall not dare to talk of it to me. That
you may have a fancy, I can quite well understand;
but a fancy, or a passion, and love are very different things. What do you, or what can you,
know of me?"

" That you are beautiful: what more is required?"

" Enough of this—I am weary. Take me instantly to my sister, or back to my friends who
are with Saleh Mohammed; for if I were to denounce you to Ackbar Khan, how much think you
your head would be worth?"

" Much less than yours, certainly."

" And at what does he—this *other* barbarian—
value me?"

" At the price of six Toorkoman horses, perhaps," was the half-angry response; " while to me

you are priceless, beyond life itself. Denounce me to Ackbar Khan—would you ? "

" Yes."

His teeth glistened under his jet moustache as he replied—

" Those stones and trees alone hear us ; so now let me tell you, Kaffir girl, that you weary me ; by the five blessed Keys of Knowledge, you do ! " and, as he spoke, he started to his feet, and by an angry twist of his embroidered girdle threw his jewelled sabre behind him.

" Oh, this is becoming frightful ! " moaned Mabel, clasping her hands and looking wildly round her; " what will become of me now ? Papa, Rose, are we never to meet again ? "

Oh, if big, burly Bob Waller, with his six feet and odd inches of stature, were only there ! Could he but know of her misery of mind—her dire extremity! but would he ever know ? God alone could tell !

There is much that is touching in the helplessness of any woman, but more than all a beautiful one, though we, whose lines are cast in pleasant places, and in a land of well-organized police, may seldom see it—a clinging, imploring expression of eye, when all is soul and depth of heart, and strength avails not. But Zohrab Zubberdust felt nothing of this. She on whom he looked might be pure as Diana, " chaste as Eve on the morning of her inno-

cence," yet, as a Mohammedan, he had a secret
contempt for her—perhaps a doubt of her—as a
Kaffir woman. He was only inspired by the emotions of triumph and passion, by the sure conviction that this fair Feringhee, this daughter of a
vanquished tribe, this outcast unbeliever, so lovely '
in her whiteness of skin, her purity of complexion,
and wondrous colour of hair, in her roundness of
limb, and in stature so far surpassing all the maids
of the twenty-one Afghan clans or races, was his—
his property—to become the slave of his will or his
cruelty, as it pleased him !

Of the paradox that woman's weakness is her
strength, with the Christian man, Zohrab knew
nothing, and felt less ; yet he tried to act the lover
in a melodramatic fashion, by making high-flown
speeches, and assuring her, again and again, that he
loved her " as the only Prophet of God loved
Ayesha, his favourite wife, the mother of all the
Faithful," and much more to the same purpose, till
amid the wind that sighed through the trees, and
shook the wild tulips and lilies by the lake, the
quickened ear of Mabel caught a distant sound; and
then one of those shrill cries of despair, that women
alone can give, escaped her.

A fierce malediction from the lips of Zohrab
mingled with it, for he dreaded Saleh Mohammed;
and in a few moments more the clink of hoofs was

heard; then Zohrab sternly drew a pistol from his girdle, and unsheathed his sabre like a flash of fire in the moonlight. The blade glittered like his own eyes, as he glared alternately from Mabel to where the sounds came; and by his keen, wild expression and fierce quivering nostrils, she saw with terror, that a very slight matter might turn his wrath and his weapons against herself.

"Here comes aid—Saleh Mohammed perhaps! Help, help, in the name of God!" she cried, recklessly.

Zohrab uttered a sound like a hiss, and placed the cold back of his sabre across her throat, implying thereby, "Silence, or death;" and at that instant, four Afghan horsemen came galloping up, and reined in their nags.

"Bismillah," said the leader, a venerable, burly, and silver-bearded man, in a huge turban.

"Bismillah," responded Zohrab, using also the expression of salutation customary to the country (and which means no more than "good evening" or "good e'en" may do with us), yet regarding the stranger with a somewhat resentful and tiger-like expression of eye for his unwelcome interruption.

"What, Zohrab Zubberdust, is this thou?" exclaimed the other.

"Shabash—it is I; and you—are Nouradeen Lal!" said the would-be lover, as he recognised his acquaintance, the hill-farmer, whose ploughman, perforce, Waller had been; "whence come you?"

"From Cabul, where I have been with many an arroba of corn for the Sirdir, who expects to be besieged by the Kaffirs from Jelallabad. Oh! and so you are at your old tricks again," continued the farmer, with a somewhat unoriental burst of laughter; "you are not content to wait for the spouses of musk and amber in their couches of pearl—the black-eyed girls with their scarfs of green!"

"Allah Keerem, but he is fortunate," said another, looking admiringly on Mabel; "most fortunate! She is fair and white as the virgins of paradise can be."

"But her cry sounded like the bay of a goorg to the rising moon; and we thought you were an afreet—the Ghoul Babian, or some such horror; for here are graves close by!"

"Nouradeen Lal is not complimentary," said the other speaker, who, by his steel cap, spear, and shield of rhinoceros hide, seemed to be a Hazir-bashi, or one of Ackbar's body-guard, "if he compare the damsel's voice to the cry of a wolf."

"But why *did* she cry? You were not ill-using her, I hope," said the old farmer, peering down at Mabel's face from under his broad circular turban.

"For the love of God—your God as well as mine—save me from this man!" said Mabel, clinging to the stirrup-leather of the farmer, whose venerable appearance encouraged her, and who placed his strong brown hand on her head encouragingly and protectingly.

"I dare you to interfere!" exclaimed Zohrab, hoarse with passion, as he drew from his girdle the long brass pistol he had just half cocked and replaced there.

"And why so?" asked the Hazir-bashi, who seemed quite ready for a brawl, and perhaps the appropriation of the girl.

"Because she is—my wife."

"Your wife!" exclaimed Nouradeen, withdrawing his hand abruptly, and swerving round his horse, so that Mabel nearly fell to the ground.

"Yes; we were married before the Cadi: and now she would seek to repudiate me, and return to her own accursed people," said the artful Zohrab; for marriage among the Mohammedans is exclusively a civil ceremony, performed before a Cadi, or magistrate, and not by an Imaum or any other minister of religion, with which it has nothing to do.

"Oh, believe not a word of this; it is false—false!" implored Mabel, with desperation in her tone.

"It is true; and thou, Kaffir, liest! Silence, silence, or I will kill thee!" hissed Zohrab in her ear; and she felt that he was but too capable of putting his threat into execution. "Interfere not with us, I charge you; but leave us, and remember what the fourth chapter of the Koran says, 'If a woman fear ill-usage or aversion from her husband, it shall be no crime in them if they settle the matter amicably between themselves; for a reconciliation is better than a separation;' therefore leave us to agree amicably, as the Prophet hath advised."

"And the same chapter, good Zohrab, tells us how we may chastise such wives as are contumacious, and those captives, too, whom our right hand may possess," said the farmer; "so farewell, and may the steps of you both be fortunate," he added, as he and his three companions galloped laughingly away, and with a wail, as if from her heart, Mabel found herself alone once more in the moonlight solitude— alone with her unscrupulous companion.

CHAPTER X.

A CHANGE had now come over him; he had grown sullen and thoughtful; but even this mood of mind she preferred to his obnoxious and intrusive tenderness. He stood silently and gloomily eyeing her for a time.

Will it be believed that, too probably, he was actually pondering whether or not policy and his own future safety required that he should pistol or sabre this helpless creature, whom a minute before he had been professing so ardently to love? He could not help speculating on what *might* have been the sequel, regarding himself, had her wild and despairing cry, instead of bringing up a stupid old mountain farmer, like Nouradeen Lal, summoned to the spot the ferocious Dooranee horsemen of Saleh Mohammed, who was bound to account for the prisoners, dead or alive, body for body, to Ackbar Khan. He knew that by this time all the roads diverging from Cabul would be beset in every direction by the horsemen of Saleh Mohammed and

the Sirdir; that, sooner or later, some of these
would meet and question the farmer returning to
his home among the hills, and the information he
and the Hazir-bashi must give, would soon bring a
mounted Rissallah round by Beymaru in search
and pursuit; so his own bold measures were instantly
taken.

In Cabul would he and his prize alone be safe,
and, as he hoped, unsought for a time at least; and
there he resolved to convey her, ere day broke, and
to conceal her in the house of one who he knew
would be faithful to him—a man named Ferishta
Lodi, who had been sutler to the Shah's Goorka
Regiment, and whose life he had spared, and whōse
escape he had connived at, when the whole of that
luckless battalion was massacred in cold blood, by
the Afghans at Charekar.

Sternly he commanded her again to mount before
him, and, aware that resistance and entreaty were
alike futile, the unhappy girl, crushed in spirit,
weeping heavily, and feeling utterly lost and helpless, obeyed; and once more their progress was
resumed, but at a slower pace, as Zohrab was
evidently husbanding the strength of his wearied
horse. Day was breaking as they passed, un-
questioned, through the Kohistan Gate of Cabul;
but its light was yet grey and dim as they traversed
the narrow, dark, and high-walled tortuous streets,

to some obscure quarter perfectly unknown to Mabel.

A few persons passed them, some going to market in the Char-chowk, others afield·to tend the trellised vines ; but she dared neither speak nor show her pallid face. She might find mercy at the hands of Zohrab, but none among the rabble of Cabul, where the miserable remains of the Queen's Envoy yet hung unburied in the great bazaar.

Mabel knew but too well, by observation and experience, the nature of the nation among whom she now found herself—alone. Nearly forty years had made no change on the people, since a Scottish traveller described them ; and his pithy account may be summed up in the following quotation :—

"If a man could be transported to Afghanistan without passing through the dominions of Turkey, Persia, or Tartary, he would be amazed by the wide and unfrequented deserts and the mountains covered with perennial snow. Even in the culti- vated part of the country he would discover a wild assemblage of hills and wastes, unmarked by en- closures, not embellished by trees, and destitute of navigable canals, public roads, and all the great and elaborate productions of human refinement and industry. He would find the towns few and far distant from each other ; he would look in vain for inns and other conveniences, which a traveller would

meet with in the wildest parts of Great Britain.
Yet he would sometimes be delighted with the fer-
tility and population of particular plains and valleys,
where he would see the productions of Europe
mingled in profusion with those of the torrid zone,
and the land tilled with an industry and judgment
nowhere surpassed.   He would see the inhabitants
accompanying their flocks in tents or villages, to
which the terraced roofs and mud walls give an
appearance entirely novel.   He would be struck
with their high and harsh features, their sun-burnt
countenances, their long beards, loose garments,
and shaggy cloaks of skins.   When he entered into
society, he would notice the absence of all courts of
justice, and of everything like an organised police.
He would be surprised at the fluctuation and utter
instability of every civil institution.   He would find
it difficult to comprehend how a nation could sub-
sist in such disorder, and pity those who were compelled to pass their days amid such scenes, and
whose minds were trained by their unhappy situation to fraud and violence, to rapine, deceit, and
cruel revenge.   Yet he could not fail to admire
their lofty and martial spirit, their hospitality,
their bold and simple manners, equally removed
from the suppleness of the citizen and the rusticity
of the clown.   In short," he adds, a stormy inde-
pendence of spirit, which leads them to declare,

" 'We are content with fierce discord; we are content with alarm; we are content with bloodshed; but we shall *never be content* with a master!' "

Mabel gave herself up more than ever for lost on finding herself within the fatal walls of Cabul; a benumbed and despairing emotion crept over her heart, and all her energies seemed away from her. She found herself lifted from horseback in a paved court that was dark, damp, and gloomy, and in the centre of which a fountain was plashing monotonously. She felt herself borne indoors somewhere, she knew not by whom, and then she fainted for a little time.

She had been carried into one of those apartments which open by a large sliding panel off the dewan-khaneh, the principal hall or receiving-room of a Cabul house. She had been there deposited at length on a soft mattrass, which was simply spread on the floor, as in that country bedsteads and sofas are unlike unknown. So people there both sleep and sit on the floor, unless in the case of persons of rank, who may seat themselves cross-legged on a divan.

Though prettily ornamented with carving, stucco, and painting, in this room there was a total absence of those invariable sentences from the Koran, woven among arabesques, which mark an Oriental mansion; but in lieu thereof were some in a language of which Mabel's weary eyes could make nothing.

These were lines from the Vedas of the Hindoos;
and in three little niches, most elaborately carved,
were the three monstrous statuettes of the god who
is worshipped by so many millions under the names
of Vishnu, Siva, and Brama; for the house to which
she had been conveyed belonged partly to Ferishta
Lodi, the ex-Sutler, who now kept a shop in the
great bazaar, and to a Hindoo, one of those same
schroffs, or bankers, through whom the luckless
General Elphinstone and his staff had negotiated
the enormous sum which was paid to procure our
peaceful march through the Passes—and paid for
our slaughtered troops—in vain.

The Hindoo banker and the Khond were alike
absent; but the wife of the former, a soft-eyed and
gentle little woman, with massive golden bangles on
her wrists and glittering anklets round her ankles,
assisted the somewhat awkward and decidedly bewildered Zohrab in the task of recovering Mabel, by
plentifully besprinkling her face, neck, and hands
with cool and delightfully perfumed water from a
large flask covered with elaborate silver filagree
work. The Hindoo woman, who knew that the
visitor was a helpless Feringhee captive, worked at
her humane duty in silence, and without venturing
to ask any questions.

A quivering of the long eyelashes, a spasmodic
twitching of the handsomely cut mouth, as she

heaved a long and deep sigh, showed that animation was returning. Slowly, indeed, did Mabel—though a girl with naturally a good physique and splendid constitution—struggle back to life and consciousness. Her beautiful face was pale as marble now; all complexion, save that of alabaster, was gone; cold and white she was, and her brilliant auburn hair in silky masses rolled over her shoulders and bosom, which heaved painfully, for every respiration was a sigh.

To the admiring and undoubtedly appreciative eyes of the enterprising Zohrab she presented a powerful contrast to the dusky little Hindoo woman, on whose ridgy shoulder her head was drooping, and whose fingers, of bronze-like hue, seemed absolutely black when placed upon the pure snowy arm of the English girl; for in aspect, race, and costume (a shapeless and indescribable garment of red cotton) the wife of the schroff was unchanged from what her ancestors had been in the days of Menou the Lawgiver.

As Mabel gradually became conscious, she sat up and gently repelled the services of the Hindoo woman. Then she burst into tears. This relieved her; and then she began to look around her, and to remember where she was—in fatal Cabul; and in whose hands—those of the lying, treacherous, and unscrupulous Zohrab Zubberdust!

For what was she yet reserved? This was her first thought. The slender chances of escape were the next; but escape from walled and guarded Cabul! and to where or to whom could she go for succour? To the bones of the dead, who lay in the passes of the Khyber mountains!

Thirst—intense thirst, the result of over-wrought emotions, of deep and bitter anxiety, and of all she had undergone mentally and bodily, made her ask Zohrab imploringly for something to quench it; and in a few moments the Hindoo woman brought her, on a scarlet Burmese salver, a china cup filled with deliciously iced water and white Cabul wine, which is not unlike full-bodied Madeira; with this refreshing beverage was a cake of Cabul apricots, folded in rice paper, the most luscious of all dried fruit, and which the Afghans have no less than fourteen distinct modes of conserving. To these she added a small slice of sweet Bokhara melon—the true melon of Toorkistan—we say a small slice, as they are of such enormous bulk, that *two* are sometimes a sufficient load for a donkey.

Revived by these delicate viands, and feeling a necessity for action, Mabel began in plaintive and piteous accents to urge upon Zohrab the chances of pecuniary reward, if he would set her at liberty near Jelalabad, or if he would even restore her to the perilous guardianship of Saleh Mohammed; for to be once more among the English hostages, his prisoners, was to be, at least, among dear friends.

But Zohrab listened in sullen and tantalising silence, gnawing the curled ends of his long moustaches the while. Now that he had her in Cabul, he saw but slender chances of getting her out of it for a time. Gossips might speak of her presence there (was it not already known to the Hindoo woman?), and so inculpate him with Ackbar Khan, whose vengeance would be swift, sharp, and sure. And now he was beginning to revolve in his own mind, whether or not his best policy would be to take his horse and quit the country for Khiva, Cashmere, or Beloochistan—all were many miles away, the latter three hundred and more—leaving Mabel in the hands of the banker and merchant, to keep or deliver up, as they chose. Yet when he thought of the peculiar *creed* of the Khond he shuddered; and she looked so beautiful, so gentle, and was withal so helpless, that he wavered in his selfish purpose, and the temptation of hoping to win her made him pause in forming any decided resolution; so the noon of the first day passed slowly and uneventfully on.

He knew that Mabel, as an European woman, dared make no attempt to escape, or even to show her face at a window; so he had no necessity either to watch or to warn her when he left her.

In tears and silence she lay on her pallet, her head propped upon pillows; near her the Hindoo woman had kindly placed a vase of fresh flowers, a feather fan, and a flask of essences; and then, left to herself for hours, she could but wait, and weep, and pray at intervals, dreading the coming night.

Some of the sounds without in Cabul were not unfamiliar to her; she had often heard them before, when driving through the central street in the carriage, or when riding with the other ladies of the garrison. Again, at stated times, she heard the shrill cries from the minarets and summits of the mosques proclaim that the hour for prayer had arrived; for the Moslems observe this frequently daily. "Glorify God," says the Koran, "when the evening overtaketh you, and when you rise in the morning; and unto Him be praise in heaven and on earth; and at sunset, and when you rest at noon, for prayer is the pillar of religion, and key of paradise."

Once she peeped forth between the parted shutters and blinds, shrinking back timidly as she did so, lest her pale white face should catch a casual passer's eye, and elicit a yell of recognition and of thirst for Christian blood. There the street below was dark and narrow; the clumsy wooden pipes projected far over, to carry off the rain from the roofs, which were flat and terraced; the walls were high, black, and almost windowless. Such was her view on one side. The other opened to a paved court, overlooked by houses built of sun-dried brick, rough stones, and red clay. Four mulberry-trees grew there, with a white marble fountain in the midst; and near it were some grizzly-bearded Afghans of mature years, in long, flowing garments, smoking and playing marbles, exactly as children do in Europe. Another party, also of full-grown men, were hopping against each other, on their right legs, grasping their left feet with their right hands. They seemed all pleasant fellows, hilarious and in high good humour; yet she dared neither to seek their aid, nor to trust to their compassion. In her eyes, they were but as so many tigers at play!

The circumstance of her being deemed the prisoner, the slave, or peculiar property of such a formidable soldier as Zohrab Zubberdust secured her from all interruption on the part of his male friends, the Khond and the Hindoo schroff, who jointly occupied the house in which he had placed her, and which was situated at the bottom of a narrow alley (opening off the main street that led to the Char Chowk, or great bazaar), a regular *cul-de-sac*, where many Khonds lived together, congregating precisely as the Irish do in the towns of England and Scotland; but this was deemed no peculiarity in Cabul, where the city was apportioned in quarters, to the different tribes of the Afghan people, the most formidably fortified being that of the Kuzzilbashes.

As evening drew on, Mabel became aware of a conversation that was proceeding in the next room; and, as she could from time to time detect the voice of Zohrab, she thought herself fully excusable in listening, which she could do with ease, as the partitions of the apartments which opened off the dewan-khaneh were all of them boarding panelled.

In one place a knot had dropped out, and to the convenient orifice made thereby, as she breathlessly applied her ear and eye alternately, she heard and saw all that was passing, and in some respects more than she cared to know, as much that she did hear only added to her repugnance and terror of those on whose mercy she found herself cast by an unhappy fate.

CHAPTER XI.

THE ABODE OF THE KHOND.

SEATED on the floor were Zohrab Zubberdust and two other men.

One was the Hindoo banker. He was slight in figure, with diminutive hands and feet; like all his vast race, he was of a dark-brown colour, with straight black hair, that seemed almost blue when the light struck it, hanging straight and lankly behind his large ears—an undoubted worshipper of Brama, of the monkey god, and of all those unnumbered idols that for forty centuries have been the objects of adoration to millions upon millions—even before the Temple of Juggernaut was built. He sat cross-legged on a *nummud*, or carpet of red frieze, above which was spread a yellow calico covering. A cushion supported his back. He had cast off his head-dress, slippers, and tunic—the day had been warm —and all save his loose dhottee, or what passed for unmentionables. He had the eye of Siva painted in the centre of his forehead (the eye that, by winking once, involved the world in darkness for a thousand years), thereby adding to the diabolical grotesquerie of his visage ; and he was occupied from time to time by indulgence in the " eighth sensual delight" of the Hindoos—chewing betel-nut, a hot and aromatic stimulant.

The other interesting native of India who sat beside him, smoking hempseed and bhang in a handsome hubble-bubble, which had snake-like coils covered with red and gold-coloured thread rising from a stem of silver, shaped like a trumpet, was Ferishta Lodi, the Khond, whose attire consisted of little more than the amount indulged in by his Hindoo friend ; but, unlike the puny latter, he was a man of powerful and muscular frame, great in stature, and terribly hideous in face and figure. He was rather pale-complexioned, for a Khond ; but his visage bars description, for ugliness of contour and expression,—it was that of a tiger, but a tiger pitted with small-pox, the few wiry bristles of his moustache that stuck fiercely out from his long, upper lip, the fiery carbuncular red of his eyes, with two long and sharp side tusks, completing the illu-sion or resemblance.

Looking wonderfully handsome by contrast to those two men, Zohrab lounged between them, propped against the wall by a soft cushion ; his bright steel cap, his beautiful Persian sabre, and gilded pistols lay near him ; he had a long cherry-

pipe stick in his mouth, and close by was a flask of
Cabul wine, in which, natheless the wise precepts of
Him of Mecca, he was indulging, greatly to Mabel's
apprehension, somewhat freely.

"And so, Ferishta," said he, "the infernal
Kuzzilbashes are in search of me too, you
say?"

"Yes—aga; three rissallahs, at least."

"From where?"

"Shireen's fort."

"And led by whom?"

"The Khan Shireen in person."

"But how know you that they are after me?"

"Because I heard Shireen say, when he met
Mohammed Saleh near Baber's tomb, that had he
not been certain that the false plotter was Over-
hearing Zohrab, he might imagine that an evil
spirit, like Sakkar, had assumed his shape and voice,
to delude them both, and the Feringhee woman
too. But that is all bosh; for who believes in such
things now?"

The dark eyes of Zohrab sparkled dangerously.
He might have pardoned some such slighting speech
in a devout Hindoo, even in a Christian; but in a
Jew, or one professing the horrible tenets of a
Khond, he could not let it pass without remark.

"Dare you say that the evil spirit, Sakkar, did not
once assume the shape of Solomon, on possessing

himself of his magic signet, and alter all the laws of the world for forty days and nights?"

"I dare say nothing about it," replied the other, sulkily: "I am a Khond."

"And, as such, accursed of God!" muttered Zohrab, under his teeth; for at that precise juncture of his affairs he could afford to quarrel with none— his present hosts least of all.

The banker looked uneasy, and crammed into his mouth an extra allowance of the eighth delight, ever the solace of the Hindoo race, and held in such estimation that Ferishta, the Moslem historian, writing in 1609, when describing the magnitude of the Indian city of Canaye, says that it contained thirty thousand shops for the sale of betel-nut alone.

Zohrab, though he sometimes broke the laws of the Koran, just as many an excellent Christian, or one who perfectly believes himself to be such, may transgress the laws of his Bible, loathed the unbelieving Khond, as he should have loathed a Jew or a fire-worshipping Gueber; but, circumstanced as he was, he felt himself compelled to listen to a speech like the following; for the Khonds are a low race of idolaters, and glory in announcing themselves as such, and in decrying the gentler creeds of others.

"The faith of your prophet would never have suited us, Aga Zohrab, though we cannot say, like

the Bedouins, we have no water in the desert, and
therefore cannot perform ablutions, as we have wells,
and to spare, in our sacred groves ; but like those
Bedouins, our people, who dwell in rocks and on
the mountains, have no money, therefore we cannot
give alms ; while the forty days' fast of Ramadan
must prove useless to poor people who fast all the
year round ; and if the presence of God be every-
where, why go all the way to seek Him in a black
stone at Mecca ? Besides, your prophet, like that
of the Feringhees, teaches, I am told, repentance—a
perilous institute, for may not a man say, 'I may
commit a thousand crimes, and, if I repent me, I
may be forgiven ; and as it will thus be no worse
for me, I may as well continue to sin and enjoy
myself even unto the end !' Is it not so, aga ?"

Zohrab, more of a soldier than a logician, and
readier with his sabre than his tongue, was unable
quite to follow the strange argument of the Khond;
he could only glare at him with bent brows and
dilated nostrils, while asserting angrily that which
had nothing exactly to do with the matter—that he
believed devoutly in the power and miracles of his
Prophet—that the waters gushed at will from the
fingers of the latter—that he was conveyed by a
mysterious animal, called a Borak, from Mecca to
Jerusalem—that in one night he performed a
journey of ten thousand years—that a holy pigeon,

sent from heaven, whispered revelations in his ear,
—not to pick peas thereat, as the accursed Kaffirs
asserted,—that he proselytised the Genii, and did
many more incredible things: to all of which the
Hindoo, whose beliefs were altogether of a different
kind, listened with the stolid aspect of one of his
own bronze idols; but the Khond did so with covert
mockery on his terrible face; while poor Mabel
dreaded a growing quarrel, as it was evident that
the fiery and impatient Zohrab abhorred the companionship and protection of Ferishta Lodi; for he
was a reckless soldier, valuing his own life little, and
the lives of others less.

It was evident that, in the heat of the present
discussion, he had forgotten all about *her*, till suddenly the Khond said—

"We talk too loud, aga, and may be overheard.
I told you who were on your track——"

"Yes; and by the eight gates of paradise, and
the seven gates of hell, I am not likely to forget
them!"

"Well, have you taken means to ensure flight?"

"Wherefor?" asked Zohrab fiercely.

"I mean, if traced."

"I have my sword and horse," was the curt reply.

"But the Feringhee woman?"

"Allah! I had all but forgotten her!" said
Zohrab, starting.

" Right: sacrifice your property for your life, and your life for your religion ; but make not yourself the captive of a woman. Now, if traced, what, I ask, of the Kaffir slave ? "

" By the soul of the Prophet!" exclaimed Zohrab, in great and sudden perplexity, "what can I do, but leave her here ? "

" Sell her to the young Shah: she is worth a thousand mohurs," suggested the Hindoo banker.

" The coward has fled," said Zohrab.

" She is beautiful as the one he lost, and whom he mourned so much that it required the whole seraglio to console him."

" Poor fellow !" sneered Zohrab.

" I will buy her of you for two hundred tomauns, paid down," said the Khond. "Money is useful to those who are fugitives."

" Buy her — for a wife ? " asked Zubberdust, changing colour. The Khond laughed; and his laugh was as the growl of some strange animal, as he replied—

" No: a Khond marries a Khond."

" For what, then ? "

" The purposes of that religion we have been discussing just now," replied the other, deliberately and in a low voice.

Mabel heard this suggestion without exactly com- prehending what it meant at the time; but she

could see that a crimson flush of shame and passion came over the dark face of Zohrab; his eyes
literally sparkled and flashed with the fury of deep
and sudden passion, as he sprang to his feet,
snatched up his sabre and half drew it, choking
with intensity of utterance, ere he could speak;
for the Khonds are a race of cruel and barbarous
idolaters, who live in the more inaccessible mountain ranges of India, and were quite unknown till
the beginning of her present Majesty's reign, when,
by the military operations undertaken in Goomsoor
and on the Chilka Lake—a long and narrow inlet
from the sea—and when our troops from thence
ascended the range of Ghauts, we made the acquaintance of this most ancient but hitherto unknown race of aborigines, whose religion, a distinct
Theism, with a subordinate demonology, requires
(as Captain Macpherson first discovered) a human
sacrifice periodically to the godhead, the fetish
or spirit whom they style Boora Penna, or the
Source of Good, who created all things by casting
five handfuls of earth around him; but, like more
enlightened folks, the Khonds have their schismatics
and sceptics, who dispute bitterly, and hate each
other as cordially as Christians can do,—but about
the origin of mountains, meteors, and whirlwinds,
where the rivers come from, where they go to, and
so forth.

It is to Tari, the wife of this Boora Penna, that the propitiatory human sacrifices are periodically offered (in groves which are dark, gloomy, and deemed holy as those of our Druids were in Europe), amid the most horrible rites, roasting over a slow fire, for one, about the time when the ground is cropped, so that each family may procure and bury a little of the victim's flesh in the soil, to ensure prosperity, and avert the malignity of the goddess, who otherwise might blast their rice, maize, or vines; and the immolation takes place amid wild jollity, deep drunkenness, and debauchery.

Aware of the complete isolation and helplessness of Mabel, the Khond saw how readily and easily he had a victim at hand; and what could prove more acceptable to Tari than the young, beautiful, and pure daughter of an alien race and creed? And the Hindoo schroff, accustomed to the incessant infanticide practised by his people, and their death-festivals at Juggernaut, saw nothing remarkable in the matter, and sat chewing his betel-nut with perfect equanimity.

Not so Zohrab Zubberdust! His passion knew no bounds. He had sprung to his feet, and fully unsheathed his sabre.

"May thy mother's grave be defiled—if indeed such be possible, O dog of an idolater!" he exclaimed, and was about to cut him down; and doubtless might have sliced his head in two, like a pumpkin, but for sudden sounds in the now partially darkened street without, that arrested the unlifted sabre.

These were the loud murmur of a multitude, the barking of pariah dogs, the trampling of horses, the voices of men in authority, and other undoubted tokens of the house being surrounded.

The glittering blade of Zohrab drooped for a moment. He passed his left hand across his brow. Then he smiled with proud disdain as he placed his steel cap on his head, and twisted the turban-cloth around it. Next he drew a pistol from his belt, while the diminutive Hindoo became pea-green with fear, and an expression of almost mad ferocity seemed to pass over the face and to swell the great chest of the Khond, Ferishta Lodi. Danger and death were at hand, he knew; but not on whom they might fall.

Zohrab rushed to a window on one side. The narrow alley was filled by a mass of armed men on foot and on horseback. He saw the mail-shirts of the Hazir-bashis, the flashing of weapons, and the red smoky light of the matches in the locks of the juzails. He hurried to another window; it opened to the court where the mulberry-trees grew. It was full of red-capped Kuzzilbashes, mounted and accoutred, some carrying red flashing torches; and

high amid the excited and bristling throng towered
old Shireen Khan on his favourite camel. He was
brandishing his long lance, and gesticulating vio-
lently to Saleh Mohammed, who was mounted on a
beautiful white Tartar horse.

The opening of the window caused them and
many others to look up. Then Zohrab was seen
and recognised by several.

"Dog, whose father has been damned! at last,
at last, we have thee!" hissed Saleh Mohammed,
through his dense beard, as he shook his sabre
upward; and a yell from his people followed,
mingled with the thunder of mallets on the entrance door.

"Dog of a Dooranee thief, take that!" cried the
reckless Zohrab, firing his long pistol full at Saleh
Mohammed (beside whom a man fell dead), and
then taking his measures in an instant, he rushed
from the room, and ascending by a narrow stair to
the roof of the house, which he knew to be flat, by
superhuman strength he tore up the ladder, cutting
off pursuit—for a mere wooden ladder it was—and
tossed it on the heads of the armed throng below.
A number of large clay vases, filled with gigantic
geraniums and other flowers, with four cross-legged
marble idols of Siva, Deva, Vishnu, and Brama, the
property of the banker, he hurled down in quick
succession also, to increase the danger and con-

fusion ; and each, as it fell crashing upon the turbaned heads, the brown upturned faces, and fierce
eyes that gleamed in the torchlight below, elicited a
storm of yells and the useless explosion of several
rifles which were levelled upward, and the balls
from which either starred upon the walls or whistled
harmlessly away into the darkness.

Zohrab, brave as a lion, now almost leisurely re-
loaded his long pistol, and felt the edge and point
of his sabre with the forefinger of his left hand.
It was an old Ispahan sword—one of those famous
blades made and tempered by Zaman, the pupil of
Asad. Formed of Akbarer steel, it rung like a
bell, and Zohrab valued this sword as second only
to his own soul. He had taken it in battle from an
old Beloochee, who was following Mehrib Khan
to the siege of Khelat, and it was valued at two
thousand rupees. Many times had that good weapon saved his life; it had ever been at his side by
day, or under his pillow by night; and now he kissed
it tenderly, with fervour in his heart and a prayer
on his lips, [for a knowledge came over him that,
though he might escape, the *end* seemed close and
nigh. He looked to the sky; it was enveloped in
masses of flying clouds.

"Ha!" he exclaimed, hopefully, "the star of
Zohrab may yet again shine out in God's blessed
firmament!"

Then he looked over the sea of flat-terraced roofs that spread around him, and from amid which the round, dark domes of the mosques and the greater mass of the Bala Hissar—rock, tower, and rampart, tier upon tier—stood abruptly up; and over these roofs he knew that he must make his way, if he would escape some dreadful death, such as impalement by a hot ramrod prior to decapitation; for Ackbar Khan and Saleh Mohammed would accord him small mercy indeed.

"Kill him!"

"Slay the ghorumsaug!"

"Drink his blood!"

"Death to the Sooni!" cried some.

"Death to the follower of Shi!" cried others, equally at random. Such were some of the shouts that loaded the night air in the streets below, where the blue gleaming of keen sabres, of tall lances, and long juzail-bayonets was incessant; for not only was the house, but even the alley itself was environed on all hands.

"A *chupao** with a vengeance!" muttered Zohrab, as by one vigorous bound he leaped from the roof on which he stood to that of the opposite street, the distance between being little more than six or seven feet. The action was not unseen; a heavy volley of rifle-shot whizzed upward—we say, *whizzed*, for

* Night attack.

the bullets were round, not conical. There was a furious spurring of horses, a rush of the crowd, and many armed men now entered the houses, to make their way upon the roofs, and to attack or capture him there; but Zohrab, light, active, and lithe, only waited to draw breath, ere he sprang across the deep, dark gulf of another narrow street, then another, and another.

Meanwhile, forgotten and left to herself, Mabel, with terror, heard all these hostile sounds dying away in the distance. Her just indignation at Zubberdust for the cruel trick he had played, and the new dangers amid which he had left her, had now passed away; and amid the fears she had for her own future fate, she was too womanly, too generous, and too tender of heart, not to feel intense compassion for a single human being—a brave young man, too—hunted in this terrible fashion from house-top to house-top, like a wild animal. Yet she could but tremble, cower on her knees, utter pious invocations in whispers, and, pausing, listen fearfully to the dropping fire of shots and the occasional yells in echoing streets without, till a firm and bold grasp was laid upon her tender arm. She looked up, and found herself looked down upon by the hideous face of the Khond, then lighted up by an indescribable expression. She remembered all she had overheard, and all she had read in "Macpherson's

Religion of the Khonds," and she became well-nigh palsied with fear.

" O my God !" she exclaimed, and closed her eyes. Then, that she might see no more of that horrible visage, being dressed like an Afghan woman, she instantly lowered her veil, according to the custom which has prevailed in the East ever since the days when "Rebekah took one, when she perceived Isaac coming towards her, and covered herself ;" but with a fierce, mocking laugh, the Khond tore it off, and, after surveying her fully and boldly, went out, securing the panel of the room behind him by a strong wooden bolt.

Four, five, even seven streets were crossed in mid air, in a succession of flying leaps, by Zohrab successfully, when, just as breath was beginning to fail him, a shot from a juzail ripped up his right thigh, rending the muscles fearfully, and the blood from a lacerated artery issued in a torrent from the wound.

" May the snares of Satan and the thunder-smitten be on the head of him who fired the shot !" moaned Zohrab, as he reeled and staggered, unable to leap again, while on the flat-terraced roof of a house he had left there came swarming up several dismounted Dooranees, armed with rifles, swords, and pistols.

He faced furiously about : the roof was perfectly

open, for there was neither cornice nor parapet to crouch behind. He fired both his pistols, and with each shot a man dropped in quick succession. At the same moment several balls were fired at him; three struck him in the body, and he sank half-powerless on his knees, but in weakness—*not* supplication. He hurled his pistols at his destroyers, and then, lest any of them should ever possess his beloved Ispahan sword, he snapped the blade across his knee as if it had been brittle glass, and cast the glittering fragments among the crowd below.

In a piercing voice he exclaimed, as he threw up his arms. "Ei dereeghâ, ei dereeghâ, oo ei dereegh! Would to Thee, O God, that I had never been tempted—had never seen her!" and then inspired by what emotion we know not, unless it were to seek succour for Mabel, and to have her saved from the terrible Khond, he took off the cloth of his turban, the *last* appeal a Mohammedan can make when imploring mercy for himself or a friend, and was waving it above his head, when a ball pierced his brain; he gave a convulsive bound upwards, and fell dead and mangled into the street below.

In half an hour after this, the head of "Zohrab the Overbearing" was placed in the public Charchowk, beside that of the unfortunate baronet, Sir William Macnaghten.

CHAPTER XII.

THE SHADE WITHIN THE SHADOW.

So one more dreadful tragedy had been enacted in that land of bloodshed!

Barbarous though she deemed the Mohammedan Afghans, she was to find herself in the grasp of those who were more barbarous still—for whose depth of cruelty there was no name—the Khonds, a race or tribe whose sacrifices of human life, though not offered up in such numbers as those of the Thugs, were done in a fashion quite as secret, and known only to themselves, and whose existence, like that of those subtle assassins, had become only known to the Indian Government of late years.

Powerless in the hands of Ferishta Lodi, the girl felt as if hovering on the verge of some death of which she knew not the form or fashion, save that it must be lingering, protracted, and horrible!

Her past life, with all its peace, happiness, and ease, its gaiety, luxury, brilliance, and good position, seemed to be, as it was indeed, like a previous state of existence—as a dream; the horrible present appeared alone the stern reality. Was her identity the same? she asked of herself many, many times, in half-audible whispers; or had she undergone that species of metempsychosis, or transmigration of soul from the body of one being to the body of another, which is a doctrine of the Indian Brahmins—of those Hindoos whom she was now beginning to loathe? Was she no longer Mabel Trecarrel, a Christian woman, a civilised European, who had a father, a sister, and so many friends? Was the existence of Waller, or was her own, a myth? She felt as if she was about to become insane, and, pressing her delicate hands upon her throbbing temples, prayed God to preserve her senses, whatever her ultimate fate might be.

Surely, unknown to herself, she must have committed some great sin, to be tortured thus, and thus punished, enduring here that she might not endure hereafter, was her next idea.

The six months or so which had elapsed since that stirring morning on which the army, under its aged and dying general, with its mighty encumbrance of camp-followers, began its homeward march for India from the old familiar cantonments seemed as so many ages to Mabel Trecarrel now! So many well-known faces and happy existences had been swept away; so complete a change had come over all the few who survived, and their prospects seemed so strange and dark. So much misery, so many sent to untimely deaths—it could not be said to their graves, as the Afghans never interred one of our dead.

What did it all mean? Why did Heaven so persecute, or leave to their fate, so many Christians in the hands of utter infidels?

Voices again roused her to action—at least to listen.

They were those of the Khond and the Hindoo conversing in Hindostanee.

"So, so," said the former, chuckling, "all is over with Zohrab; he can 'overbear' no longer."

"Yes; the head he carried so proudly is gone to the gate of the Char-chowk; but the Kuzzilbashes are still in the street, and I wish they were gone to their own quarter."

"Why?"

"They may take a fancy to our heads, too."

"Why, I say?" asked the Khond, fiercely.

"Can you ask?—if the Feringhee woman is not forthcoming."

"She is mine, and I have saved my two hundred tomauns."

"How yours?"

"Zohrab is gone; none seem to know that she is here; and you will be silent, if you are wise.

Ackbar Khan would like an excuse to plunder a schroff so rich as you; hence you must, I know, be silent."

The last words sounded more like a threat than an advice or an entreaty, as the voice of the fierce Khond accentuated them; the sly Hindoo, however, made some evasive response, and then Mabel heard him draw on his slippers and tunic and shuffle from the room. Where he went she knew not; but, after a time, with an exclamation of anger and mistrust, the Khond tossed aside the mouth-piece of his hubble-bubble, and followed him.

So the Kuzzilbashes were still in the adjacent streets! Could she but reach them! They were gallant and soldierly fellows, though, till of late, as bitter foes of the British troops as any tribe in the country. But now the politics of their Khan had begun to change, and he had kept aloof from Ackbar and his interests. She once more applied herself to the windows. Many dark figures were hovering about in the street, and looking up at the house. Who or what these people were she knew not. The courtyard was quite empty; but she heard the clatter of hoofs and the clink of arms, as horsemen rode hastily to and fro in the main thoroughfare that led to the bazaar.

She was in perfect darkness now.

She sought feebly to draw or push down the panel that separated her from the dewan-khaneh; but the wooden bolt secured it beyond all the efforts of her humble strength to force a way; and she feared to make the least noise, lest, by being caught in the act of escaping, she might only accelerate her own fate.

Breathlessly she listened!

Sounds passed at intervals through the large and scantily furnished chambers of the slenderly built house. The floors being all uncarpeted, and the windows without draperies, in the fashion of the country, the edifice was liable to produce strange echoes, and Mabel strove to gather from these something of good or bad augury as they fell on her overstrained ear.

Ah, were she but once more back in the hitherto abhorred fort of Saleh Mohammed—back to the sad companionship of the hostages—to the shelter and counsel of her own sex and people! In the power of the Khond she felt, truly and terribly, that if they had much to dread and to anticipate when in the fort, she had much that was more immediate to dread now; that within every shade there may be a deeper shadow. Rose could never know her fate, or how she had perished in seeking to rejoin her; and she might have to die and never know the story of the younger sister she loved so dearly.

Suddenly, amid her sad reverie, she heard the sound of heavy boots, the brown-tanned jorabs of Afghan horsemen, and the cadence of various guttural voices in the dewan-khaneh. Then a red light streamed through the jointings of the panelled wall. The wooden bolt outside was shot back; the great central panel slid down in its grooves, and within the square outline it left, framed as if in a picture, with the red smoky glare of an upheld torch falling strongly upon him, stood the tall and grim but most picturesque figure of the old Khan of the Dooranees, Saleh Mohammed, with one brown bony hand thrust into his yellow Cashmere girdle, and the other resting on the jewelled hilt of his sheathed sabre.

His bushy beard concealed alike the form of his mouth and chin; but his slender hooked nose, with arching nostril, his shaggy brows, and keen eagle-like eyes indicated firmness, decision, and rapidity of thought and action. He wore a loose and ample chogah of scarlet cloth, lined with fine fur, and richly embroidered; a short matchlock, beautifully inlaid with mother-of-pearl, was slung upon his back, with a silk handkerchief bound over its lock for protection; his girdle bristled with the usual number of elaborate knives, daggers, and pistols;

and he wore a green turban to indicate his assumed or acknowledged descent from the Prophet.

With something of kindness mingled with sternness, he held out a hand to the drooping Mabel, and raised her from her knees; for she was half sitting and half reclining, hopelessly and weakly, against the wooden partition; and he saw how pale and piteous she looked. Now old Saleh had several wives and daughters of his own in a secluded fort among the Siah Sung Hills, and he was not without some promptings of human sympathy in his heart.

"Come," said he; "with me you are safe, and shall go back to your friends. From Shireen Khan I have been told how Zohrab, that liar who is now hanging over hell by the tongue, deceived you."

She thankfully placed her hand in that of the Dooranee chief, for, after the tiger-like visage of the Khond, his bearded face and venerable aspect were as those of a father to her, and most gratefully she welcomed him.

The hint of the Khond, that Ackbar Khan, or some of the other Khans, whose number was legion in Cabul, might confiscate his substance and appropriate his hard-won mohurs, tomauns, rupees, and good English guineas, had not been lost on the quiet and acquisitive Hindoo banker, who had straightway betaken him to Mohammed Saleh in the street, just as he was collecting his men to depart, and, to make his peace with all, had surrendered Mabel, while, for some reason known to himself alone, he had no future fear of Ferishta Lodi's anger.

As Mabel was too weak to ride on a side-saddle, and to walk was, of course, impossible, a palanquin was soon procured, and in that she was rapidly conveyed by four bearers in the fashion to which she was quite accustomed, away from the city, under the shadow of the great Bala Hissar, past the tomb of Baber, and round between the Siah Sung Hills and the Cabul river, once more to the fort of Saleh Mohammed, where, just as day was breaking, she was roused from a slumber that was full of painful visions and nervous startings, to find herself welcomed by pure English tongues and by the embraces of her companions in misfortune, the lady hostages of Elphinstone's hapless army.

A severe illness, consequent on all her delicate frame had undergone, now fell upon Mabel—a nervous illness, which her friends were without the means of alleviating, when on the, to them, most memorable 25th of August, came the cruel order of Ackbar Khan for the immediate transmission of all to Toorkistan, where he had condemned them all to sale and slavery—an order consequent on his fury at the retention of Jelalabad, and the combined advance of General Pollock and Sir Robert Sale upon Cabul.

So on that day, by horse, on foot, on camels, or in dhooleys, the hapless females and children, a few accompanied by husbands and fathers, the sick, the wounded, and the ailing, all in misery, in tears, and despair, under Saleh Mohammed and a strong guard of Dooranees, set forth towards the frontier of the land where they were to be scattered and lost to their friends and to freedom for ever—the land of Toorkistan, a name so vaguely given to all that vast, lawless, and uncivilized region that lies between the plateau of Central Asia and the shores of the Caspian Sea!

CHAPTER XIII.

ROSE IN A NEW CHARACTER.

LOVERS are more interesting to each other than they can ever possibly prove to third or fourth parties; yet we cannot preserve the unity of our story and lose sight of Denzil and Rose Trecarrel, whose case and circumstances were altogether exceptional; for, certainly, few lovers have been precisely situated as they were, in this age of the world at least.

Yet the course of their love was not fated to "run smooth," though, in the care of Shireen Khan, no such perils menaced them as those which beset Mabel and her companion, or, still more, those who were the immediate prisoners of Ackbar, unless we refer to the watch kept on the Kuzzilbash fort, by some of the fanatical Ghazees, who, on discovering that Feringhee prisoners were there, thought to add to their own chances of salvation by cutting them off.

In this late affair with Zohrab, Shireen had permitted Denzil to go, armed and mounted, with a party of twenty Kuzzilbashes in search of him and

Mabel, round by the hills of Beymaru, the borders
of the Lake of Istaliff, and other places over which
he and Waller had hunted and shot together, often
in the more peaceful time that was past. After his
months of seclusion and useless inactivity, Denzil,
apart from the natural excitement and anxiety re-
sulting from the object in view—the rescue of Mabel
and reunion of the sisters—felt a joyous emotion on
finding himself once more an armed man, astride a
magnificent horse, and spurring like the wind along
the steep mountain slopes, through fertile valley
and foaming river, at the head of twenty soldierly
fellows, in fur caps with red bags, flaming scarlet
chogahs, and glittering lances.

Shireen had perfect confidence in according to
him this unusual liberty, knowing, as he said drily
to the Khanum, his wife, that "while they retained
the hen in the roost, the cock-bird would not go far
off." He was surprised, however, that Denzil, when
on this expedition, could by no means be persuaded
to wear his remarkable yellow silk robe, with the
embroidered letters and sphynxes, which was supposed to be his war dress, or to indicate his rank
as a great Nawab or Bahadoor of the Queen of
England.

In the ardour of the chase, Denzil took a wrong
direction, and over-exerted himself to repair the
error; he rode with his party beyond Loghur, and

the reach of all probable places where the abductor was likely to be found; and then, at a time when the midsummer sun was intensely hot, and the atmosphere filled with steamy and miasmatic exhalations from the rice-fields, he swam his horse through three rivers, at points where the water rose nearly to his neck.

A fever and ague—nearly regular jungle-fever—combined with some other ailment, were the result of this rashness; and on the second day after, Denzil found himself prostrate on a bed of sickness.

By the Khan, he and Rose had been duly informed of the narrow escapes of her sister; of the wile by which she had been lured from the fort of Saleh Mohammed, at whose rage and want of circumspection the more wary Shireen laughed heartily; of the trickery and reckless valour of Zohrab Zubberdust, and the horrible schemes of the Khond, happily averted by the timidity and avarice of the Hindoo schroff; and Rose felt grateful to Heaven—intensely so in her heart—that her " dear, dear Mab " was safe once more, or comparatively so, in the companionship of sorrow—for such she knew it must inevitably be, with Lady Sale, her widowed daughter, the widow of the Envoy, and other captives of Ackbar; though, by chances she had not foreseen, their meeting was delayed—she could only hope and pray, for a time.

These episodes and the tenour of the life they all led in the sequestered fort, with the daily looking forward to some startling event or catastrophe, a battle, a revolution, even an earthquake, as a means to set them free, seemed to tame down and sadden much of Rose's constitutional heedlessness; besides, the illness of Denzil was a genuine source for present sorrow and growing anxiety.

He was alternately in a burning fever and then in icy perspirations; he had intense pains in the head and loins, a heavy sickness, a weariness over all his limbs, a listlessness of spirit, a general sinking and rapid wasting of the whole system, with a thirst that at times could not be alleviated by the simple sangaree or sherbet, i.e., lime-juice and sugar, prepared for him by the Khanum. Denzil inherited from his mother, Constance Devereaux, a more delicate physique and nervous organisation than that possessed by his hardier father; hence he was the more calculated to succumb to the subtle ailment that had fastened on him now; but neither he nor those about him thought of danger yet.

The old white-bearded and black-robed Hakeem, Aber Malee, who attended the inhabitants of the fort, and came thither from the city every other day, on his donkey, prescribed decoctions of honey, which is recommended by the Koran as a sovereign " medicine for man." He did more: with intense solemnity, he copied many texts or prescriptions from the pages of the same book, on strips of parchment, then washed them off into a cup of water from the holy well at Baber's tomb, and gave it to his patient to swallow; but whenever he departed, Rose or Denzil tossed them over the window; so, left thus, altogether without medical attendance, the disease took a deeper and more permanent root.

Rose had now gladly relinquished the Afghan female dress. Amid the plentiful supply of plunder of every kind gleaned up by the Kuzzilbashes in the track of the retreating army, were several overlands bullock-trunks and portmanteaus filled with clothing. Among these, some of which had doubtless belonged to her own lady friends, Rose was fain to make selections; thus, one evening in June, when the sun was setting behind the black mountains, throwing across the broad green valley where the Cabul winds, their shadows to where the old cantonments lay, and tipping with fire the conical hill that overhangs the distant city, while Denzil, who had been dosing uneasily on his hard native bed, was looking with a haggard eye about him, he saw Rose seated near, at an open window, on a low divan, dressed in a most becoming fashion, and consequently looking much more like her former self.

And as his bed, in the usual Afghan fashion, lay simply on the floor, which had no covering but a *satringee,* or piece of cotton carpet, he could see the whole of her handsome figure, as she reclined a cheek upon her dimpled hand, showing one lovely taper arm bare to the white elbow, while alternately idling over the pages of a European book and furtively watching him, as he had slept, lulled over by the drowsy hum of myriad insects at the open casement, and among the brilliantly flowered creepers that clambered round it, a sound like the murmur of distant water, or of the wind in an ocean shell, but very suggestive of heat, of lassitude, and repose; yet Denzil, though he had slept, felt more weary than ever.

"Rose," said he, faintly.

"Dear Denzil—you are awake again, my poor pet; you sleep but by snatches," said the girl, closing her book and sinking on her knees beside his pillow, which, with ready and gentle hands, she noiselessly rearranged.

"I have been thinking, Rose—that—that——" he paused.

"What? Do not exert yourself."

"That my presence must be full of peril to you!"

"To me—how?"

"This illness may be an infectious one."

"I scarcely think so, Denzil; and if it were," she added, with a smile of inexpressible tenderness, "if it were—what then?"

"It might seize on you, darling Rose. Let one of those Kuzzilbash fellows attend me; their lives are of no consequence, while yours——"

"Is of value only to myself."

"And to me, Rose—to me; how unkind!"

He raised himself feebly on his elbow, and gazed at her with eyes expressive of love and admiration.

"Why, Rose, how well you are looking this evening—quite a belle too, or a 'swell,' if one may speak slang," said he, with affected cheerfulness.

"And you, too, Denzil," said she in the same manner, kindly assumed, but with an arrested sob in her throat, for she saw that in reality he was more and more wasted, hollow-cheeked, and large-eyed than ever, and that the tendons of his hands stood sharply out in ridges, distinct to the eye, quite like those of an old man.

His full, deep, dark blue eyes had in them an unnatural lustre; his fair, curly hair had the same golden tint as usual, when the falling sunlight touched it; but the Indian brown and the jolly English bloom had left his once-rounded cheeks together, and they were now pale and hollow indeed; and though he was very fair, and his mother had been dark in eye and jetty in tress, something in his face and expression recalled her now to Rose's memory, as she had seen her on that day, when she and Mabel had visited the villa at Porthellick, and, in the vanity of the hour, flattered themselves that they had condescended mightily in so doing. Could they then have foreseen the present time and circumstances?

She gazed at him with great sadness, and great love, too, in her eyes and in her heart; while he, in turn, looked up to her with love and admiration too, and with somewhat of anxiety for her future.

She was attired so prettily and suitably; for the season was summer, and the month was June.

No longer hanging dishevelled in the Afghan fashion, the splendid ripples of her bright auburn hair were coiled up by her own clever fingers in the European mode, and smoothly braided, as she was wont to have them in happier times, showing all the contour of her fine head, her slender neck, and delicate ears. She wore a simple loose dress of white muslin, spotted with the tiniest of red rose-buds; and through the delicate texture of this fabric the curved outline of her shoulders and her tapered arms could be traced, whiter than the gauzy muslin itself—a piquant species of costume, which made old Shireen stroke his beard and mutter, "*Bari-killah!*" (excellent!), as expressive of great satisfaction, not unmixed with more admiration than the Khanum relished.

Rose was destitute of all ornaments, for every-

thing she once possessed of that kind had long since
been lost or taken from her. Her feet were cased
in tight silk stockings and beautiful little kid boots,
laced up in front, and they peeped from amid a
wilderness of white-edged petticoats, that lay wreath
upon wreath like the leaves of a rose in full bloom;
and, altogether, she was such a figure as Denzil had
not seen since the jovial days when he and Bob
Waller had smoked the calumet of peace together in
the old cantonments, and were wont to promenade at
the band-stand which stood in the centre thereof;
certainly she was quite unlike what one might
expect to see in the residence of the Khan of the
Kuzzilbashes, where the ideas of the middle ages,
and darker epochs still, have not passed away, and
things are pretty much as they were in the days of
Timour the Tartar.

Rose seemed intuitively to read something of all
this in the expression of Denzil's face; for she
smiled, and, with one of her old coquettish glances,
kissed the tips of her fingers to him.

Circumstanced as they were, Rose, no doubt, in
time past had talked a great deal of nonsense, and,
seeing how necessary she was to Denzil's happiness,
Shireen Khan had relinquished much of her society
at chess in his favour; but who ever scrutinises very
closely all that a pretty girl talks about, or what
male listener, or lover especially, would care to

analyse the logic thereof? The parting of charming lips is ever pleasant to look upon, and the music of a sweet English female voice is ever pleasant to hear, and never so sweet or so seductive as when far away from home. And so thought Denzil, as he lay upon his pillow, with heavy eye, with aching temples, and throbbing pulses, listening to the prattle of Rose Trecarrel.

Some books, picked up in the burned cantonments, had also been brought to Rose by the Khan, though he suggested that the Koran, with its hundred and fourteen chapters, ought to suffice for all the literary, legal, and medical necessities of mankind, and womankind too. Among those stray volumes was a copy of "Lalla Rookh," with poor Harry Burgoyne's autograph on the fly-leaf, and with this she had read Denzil asleep, reading steadily on afterwards, and kindly fearing to stop, lest by doing so she might awake him; but now, without her ceasing, he had restlessly stirred and roused himself.

He grudged, even by necessary sleep, to lose by day a moment of her society; for they could converse silently, eye with eye, without speaking; for to lovers there is a dear companionship, an eloquence even, in silence; and now the girl gazed upon her care with her eyes and her heart full of love and tenderness, all the more that he, by perfect isolation,

M 2

was so completely her own, and that she could minister unto him, as only a woman, a loving and tender one, can tend and minister to the suffering.

It was very strange, all this !

To Rose Trecarrel it had seemed as if, once upon a time, the world was quite running over with lovers. Now, her world was, oddly enough, narrowed to the boundary wall and grassy fausse-braye of Shireen Khan's fort. That a girl, in her extreme youth, chances to have been, like Rose, a flirt, is no· proof that she is incapable of a very deep and enduring affection; it is often quite the contrary, and Rose was just a case in point. Here, with her and Denzil, the pretty biter was *bitten*. " A flirt," says one, who wrote long ago, " is merely a girl of more than common beauty and amiability, just hovering on the verge which separates childhood from womanhood. She is just awakening to a sense of her power, and finds an innocent pleasure in the exercise of it. The blissful consciousness parts her ripe lips with prouder breath, kindles her moist eyes with richer lustre, and gives additional buoyancy and swan-like grace to all her motions. She looks for homage at the hands of every man who approaches her, and richly does she repay him with rosy smiles and sparkling glances. There is no passion in all this." It is the first trembling, unconscious existence of that sentiment which will become love in time. And Rose's time had come!

So had it been with her, though her flirtations had bordered too often on actual coquetry, thereby overacting the flirt, incurring the sneers of the piqued, and accusations of heartlessness and vanity, as one who loved the love-making, but *not* the lover. She had now become a veritable Undine—the type of everything that is amiable and beautiful, tender and true, in her sex. Yet we are constrained to admit that much of this sudden change *might* have been brought about by the dire pressure of unforeseen events and calamities. In her late term of bitter experiences, she, and all about her, had learned palpably, that those they loved most on earth were merely mortal, and might be, or had been, torn from them by cruel and sudden deaths.

In her new phase of life, how completely her former had passed away—been forgotten, with its balls, parties, picnics, déjeuners, and promenades; its selection of dresses and colours, flowers and perfumes; its promenades and drives; its fun and jollity; its gossips, flirtations, and folly! All existence seemed merged or narrowed now in two circles or hopes—the health of Denzil, and their mutual restoration to liberty and safety!

All her girlish foibles had passed away, and the genuine woman came to the surface, when perhaps too late; for Denzil seemed too surely to be sinking fast, and unwittingly, when his mind wandered in the delirium of fever, he murmured things that he had heard amid the banter of the mess-bungalow, and elsewhere, that stung her repentant heart, and drew tears from her eyes.

"Rose—oh Rose," he would say, "it can't be true all that Jack Polwhele said, and Harry Burgoyne, of the 37th, too—but they are dead, poor fellows!—and Grahame, and Ravelstoke, and ever so many more."

"What did they say, Denzil?"

"That you flirted with them all—oh, no, no, no! And then there is my cousin Audley—if indeed he *is* my cousin," he added, through his chattering teeth, "he cannot love you as I love you! He must have made a fool of many a girl in his time, while I—I love but you—even as I told you on that day by the lake, when you—you said—what did *she* say?—ask her, Sybil," he would add, looking up vacantly, yet earnestly; and then the conscience of the listener would be stirred to find that her thoughtless follies were remembered at such a time.

"In his soul, he doubts me still," she thought. "My poor Denzil, I was only flirting, as most girls do. It was only fun," she added, aloud.

"Yes, I am *poor*, and junior in rank, I know," he

replied, catching a new idea from her words, "too poor for her to love me, Sybil; I heard her tell that fellow, Audley, so; and he—ah! he is the heir of Lord Lamorna!"

"Denzil, dearest Denzil!" then Rose exclaimed, in a low and earnest whisper, putting an arm caressingly round his neck, and her tremulous lips close to his ear, "you are certain to have been promoted by this time, and doubtless the Queen will give you the Order of the Dooranee Empire. I feel sure of it," she added, little knowing that all this had already taken place.

But, at the moment she spoke, an access of fever and weakness came over poor Denzil; his bloodshot eyes moved, but he made no response; and a fear began to come over her that he was passing away— slipping from her love and her care—perhaps already far beyond caring now either for promotion or "a ribbon at the breast."

How she repented the past pangs her heedlessness had cost this honest heart, we need not say; but as her eyes fell on a verse of "Lalla Rookh," under- lined in some old flirtation of Burgoyne's, she applied it to herself; for now

> "Far other feelings love hath brought;
> Her soul all flame, her brow all sadness;
> She now has but the one dear thought,
> And thinks that o'er almost to madness."

On one occasion he became almost insensible; but whether he slept or had swooned, she knew not in her despair of heart; and none of Shireen's household could aid her, by advice or otherwise. At dressing a sabre-cut with myrrh, or stanching a bullet-hole with a bunch of nettle-leaves as a styptic, any of them would have been ready and skilful enough; but with such an ailment as that of Denzil, they were as useless as children, and apt to attribute it to magic, or the spell of some unseen and offended genii; while, as fatalists, they were disposed to commit the event to God alone.

So the sorrow and apprehension of the lonely girl grew daily greater.

"And this is the only man I ever loved; yet through me, or my sister's cause—through us—has death, perhaps, come untimely upon him!" Rose would say, wildly and passionately, and in a low, concentrated voice, as she flung herself at the foot of Denzil's bed; while all the horror of anticipated loneliness, if he should be taken away, and she left, came upon her. How bitterly now she felt punished for all the little follies of the past!

His ailment was, certainly, one under which a patient may linger a long time—nay, may seem to get well, and then again be worse than ever, but which, in the end, too often slays. Hence, it is no wonder that the humble Hakeem, Abu Malec—who

believed that a verse of the Koran written, washed
off, and swallowed with reverence, must form a
sovereign remedy, even for an obstinate and be-
nighted infidel—should stroke his beard in sore perplexity and great wonder, and mutter—

"Thus it is that Allah seals the hearts of those
who are steeped in ignorance! Their doctrines are
as a worthless tree, the roots of which run on the
surface of the ground, and hath no stability, and the
blast of heaven will overturn."

"A tiresome old pump! For Heaven's sake, keep
him away, Rose!" would be the comment of the sick
subaltern.

And the latter had at times a secret presentiment
that he would never leave the fort of Shireen Khan
alive; yet the conviction was sweet that Rose had
loved him, ere he passed away. She would never
forget him now: he felt sure of that. She might
love *another* in time; but would that matter to him?
To die, ere she was restored to the society and protection of Europeans, was to leave her most lonely
and widowed in heart, and was his keenest affliction;
yet he kept it to himself, having no desire to distress
her unnecessarily, though his ravings sometimes
indicated the prevailing thought, and the fear he
saw was in her.

"I don't think I shall die this bout, Rose darling.
I cannot have a very deadly fever! I rode only

forty miles—twenty to Loghur, and twenty back—on Shireen's old brute of a Tartar horse, and smoked about ten cheroots ; but they were execrable— picked up among the lost baggage; and—and you know, dear mother, they are thorough disinfectants any way. Oh, no—I can't have a deadly fever. I shall soon be better, dear, dear mother !"

Thus, Rose would learn that his wandering thoughts had flashed far, far from her, till the clouds that oppressed his brain would pass away, and, all ignorant of past delirium, he would welcome her presence with loving yet forced smiles, and seek to assure her, in a voice that grew more husky and more weak daily, "that he was better—oh, so very much better;" adding, "Ah, if we had but Sybil here—or, rather, if we did but know what has become of her ! "

"Sybil—ah, would that I could but know of her ! But she shall be my sister, Denzil; for too surely, I fear, we shall never see Mabel more ! "

"Don't say so. You and Mabel shall both be happy, I hope, long, long after——" he paused.

"After what, darling?"

"After all these sorrows have passed away," said he; and though it was not thus he had meant to close the sentence, Rose read his secret meaning in his mournful eyes.

There were times when he lay quiet, breathing

hard and shortly, but quite apathetic to all around him; and other times when he moaned and muttered of his broken and desolate home—a home now no more; of Cornwall, its moors and cliffs; of wanderings in Italy—the peaks of the Abruzzi and the banks of the Arno; of his parents and sister; of Rose—ever and anon it was Rose, and the day by the Lake of Istaliff; all oddly confused together, till the listener's heart was crushed, and she prayed on her knees, with bowed head, that he might be spared for her, or that, while her unfelt kisses were pressed upon his brow and cheek, she too might catch the same fever, and that they might die and be buried together under the green turf, outside the Afghan fort, where the acacia-trees were tossing their light, feathery foliage in the wind.

So thus would the sleepless hours of many a weary night of watching pass away; the boom of brass cannon, mellowed by distance, would come from the far-off Bala Hissar, indicating that dawn was breaking, and pale Rose Trecarrel would know that the slow lingering hours of another day of heartless sorrow were before her.

One noon, however, a little hope dawned in her breast! The Hakeem, Abu Malec, arrived with a stranger, whose fair European face belied his Afghan camise and brown leather boots.

"A Feringhee doctor Sahib has come from

Cabul," said Abu Malec, not without a spice of professional jealousy in his tone, while, to the infinite joy of Rose, he introduced Doctor C——, of the 54th Infantry, one of those gallant and devoted medical officers, who volunteered by lot cast on the drum-head, to remain behind in that place of peril, and attend to the wants of our sick and wounded soldiers; so now she devoutly hoped that Denzil would have some better treatment than that which resulted from mere superstition and a dogged belief in that fatalism which is eminently Mohammedan.

The doctor, an old friend, greeted Rose kindly, and with genuine warmth—to exist was cause for congratulation then; next he turned to Denzil, and, after a brief examination, shook his head despondingly, to the intense satisfaction of the Hakeem, Abu Malec.

CHAPTER XIV.

WITH SALE'S BRIGADE.

SINCE that ill-omened hour and time of dread excitement, when on the disastrous day in January the ladies and other hostages were handed over to Ackbar Khan, their friends and relatives even in Afghanistan knew nothing of their actual safety—who were living, who were dead, or who were mutilated or disgraced by insults worse than death, on the route towards Toorkistan; and now the beginning of September had come.

It was only known that Ackbar's orders to Saleh Mohammed were, " to hurry them on their journey, and to butcher all the sick, and those for whom there might be no speedy conveyance."

Eight months—eight weary and harassing months of eager longing, of fierce excitement, and impatience to avenge the fallen and rescue the helpless— had passed ere the junction between General Pollock's troops and those of Sir Robert Sale was fully effected, and the advance upon Cabul, so long resolved upon, was once more begun, while Nott was pushing victoriously from Candahar on the same point, leaving Ghuznee in smoking ruins behind him.

To Waller's mind, Mabel, though an ever-prevailing thought, had become a kind of myth by that time—existent, yet non-existent, for separation was a species of living death; and he could but pray that she was still living, though in the hands of Ackbar Khan. So a sad memory to many a husband was the face of his wife; so to many a father were the voice and smile of his child; and all knew that on their own swords, and the valour and resolution of their comrades, depended the chance of their all being ever reunited again.

Waller looked older than he was wont to do—older than his years; for he had become, like many others serving there, more grave and more thoughtful now. Fun and merriment were unknown in Pollock's army, and laughter, like many another luxury, was as scarce. With haversacks, canteens, and purses empty, and hard fighting in front, life looks far from rosy. Waller had more than once detected a most decided and long grey hair in his carefully cultivated whiskers. A grey hair!—when improvising the back of his hunting-watch as a mirror: his own elaborate rosewood dressing-case, with silver-mounted essence bottles—the parting gift of a rich aunt, from whom Bob had " expectations," was now degraded to the duty of holding cooking-spices and stuffs for pillaus and kabobs in the kitchen of a Khan; but the grey hairs—once upon a time he should have twitched them out.

"Bah! what do they matter now?" said he, and finished his toilet by clasping on his waist-belt.

Waller felt more than ever, from personal causes, inspired by an ardour in the performance of his duty, and speedily became distinguished as one of the most active and gallant officers on the staff of Sir Robert Sale, a veteran whose uninterrupted career of service dated back to the battle of Malavelly, where Harris defeated Tippoo Saib, and the storming of Seringapatam, in the closing year of the preceding century. Sale commanded one division in our Army of Vengeance,—for such it deemed itself; General M'Caskill, a stern and resolute Scotsman, led the other; and the whole under General Pollock, on being reinforced by Her Majesty 31st, the 33rd Native Light Infantry, the 1st Light Cavalry, all clad in silver grey, and a train of mountain guns (the ghalondazees of which wore picturesque oriental dresses), commenced the march towards the mighty range of mountains that lie between Jelalabad and Cabul.

McCaskill was in such feeble health that the brave old fellow had to proceed at the head of his division in a litter borne by four Hindoos.

Experience had taught our leaders the mistake of having the usual mighty encumbrances of camp-followers, the tenting and feeding of which formed the curse of our Indian armies; so, in this instance, such appendages were greatly reduced. For tents, the palls or little marquees of the sepoys were substituted. Save a single change of linen, the soldiers carried nothing in their knapsacks; the baggage of the officers was cut down to the smallest extent—Waller carried his in a valise at his saddle—and three or four had to sleep under one marquee. All the sick and wounded were left under a guard in Jelalabad; and thus the army was trimmed, pruned, and fined down to the active, well-armed, and lightly accoutred fighting-men alone.

Hence the camp had no longer the aspect usually presented by those of our Indian forces, as these usually exhibit a motley collection of coverings, to ward off the baleful dews of night or the scorching sun by day. Here and there a superb suite of tents or marquees, surrounded by squalid little erections of coloured calico, tattered cloths and blankets stretched over sticks and poles, even palm leaves being improvised when they could be had; and amid all these congeries of variously coloured masses, the flags of chiefs and colonels, the bells of arms, horses, oxen, camels, and elephants, pell mell!

A final act of individual cruelty, perpetrated by

Ackbar Khan on a poor Hindoo—the same schroff, or banker, whom Mabel had seen in Cabul—greatly exasperated all ranks against him.

Hearing that our troops had begun their march, this man, whose nationality and sympathies led him to favour their interests, when making his way towards them, was overtaken, and brought before Ackbar in the castle of Buddeeabad, and was there bitterly upbraided as a traitor.

" Throw him down," he cried to his Haozir-bashes, and then drew his sabre.

Believing he was about to be beheaded, the wretched Hindoo implored mercy.

" Hold him fast," said Ackbar, baring his right arm to the elbow. " What, dog of an idolater, you wish to see the Feringhees, do you ? "

By two blows of his heavy sabre, which was inscribed by a verse from the Koran, he hacked off the feet of the Hindoo above the ankles, and said mockingly—

" *Now* you may go where you will : throw him out of doors."

Cast forth, faint and bleeding, the poor wretch, tore his turban-cloth into strips and staunched with them the hemorrhage, enabling him actually to crawl on his hands and knees to our outposts, where his appearance excited the bitterest feelings in the breasts of all the troops, European as well as native.

Rumour stated that Ackbar Khan was filled with alarm and rage, either of which might prompt him to execute some of his terrible threats on the helpless hostages; and that he was prepared for any extremity, and to lay the land waste, was evinced by the alarming noises that were heard in the Passes, ere our march began, and by the sky above the mountain-tops being nightly reddened by the blaze of burning villages which he destroyed, so that neither food nor shelter might be found by an advancing foe.

At the hill of Gundamuck, where there is a walled village surrounded by groves of cypresses, Waller saw, with some emotions of interest, the cave in which he lurked after the last fatal stand was made there, and vividly came back to memory the despair of the final struggle.

As our troops began to penetrate into the recesses of those mountains, whose names and features were so calculated to inspire mournful thoughts in all who looked on them (for there had a British army marched *in*, never more to come forth, being literally swallowed up), they found, as before, the ferocious Ghilzies again in position, and in thousands ready to defend their native rocks with all their native ardour, inflamed by past triumph, the hopes of future plunder, by fanaticism and pleasant doses of bhang; and from steep to steep, and from ridge to ridge, from tree to tree, and hill to hill, they defended themselves, and fought or died with stubborn and resolute bravery, harassing our troops in front, in rear, and on both flanks. Yet on pushed our columns: the dying and the dead fell fast, and remained a ghastly train to mark the rearward route; but every life lost seemed but to add to the pluck and hardihood of the survivors.

The sputtering fire of the long juzails, concentrating to a roar at times, filled all these savage defiles with countless and incessant puffs of white smoke, that started from among the grey impending rocks, where the great yellow gourds, the purple grapes, and the scarlet creepers grew in wild luxuriance; from dark and cavernous fissures and the green groves of the pine and the plane tree. Every beetling crag was fringed with curling smoke, and streaked with fire, scaring the mountain eagles high into mid air, while with every shot that helped to thin our ranks the shrill cry of *Allah Ackbar!* (God is mighty) was echoed from side to side, to die upward, yet, we hoped, to find no echo in heaven.

A little way within the eastern entrance to the series of defiles, at the village of Jugdulluck, where the mountains are between five and six thousand feet above the sea's level, there was a peculiarly fierce encounter; for there the Afghans, led by the Arab Hadji Abdallah Osman, and inflamed to religious fury by his precepts and mad example,

N 2

had fortified the summit of the Pass by earthworks
and some of our own captured cannon ; but, mounting
the steep heights on each side, the 9th and 13th
Regiments turned the flank of their position, and
by the bayonet drove away the defenders amid terrible slaughter, neither side asking or hoping for
quarter.

From point to point at other places were fierce
contests; and now, as our soldiers opened up with
the cold steel those Passes which had been closed
to all Europeans for the past eight months, their
onward march—a series of prolonged conflicts, in
fact—exhibited to them an awful and harrowing
scene.

CHAPTER XV.

FROM out of the Passes, dark and shadowing, the reverberating echoes of the adverse musketry roused black clouds of vultures, with angry croak and flapping wing. It would seem almost as if all the obscene birds of Asia had been wont to seek, for months past, this ghastly place—to make it their undisturbed rendezvous; and such, no doubt, it had been, for there,

"Without a grave, unknelled, uncoffined, and unknown,"

all belted and accoutred in the rags of their uniform, just as the death-shots had struck them down, and as they had fallen over each other in piles, lay the remains of Elphinstone's slaughtered army.

Close in ranks, as when living, in some places lay the ghastly relics of the dead. In one spot, where the last stand had been made by Her Majesty's 44th Regiment, more than two hundred skeletons lay in one horrid hecatomb; and in the shreds of red cloth that flapped in the wind,

the buttons and badges, sad and agonizing were
the efforts made by officers and men to recognise
the remains of some dear and jovial friend, some
true and gallant comrade in the times that were
gone; and it was all the sadder to reflect that most
of the fallen had been cut off in their prime, or even
before it, as from eighteen to twenty-six years is the
average age of our soldiers on service.

In too many, if not nearly all, instances the
remains were headless, the skulls having been borne
off as trophies by the various mountain tribes; and
in some places the white bones lay amid purple,
crimson, and golden beds of those sweetly scented
violets which the Orientals so often use to flavour
their finest sherbets.

For miles upon miles it was but a sad repetition
of whitening bones, fragments of uniforms, and ammunition paper, bleached by the wind and rain
and the snows of the past winter, together with the
shrunken remains of camels, horses, and yaboos,
from which the baggage and other trappings had
long since been carried off; and ever and always in
mid air the croaking and flapping of the ravening
vultures, long unused to be disturbed by the living,
in that valley of solitude and silence, death and
desolation.

Like many others, with a swollen heart, set lips,
and stern eyes, Waller reined in his horse, and

would look round him from time to time, in places where the dead lay thicker than usual. Our now victorious army was marching in thousands over their fallen comrades, yet with them Waller felt himself *alone*, and a man possessed by one harassing thought.

His comrades were lying among those bones, through which the rank dog-grass was sprouting—the companions of many a pleasant hour, the sharers of many a past danger. The object of the loving, the gentle, the tender, and the peaceful in England far away lay there, abandoned skeletons, exposed to the elements, to whiten and decay like the fallen branches of the forest.

Orderly and quiet at all times, a deeper silence fell upon our advancing troops as they traversed this terrible scene, a silence broken only by the dropping fire maintained by our advanced guard with the enemy's rear, under Amen Oolah Khan, till the leading brigade of the first division on the road from Khoord Cabul to Tizeen began to ascend the shoulder of a vast green mountain, named the Huft Kothul, where the narrow and tortuous pathway reaches its greatest altitude, rising above even the white mists of the deep and dark green valleys.

Even there, a portion of the path is overlooked by the Castle of Buddeeabad, which has a frontage of nearly eighty feet, and walls so lofty that the mountaineers attributed its erection, of course, to the genii, under Jan Ben Jan, who ruled the world before Adam came. It belonged to the father-in-law of Ackbar Khan, a Ghilzie chief; and there had the unfortunate old General Elphinstone looked his last upon the setting sun.

Under the immediate directions of Ackbar and of Amen Oolah, the Afghans, particularly the Khyberees, in their yellow turbans, the Ghilzies and others, were in vast force, and they poured down such a storm of bullets from rock and bank, cleft and fissure, that the whole air seemed alive with the hissing sound, as they passed over and, too often fatally, through our ranks.

"Thirteenth Light Infantry to the right!—Second Queen's to the left—extend!" were the instant orders of Sir Robert Sale to Waller and his other aide-de-camp or secretary, Sir Richmond Shakespere, a gallant and enterprising officer, of whom more anon; and away they galloped to have them executed. Waller rode, like most of the cavalry men, with a bundle of green corn over his horse's flanks, to serve alike as provender and to keep off the flies; but, as he spurred on to the head of the 13th Regiment, a shot from a jingaul tore it away, and scattered it to the wind. By the bad gunnery of the Afghans, their cannon-balls ricocheted in a way that would have delighted Marshal Vauban, who originally invented that mode of rendering a round shot doubly dangerous, a half-charge causing it to roll, rebound, maim, kill, and cause more disorder than if fired point blank; and hence the origin of the name, as *ricoche* signifies simply " duck and drake," the name given by boys to the bounding of a flat stone cast horizontally on the water.

The two aides delivered their orders in safety to the advancing battalions, and the commander of each gave his orders for " three companies on the right (it was the left for the 13th) to extend from the centre." Cheerily rang out the Kentish bugles, and away went the skirmishers, confident in their supports, with wonderful rapidity, though the men were falling fast on every hand. They spread over the green sunny slopes to the right and left, firing as they proceeded upward, and swept over the hills in beautiful order, till the central gorge was passed; then closing in by companies, and then in line, each regiment began to fix bayonets, and mutually to utter that hearty " hurrah !" which is ever the inspiring prelude to a charge of British troops.

Brightly flashed the ridge of bayonets in the sunshine, as on right and left the red battalions came wheeling down the grassy slopes at a resolute and steady double. The Afghans, though armed with bayonets too, never waited to cross them, but turned and fled, with howls of rage and terror, abandoning two English pieces of artillery.

Then rang out the trumpets sharp and shrill, and giving the reins to their horses, the 3rd Light Dragoons, all in blue uniform, with white puggerees over their shakos, their long, straight sword-blades flashing and uplifted, their heads stooped, their teeth set with energy, and every bronzed face flushed with ardour, spurred on their way; and as they rushed past at racing speed, Bob Waller, impelled by an irresistible impulse, joined them. It was, indeed, a race to be the first in the task of vengeance; for here and there, unchecked and un-restrained, the privates, if better mounted, would dart in front of the officers, as the true English emulous spirit broke out, each seeking madly to outride his comrades, and be passed by none—so on swept our Light Dragoons like a living flood.

Right and left the trenchant sword-blades went flashing downward in the sun, only to be uplifted for another cut or thrust, the blood-drops flying from them in the air.

In the scattered conflict—for such it became, when the ranks of the charging cavalry were broken open and loose, every file acting in the slaughter in-dependently for himself, and keeping but a slight eye on the motions of his squadron leader—Waller's attention was attracted by a horseman who seemed to be in high authority, and whose figure, arms, and equipment were not unfamiliar to his eye. The Afghan was undoubtedly a brave fellow, and splendidly mounted on a spirited horse, the saddle and trappings of which were elaborately embossed and tasselled with gold, while at his martingale were four long flying tassels of white hair taken from the tails of wild oxen. He had on his left arm a small round shield, adorned by four silver knobs; a dagger was in his teeth, and in his right hand a long and brightly headed lance, with which he had succeeded in unhorsing and pinning more than one of the 3rd Light Dragoons to the earth. He was just in the act of cruelly repassing this weapon through one who had fallen on his face, and who, in his dying agony was tearing up the turf with his hands and feet, when both Waller and Shakespere rode at him simultaneously, and sword in hand.

From the writhing and convulsed body he extricated his spear with difficulty, and turned furiously to face them, glancing and pointing it at each alternately. He wore a steel cap, engraved with gold; a sliding bar through the front peak, fixed there with a screw, protected his face; and in the knob that held his plume—a heron's tuft—there gleamed a precious stone of great value.

For an instant, quick as lightning, he relinquished his lance, letting it drop in the sling behind, while he drew a pistol from his scarlet silk girdle, and firing it at Shakespere, he hurled it dexterously at Waller, who ducked as it whizzed over his head. Recognising now, however, with whom he had to deal, he cried, fearlessly and confidently—

"Shakespere, as a favour, leave this fellow to me, and, with God's help, I shall polish him off as he deserves!"

"Shumsheer-bu-dust! (come on, sword in hand). Dog! thy soul shall be under the devil's jaw to-night!" cried the Afghan with fierce defiance, as his horse curveted and pranced.

He was Amen Oolah Khan, and a splendid and picturesque figure he presented in his brightly coloured and flaming dress, through the openings of which his shirt and sleeves of the finest chain-mail, bright as silver or frostwork on a winter branch, were visible, and, as Waller knew, impervious to the swords used in our service; at the same time he remembered that his pistols had both been discharged, and were still unloaded.

Shakespere reined back his horse, ready, if necessary, to second Waller, to whom he handed a pistol, on the Khan firing a second at him. Thus armed, Waller took a steady aim and fired straight at the head of his antagonist. The latter, to save himself, by a sharp use of the spur and curb, made his horse rear up, so that the bullet entered the throat and spine of the animal, which toppled forward with its head between its knees, just as Amen Oolah was coming to the charge with his lance, the point of which, by the downward sinking of his horse, entered the turf so deeply, that, by the consequent breaking of the shaft, he found himself tumbled ignominiously in a heap from his saddle, and at the mercy of Waller, who, dashing at him, rained blow after blow, without avail, upon his steel cap and mailed shoulders.

The sabre of Amen Oolah had been broken in some previous conflict; he had but one weapon left, the long and deadly Afghan knife, which, as a last resort, he had clenched in his teeth, and with this, while uttering a hoarse cry of rage and defiance, mingled with a rancorous malediction, he rushed at Waller, and strove to drag him from his saddle, spitting at him like a viper the while, and adding, exultingly,

" Ha!—your women are away to Toorkistan, to be the slaves of the Toorkomans—their slaves of the right hand!"

Waller, a finished horseman, was not to be easily dislodged, for he had twice the bulk and strength of his adversary. Twisting the reins round his left arm, he grasped the wrist of the hand which held the menacing knife, and by a single blow of his

sword across the fingers, compelled the Khan to
drop it. Heavy curses came from his lips, but
never once the word *amaun* (quarter); he knew it
would be useless, and he disdained to ask it. No
thought of mercy had Waller in his heart, for he
knew that if defeated he should have met with none;
and on this man's hands there might be, for all he
knew, the blood of Mabel Trecarrel, perhaps, of
others certainly, and such surmises, at such a time,
were maddening.

Barehanded now, the Afghan struggled like a
tiger with his powerful adversary, whom he strove
to unhorse. Waller endeavoured again and again
to run him through the body; but the Sheffield
blade bent, and failed to pierce the fine rings of the
Oriental shirt of mail, so to end the affair, he
smote the Khan repeatedly on the face with the hilt
of his sword, but the helmet bar protected him;
then, by making his horse rear, he endeavoured to
cast him off, or kick him under foot.

Stunned and confused, the savage Afghan at last
sank downward, and by some mischance got his
head into the stirrup-leather of Waller, whose left
foot was unavoidably pressed upon his throat; and
as the horse, terrified by this unusual appendage,
plunged wildly, and swerved round and round, the
wretched Khan was speedily strangled, and sank
into a state of insensibility, from which he never

recovered, as a couple of the 13th passed their fixed bayonets through his body, and one tore off his beautiful steel cap, from which Waller afterwards obtained the jewel—a sapphire of great value.

The cap itself, which was studded with those turquoises that are found in the mountains of Nishapour, in Khorassan, he tossed to the two soldiers, who proceeded at once to poke them out with their bayonets.

"If I ever meet my Mabel again, this sapphire shall be a gift for her!" thought Waller, with a sigh of weariness, for his victory brought neither triumph nor regret to his heart.

It was afterwards remembered, as a curious instance of retributive justice, that Amen Oollah Khan should die in the battle of Tizeen, almost by the same death as that to which he put his luckless elder brother, that he might succeed to his inheritance—strangulation.

The whole affair occupied only a few minutes; but, long ere it was over, the cavalry had swept far in pursuit, and Waller found himself almost alone. On one side was savage terror; on the other, civilized men thirsty for justice and vengeance; and so on all sides the turbaned hordes were stricken down by those who felt that to them was left the task of atoning for the betrayal and death of friends, comrades, and relatives; and there, on the heights of Tizeen, the standard of Ackbar Khan was trod in the dust, never to rise again !

Once more the sun went down in blood upon the passes of the Khyberees; but once again they were open, and the way to Cabul was clear.

Resistance had ceased; scarcely a single juzail shot was fired next day, when, after halting for the night, our infantry began their march beyond Tizeen, traversing, as the despatch has it, "those frightful ravines, now doubly frightful because of the heaps of dead bodies with which the narrow way was choked."

Another junction was made with the victorious troops of General Nott, advancing from Candahar and Ghuznee; and once more the green and lovely valley of Cabul, bounded by the snow-clad peaks of Kohistan, and threaded by its blue and winding river, came into view beyond the black rocky gorges of the Siah Sung; and the morning sun shone red and brightly on leaden dome and marble minar, on the walls of the city, and the vast castellated masses of the Bala Hissar. The uncased colours of horse and foot, European and Native, rustling in silk and embroidery, were given to the pleasant breeze; the fixed bayonets in long lines came like a stream of glittering steel out of the dark mountain passes; the bands struck up, and once again the merry British drums woke the same.

echoes that, ages upon ages ago, had replied to the clarions of the conquering Emperor Baber, of Mohammed, of Ghuznee, and even of Alexander and his bare-kneed Macedonians.

But still where were the captive hostages—the women and children?

CHAPTER XVI.

TO TOORKISTAN!

THE pen of Scott would have failed to describe, and the pencil of Gustave Doré to depict, the anguish of the poor hostages, when, at the behest of Ackbar, and at the very time the long prayed-for succour was coming, they were compelled to set out on their sorrowful journey towards the Land of Desert.

"Oh, my poor children—my helpless lambs—my fatherless little ones!" one would cry, folding in her loving arms her scared, pale, and half-starved brood, gathering them to her while they were yet *her own*, "even as a hen gathereth her chickens."

"My husband—my husband! shall we never meet again?"

"My poor 'Bob,' or 'Bill,' or, it might be, 'Tom,'" some soldier's wife would exclaim, "I shall never see the likes of you more, darling;" for though Tom perhaps drank all his pay, and gave Biddy now and then "a taste of his buff belt," he "was an angel, compared to a naygur, anyhow!"

But the majority of the hostages were ladies, and some of them were like Lady Macnaghten and Sir Robert Sale's daughter, who were widows—who had lost alike husband and children, and mourned as those only mourn who have no hope. And now many a quaint pet name, known best in the nursery and to the playfulness of the loving heart, was mingled with the most solemn of prayers.

"Death—death were better than this!" would be the despairing cry of some; and, ere their sad journey ended, death came to more than one of that devoted band.

For in one or two instances, despite the piteous entreaties of the ladies, some soldiers—those very men whom the 13th had subscribed their rupees at the drum-head to ransom—whose weakness from wounds or bodily illness rendered them incapable of riding or marching were shot by the wayside, and left unburied, even as so many lamed horses or diseased dogs which were useless might have been. One or two, who were weary of life, entreated to have it ended thus, and all whom the Dooranees destroyed thus in obedience to Ackbar's orders and the grim law, perhaps, of necessity, died peacefully and piously—sick of their present existence, and hopeful of the future; but the women screamed, lamented, and prayed, seeking to muffle their ears when the death-shots rang in the mountain wilderness.

Mabel Trecarrel was weak and ailing too, but she was much too valuable a species of commodity to be shot out of hand, like a poor Feringhee soldier, even though quite as much a Kaffir and infidel as he might be; so she was tenderly borne in a palanquin which had been found in the cantonments, and which contained every comfort and appliance for travelling—little drawers for holding clothes or food, and even a mirror, though she never looked at it.

Like a few more, she was silent in her grief, and found a refuge in tears.

The wedded wife might utter loudly and despairingly the name of her husband, and the parent that of the dead or absent child, finding a relief for the overcharged heart in sound; but, even in that terrible time, the poor betrothed girl could only whisper, in the inmost recesses of her breast, of the lover she never more might see, and gaze backward with haggard eyes on the features of the landscape with which they had both become familiar—the hills of Beymaru, the ridges of the Black Rocks, and the smiling valley of Cabul, as they all lessened and faded away in the distance, while slowly but surely, under a watchful and most unscrupulous guard, the train of prisoners, on active Tartar horses or plodding Afghan yaboos, in swinging dhooleys and curtained litters of other kinds, wound among the mountains on their way to Toorkistan, the frontiers of which were only about a week's journey distant.

And what was the prospect before them?

Separation and distribution, to be bartered for horses, or sold into slavery and degradation; the few men among them, irrespective of rank, to be the bondsmen, syces, carpet-spreaders, and grooms, hewers of wood and drawers of water: the women, if young, to be the veriest slaves of ignorant and unlettered masters, as yet unseen and unknown; if old, to become nurses and drudges to the women of the Usbec Tartars: and all these were Christians, and civilised subjects of the Queen; many of them accomplished, highly bred, nobly born, and tenderly nurtured.

Terrible were the emotions of the English mother, who, circumstanced thus, looked on her pure and innocent daughters and thought of what a week might bring forth!

Yet such were the fates before them—the fates that even the quickest marching of our troops might fail to avert; for were not the Afghans, as they heard, again disputing every inch of the Passes with a desperation which proved that Lord Auckland's policy, and that of the " peace at any price party" at home, would never have availed with those who deemed diplomacy but cowardly cunning, treaties as trash, bribes as fair "loot," and all war as legal fraud?

The lamentations of the women at times, when mingled and united (for grief is very infectious), roused even the usually phlegmatic Saleh Mohammed, who rode in the centre of the caravan, perched between the humps of a very high camel.

"In the land to which you are going, of course, you shall find neither Jinnistan, the Country of Delight, nor its capital, the City of Precious Stones; neither will fruits and sweet cakes drop into your mouths, as if you sat under the blessed tree of Toaba, which is watered by the rivers of paradise," said he, half scoffingly; "but you will see the vast sandy waste of the Kirghisian desert, which to the thirsty looks like a silvery sea in the distance; and some of you may happily see the city of Souzak, which contains five hundred houses of stone, and I doubt if the Queen of the Feringhees has so many in her little island. Barikillah! and you will see the black tents and the fleecy flocks of the Usbec Tartars, for they are numerous as leaves in the vale of Cashmere."

And thus he sought to console them when, on the evening of the first day's journey, they halted at Killi-Hadji, on the Ghuznee road (only seven miles westward from Cabul), and so called from the killi, or fort of mud that guards its cluster of huts. It

was approached by narrow and tortuous lanes overhung by shady mulberry-trees; and there, beside
the walls of the fort, they bivouacked for the night.

The deep crimson glory of sunset was over; but
the flush of the western sky lengthened far the
purple shadows of tree, and rock, and hut, even of
the tall camels, ere they knelt to rest, across the
scene of the bivouvac, which was not without its
strong aspect of the quaint and picturesque, albeit
the sad eyes of those who looked thereon were sick
of such elements, as being associated with all their
most unmerited miseries.

Unbitted, with leather tobrahs, or nose-bags filled
with barley, hanging from their heads, the patient
horses were eating, while the hardier yaboos grazed
the long grass that grew in the lanes and waste
places.

Fires were lighted, and around them all of the
Dooranee guard, who were not posted in the chain
of sentinels, sat cross-legged, smoking hempseed,
cleaning their arms, fixing fresh flints or dry
matches to their musket-locks; others were indus-
triously picking out of their furred poshteens those
active insects of the genus *pulex*, called by the
Arabians "the father of leapers," while the flesh of
a camel, which had been shot by the way, as useless
—its feet being wounded and sore—sputtered and
broiled on the embers for supper, and the light from

the flames fell in strong gleams and patches on the strange equipment, the swarthy turbaned faces, and gleaming eyes of those wild fellows, whose shawl-girdles bristled with arms and powder-flasks, and some four hundred of whom were furnished with muskets and bayonets.

A spear stuck upright in the earth—its sharp point glittering like a tiny red star—indicated the head-quarters, where, muffled in his poshteen and ample chogah, with a piece of thick xummul folded under him, Saleh Mohammed Khan, propped against the saddle of his camel, prepared, with pipe in mouth, to dose away the hours of the short August night.

Most, if not nearly all, the lady captives, wore now, of necessity, the Afghan travelling-dress, a large sheet shrouding the entire form, having a *bourkha*, or veil of white muslin, furnished with two holes to peep through; and with those who, muffled thus, sat in kujawurs, or camel-litters, the semblance of their orientalism was complete.

From time to time, dried branches or cass—a prickly furze grass which grows in bunches—were cast upon the fire, causing the flames to shoot up anew, on the pale faces of the prisoners and the dark faces of their guards, till at last the embers died out and the white ashes alone remained; and such was the scene which, like a species of phantasmagoria, met the eyes of Mabel Trecarrel, when, in the still watches of the night, she drew back the curtains of her palanquin and looked forth occasionally. But the stars began to pale in the sky; its blue gave place to opal tints; the sun arose, and after the Mohammedans had said their prayers with their faces towards Mecca, and the Christians with their eyes bent towards the earth or to heaven, once more the heartless march was resumed, in the same order as on the preceding day, through a pass in the mountains, and from thence across the beautiful valley of Maidan.

Saleh Mohammed, though a Khan, having once been a Soubadar in Captain Hopkins's Afghan Levy (from which he had deserted to the party of Ackbar Khan, at the beginning of the troubles), had some ideas of military order and show: thus he had at the head of the caravan—for it resembled nothing else—six Hindostanees, furnished with some of our drums and bugles gleaned up in the Khyber Pass, and with these they made the most horrible noises for several miles at the commencement and close of each day's march; but even this medley of discordant sounds failed to extract the faintest smile from the hostages—even from Major Pottinger and the few soldiers—so sunk were they in heart and spirit now.

In the Maidan valley they rode between fields of

golden grain bordered by towering poplars and pale willows. Bare, bleak-looking mountains undulated in the distance, and the poor ladies eyed them wistfully.

Were these the borders of dreaded Toorkistan ?

They proved, however, to be only a portion of the Indian Caucasus, the extremity of which, the Koh-i-baba, a snow-clad peak, rises to the height of sixteen thousand feet above the level of the Indian Sea.

That night Saleh Mohammed chose a pleasant halting-place for them, influenced by some sudden emotion of pity. There they were supplied with plums, wild cherries, peaches, and the white apricot which has the flavour of rose water. But ere morning there was an alarm ; a confused discharge of musketry was fired in every direction at random, all round the bivouac ; one or two bullets whistled through it. A dhooley-wallah was shot dead, and several red arrows, barbed and bearded, stuck quivering in the turf; yells were heard, and then a furious galloping of horses passing swiftly away in the distance.

It was a *chupao*—a night attack planned by some of the Hazarees, a wild and independent Tartar tribe, whose thatched huts lie sunk and unseen on the hill slopes, and on whose confines they had halted. They are all good archers, and, though armed with the matchlock, usually prefer the bow.

They are bitter foes of the Afghans, and had hoped, by making a dash, to cut off some of their prisoners; but Saleh Mohammed was too wary for them, and on that evening had doubled his guards ere the sun went down.

The 2nd of September found the train traversing the Kaloo Mountain, one in height only inferior to the Koh-i-baba. From thence, over a vast chaos of wild and terrific hilly peaks that spread beneath them like the pointed waves of a petrified sea, they could view, at last, and afar off, the plains of Toorkistan—the land of their future bondage; and anew the wail of grief and woe rose from them at the sight.

The following day, that the absurd might not be wanting amid their misery, to the surprise of all, Saleh Mohammed appeared mounted on his camel, not in his usual amplitude of turban, with his flowing chogah and Cashmere shawls, but with his lean, shrunken, and bony figure buttoned up in a tight regimental blue surtout, with gold shoulder-scales, and crimson sash, frog-belt, and sword, all of which had whilom belonged to Jack Polwhele, of the Cornish Light Infantry, a tiny forage cap (which Jack used to wear very much over his right ear) being perched on the back of his bald head, while the chin-strap came uncomfortably only below the tip of his high hooked nose; and thus arrayed he prepared to meet and, as he hoped, duly to impress Zoolficar Khan, the governor of the town of Bameean, where the first halt was to be made for further and final orders from Ackbar, as to whether the hostages should be sold or slain; for now their custodian began to have some strange doubts upon the subject, and now his victims were fairly out of Afghanistan and in the land of the Tartars, nine days of monotonous and arduous journey distant from Cabul.

We have lately seen the kind of mercy meted out to helpless hostages by Communal savages in the boasted city of Paris—the self-styled centre of civilization—and so may fairly tremble for the fate of those who were in the hands of Asiatic fanatics on the western slopes of the Hindoo-Kush.

CHAPTER XVII.

MABEL'S PRESENTIMENT.

MABEL TRECARREL seemed to see or to feel the image of Waller become more vividly impressed upon her mind, now, as every day's journey, as every hour, and every mile towards the deserts of Great Tartary, increased the perils of her own situation, and seemed to add to the difficulties, if not entirely to close all the chances, of their ever meeting again on this earth; and as Bameean, a rock-hewn city, the Thebes of the East, and geographically situated in Persia, began to rise before the caravan, when it wound down from the Akrobat Pass, a deeper chill fell on her heart, for she had a solemn presentiment creeping over her that *there* all her sorrows, if not those of her companions too, should be ended.

A laborious progress of several miles, during which her now weary dhooley-wallahs staggered and reeled with fatigue, brought them from the mountain slopes into a plain, damp, muddy, and marshy, where from the plashy soil there rose a mist through which the city seemed to shimmer and loom, shadowy and ghost-like. A great portion of this plain was waste, and hence believed to be the abode of ghouls, afreets, and demons, who, in the dark and twilight, sought to lure the children of Adam to unknown but terrible doom.

A gust of wind careering over the waste from the Pass, rolled away, like a veil of gauze, the shroud which had half concealed the place they were approaching; and with a mournful and sickly interest, not unmixed with anticipated dread, Mabel and her friends surveyed the city of Bameean.

Rising terrace over terrace on the green acclivities of an insulated mountain, the bolder features and details shining in the ruddy sunlight, the intermediate spaces sunk in sombre shadow, it exhibited a series of the most wonderfully excavated mansions, temples, and ornamental caverns (the abodes of its ancient and nameless inhabitants), to the number of more than twelve thousand, covering a slope of eight miles in extent.

Many of those rock-hewn edifices, carved out of the living stone which supports the mountain, and are the chief portions of its foundation and structure, have beautiful friezes and entablatures, domes and cupolas, with elaborately arched doors and windows. Others are mere dens and caverns, with square air-holes; but towering over all are many colossal figures, more particularly two—a woman one hundred and twenty feet high, and another of a man, forty feet *higher*—all hewn out of the face of a lofty cliff.

By what race, or when, those mighty and wondrous works of art were formed, at such vast labour, no human record, not even a tradition, remains to tell; their origin is shrouded by a veil of mystery, like that of the ruined cities of Yucatan; so whether they are relics of Bhuddism, or were hewn in the third century, during the dynasty of the Sassanides, has nothing to do with our story. But the poor hostages, as they were conveyed past those silent, dark, and empty temples, abandoned now to the jackal, the serpent, and the flying fox, with the towering and gigantic apparitions of the stone colossi lookingly grimly down in silence, felt strange emotions of chilly awe come over them—the ladies especially. To Mabel Trecarrel, in her weak and nervous state, the scene proved too much; she became hysterical, and wept and laughed at the same moment, to the great perplexity of Saleh Mohammed, who was quite unused to such exhibitions among the ladies of *his* zenanah.

Though stormed by Jenghiz Khan and his hordes, in 1220, after a vigorous resistance, this rock-hewn city, by its materials and massiveness, could suffer little; yet it was subsequently deserted by all its inhabitants, who named it "Maublig," or the *un-*

fortunate. After that time, its history sank into utter obscurity; its once-fertile plain reverted to a desert state once more; yet unchanged as when Bameean was in its zenith, its river of the same name flows past the caverned mountain, on its silent way to the snowy wastes where its waters mingle with those of the Oxus. ·

In this remote place the captives were all, as usual, enclosed in a walled fort which contained a few hovels of mud, where in darkness and damp they strove to make themselves as comfortable as circumstances permitted, with blankets, xummuls, and the saddles on which they had ridden.

The Dooranees of Saleh Mohammed had to keep sure watch and ward there, for the Usbec Tartars are the predominating people, and, though divided into many tribes, they are all rigid Soonees, with but small favour for the Afghans; and the prisoners soon learned that the unusual costume of Saleh Mohammed, instead of inspiring Zoolficar Khan, as he had expected, with wonder, only excited in that sturdy Toorkoman an emotion of contempt, that a Mussulman should so far degrade himself by adopting, even for a day, the dress of a Feringhee—a Kaffir; and they had something approaching to hasty words on the subject, when, on the first evening of their meeting, those dignitaries sat together on the same carpet

under a date tree in the garden of the fort, while
slaves supplied them with hot coffee, wheat pillau,
pipes, and tobacco.

There, too, had Mabel been borne on a pallet, by
the express permission of the Khan, that she might
enjoy the sunshine; there was, he knew, no chance
of her attempting to escape; and to prevent any
covetous Toorkoman from playing tricks with the
tender wares entrusted to him, he had a double
chain of sentinels with loaded muskets planted
round them, as Zoolficar Khan could perceive when
reconnoitring the place, which was outside the city
of Bameean, but immediately under the shadow of
its temples and rock-hewn giants; for Zoolficar,
having learned that Saleh Mohammed was proceeding towards the deserts with the captives to
sell, to punish the men of their tribe for interference in the affairs of Afghanistan, was not in-
disposed to have the first selection from among
them, and had resolved to look over "the lot" with
a purchaser's eye.

He had already, over their pipes and coffee,
broached the subject to Saleh Mohammed; but the
latter, undecided in everything, save that he had to
halt where he was for fresh orders from the Sirdir,
Ackbar Khan, would not as yet listen to any proposals for selling or bartering, and eventually dozed
off asleep, with the amber mouthpiece of the bubble-

bubble in his mouth, leaving Zoolficar Khan to amuse himself as best he might.

Mabel, weary and faint with her long journey of nine consecutive days, though borne easily and carefully enough in a palanquin, lay listlessly and drowsily pillowed on her pallet, under the cool and pleasant shade of an acacia tree. Near her stood a tiny pagoda of white marble, carved as minutely and elaborately as a Chinese ivory puzzle; and before it was a tank wherein were floating some of the beautiful red lotus, the flowers of which far exceed in size and beauty those of the ordinary water-lily.

The slender, drooping, and fibrous branches of the acacia tree, so graceful in their forms and so tender in their texture, cast a partial shadow over her, and, as they moved slowly to and fro in the soft evening wind, by their rocking or oscillating motion predisposed her to slumber; and so, ere long, she slept, but slept only to dream of the past—the happy, happy past, for keenly did she and all who were with her realise now that "it is the eternal looking-back in this world that forms the staple of all our misery."

Anon, she dreamed of the monotonous swinging of her palanquin, and the doggrel songs by which the poor half-nude bearers sought to beguile their toil and cheer the mountain way; now it was of Waller,

with his fair English face, his handsome winning
eyes, and frank, jovial manner, retorting some of the
banter of Polwhele or Burgoyne. She was at her
piano; he was hanging over her as of old, and their
whispers mingled, though fears suggested that the
horrible Quasimodo, the Khond, with his cat-like
moustaches and mouth that resembled a red gash,
was concealed somewhere close by; then she heard
cries and shots—they were attacked by Hazarees,
Ghazees, Ghilzies, or some other dark-coloured
wretches; and with a little scream she started and
awoke, to find that her veil had been rudely withdrawn—uplifted, in fact—in the hand of a man who
stood under the acacia tree, and had been leisurely
surveying her in her sleep with eyes expressive of
inspection and satisfaction.

She shuddered, and a low cry of fear escaped her;
for she knew by the cast of his face, by his air and
equipment, that the stranger was a Toorkoman—the
first who had come—by his unwelcome presence
bringing fresh perils, as she knew, to all the English
ladies; yet he was a handsome fellow, not much over
five-and-twenty, and so like Zohrab Zubberdust in
aspect and bearing, that they might have passed for
brothers.

Mabel feebly struggled into a sitting posture, and,
snatching her veil from his hand, looked steadily,
perhaps a little defiantly, at Zoolficar Khan; for he it

was who, when his older host dozed off, to dream
of plunder and paradise, had proceeded to make a
reconnaissance of whatever might be seen of the
prisoners and their guards; for it might yet suit his
interests or his fancy to cut off the whole caravan
in a night or so. Thus, a few paces from where Saleh
Mohammed was sleeping in the sunshine had
brought him unexpectedly on Mabel!

He was a dashing fellow, whose dress was not the
least remarkable thing about him. His trowsers, of
ample dimensions, were of bright blue cloth, very
baggy, and thrust into short yellow boots; he had
on three collarless jackets, all of different hues,
and richly fringed and laced; a large turban of
silk of every colour, with a white heron's plume, to
indicate that he was a chief; a shawl girdle, with
sword, dagger, and long-barrelled awkward Turkish
pistols stuck therein, completed his attire. His
keen, sharp Tartar features, though suggestive of
good humour by their general expression, were not,
however, without much of cunning, rakish insolence,
and the bold effrontery incident to a lawless state of
society, a knowledge of power, and much of contempt or indifference for the feelings of others. He
looked every inch one of those wild

"Toorkomans, countless as their flocks, led forth
From th' aromatic pastures of the north;

Wild warriors of the Turquoise hills, and those
Who dwell beyond the everlasting snows
Of Hindoo Koosh, in stormy freedom bred,
Their fort the rock, their camp the torrent's bed !"

He simply gave the scared Mabel a smile, full of
confidence and saucy meaning, and then turned
away, leaving her a. prey to emotions of fear—a
fear that might have been all the greater had she
heard what passed between him and Saleh Mohammed at the time when she, trembling in heart
and feeble in limb, crept back to the ladies' huts to
tell them, with lips blanched by terror, that "the
first Toorkoman had come !"

And stronger than ever grew her presentiment
within her.

The craving to hear of the movements of the
three British armies which they knew to be still in
Afghanistan was strong as ever in the hearts of the
captives—to hear the last, ere a barrier rose between them and their past life ; and that barrier
seemed now to be the mighty chain of Hindoo Koosh
rising between them and the way to India and to
home. Long had they hoped against hope. Nott,
and Pollock, and Sale—where were they and their
soldiers? What were they doing? For the Dooranees
would tell nothing. Had they and their forces been
destroyed in detail, even as Elphinstone's had been?
Those yells and noisy discharges of musketry, in

which the captors at times indulged in honour of alleged victories over the three Kaffir Sirdirs, on tidings brought by wandering hadjis, filthy faquirs, and dancing dervishes, could they be justified? Alas! fate seemed to have done its worst!

Surmises were become threadbare; invention was worn out. Each of the poor captives had striven, by suggestions of probabilities and by efforts of imagination, to flatter themselves and buoy up the hearts of others; but all seemed at an end now.

CHAPTER XVIII.

THE GOVERNOR OF BAMEEAN.

WAKING up Saleh Mohammed without much ceremony, the young Toorkoman chief proceeded to
business at once, but in a very cunning way, com-
mencing with another subject, like a wily lawyer
seeking to lure and throw a witness off his guard.

"After a nine days' journey, Khan, you must be
short of provisions?" said he.

"Oh, fear not for our presence here in Bameean,"
replied Saleh Mohammed, leisurely sucking at his
hubble-bubble, the light of which had gone out;
"every tobrah full of oats, every maund of ottah
and rice, we require shall be duly paid for."

"You mistake me; I did not mean that."

"What then? Bismillah! we are rich: the spoil
of the Kaffir dogs who come to Cabul has made us
happy."

Zoolficar's almond-shaped eyes glistened with
covetousness on hearing this. He reflected: the
Dooranees were not quite five hundred strong, and
he could bring a thousand Tartar horsemen into the

field; hence, why might not all this plunder so freely spoken of, and these slaves, two of whom he had seen (and they *were* so white and handsome!), be his?

"You propose to remain here for some days, aga?" he resumed, seating himself cross-legged, and playing with the silken tassel of his sabre.

"Yes."

"Waiting for orders from Ackbar Khan?"

"Yes."

"His final firmaun, I think you said?"

"Yes."

"To advance or retire?"

"Yes."

"If he has proved signally victorious?" queried Zoolficar sharply, as he grew impatient of these mere affirmatives, which were resorted to by the other merely to give him time to think and sift the other's purpose.

"Wallah billah—victorious."

"Yes—which, under Allah, we cannot doubt?"

"Well, aga."

"Then his orders will be to sell these hostages, I suppose?"

"Yes—perhaps."

"Where, Khan?—here in Bameean?"

"No; they will bring larger prices nearer Bokhara."

"But if he is *not* victorious?" suggested Zoolficar.

"Staferillah! Then we must leave the event to fate; or my orders may be——" and here even Saleh Mohammed paused ere he made the atrocious admission that hovered on his tongue.

"What—what?"

"To behead them. Ackbar has sworn that none should live to tell the tale of those who came up the Khyber Pass; and I must own that his sparing these surprised me."

There was a pause, after which the Governor of Bameean said—

"And when may you expect those final orders?"

"Or tidings, let us call them."

"Well, well, aga, this is playing with words."

"Tidings that shall guide me may come without orders," replied Saleh Mohammed, glancing at the green flag of Ackbar which was flying on the fort, and then half closing his eyes to watch the other keenly, and as if to read in his face the drift of all these questions. "You surely take a deep interest in these Kaffirs, Zoolficar Khan?" he added.

"I take an interest, at least, in two whom I have seen—in one particularly."

"The Hindoo ayah in the red garment?" suggested Saleh, pointing with the amber mouthpiece of his pipe to an old nurse who was passing, with two of the captive children.

" The devil—no! One who is beautiful as the rose
with the hundred leaves—one with a skin as fair as
if she had bathed in the waters of Cashmere; an
idol more lovely than ever adorned the house of
Azor! She was under yonder tree asleep, when I
lifted her veil and looked on her."

" Allah Ackbar—now we have it!" exclaimed
Saleh Mohammed, with something between irritation and amusement. " Well, know, aga, that to
quote a Parsee or Hindoo banker's book in lieu of
Hafiz might be more to the purpose."

" Perhaps so : we have more metal in our scab-
bards than in our purses, in the desert here."

" They have tempers, these Feringhee women, I
can tell you," said the Dooranee, with a quiet laugh.

" So have ours, for the matter of that, and are
free enough with their slipper heel on a man's beard
at times."

" Ah! all women, I dare say, are like the apples
of Istkahar, one half sweet and one half sour," said
the old Khan, shaking his long beard.

" You must seek the well of youth again," rejoined
the young Toorkoman, laughing. " There is another
Kaffir damsel whose voice sounded sweetly, as if she
had tasted of the leaves that shadow the tomb of
Tan-Sien," he continued, using in his ordinary conversation figures and phraseology that seem no way
far-fetched to an Oriental; " yes, aga, tender and

soft, for I heard her sing her two children to sleep in yonder hut. Yet she may never have been in Gwalior," added Zoolficar; for the lady was an officer's widow, young and pretty, with two poor sickly babes; and the *tomb* he referred to was that of the famous musician, who once flourished at the court of the Emperor Ackbar, and the leaves of a tree near which are supposed to impart, when eaten, a wondrous melody to the human voice.

" Then am I to understand that you have set eyes upon both these prisoners ? " asked Saleh Mohammed, his keen black eyes becoming very round, as he seemed to make up more fully to the matter in hand.

" Please God, I have. In a word," said Zoolficar Khan, lowering his voice, "I shall give you a purse of five hundred tomauns for them both—peaceably, and help you to plunder the Hazarees on your way home."

" And what of the Sirdir ? "

" Tell him they died on the way: moreover, I don't want the two children—you may keep them."

This liberality failed to find any approbation in Saleh Mohammed, who affected to look indignant, and exclaimed—

" I am Saleh Mohammed Khan, chief of the Dooranees, and *not* a slave-dealer, staferillah!—God forbid ! "

"Neither is Ackbar Khan—a son of the royal house of Afghanistan; yet he has sent hither those people for sale, in *your* charge—for sale to the Toorkomans; and what am I?"

"I have no final orders—as yet," replied the Khan, doggedly.

"For their disposal, you mean?"

"No."

"For what, then?"

"Simply to halt here; to act peaceably, but watchfully, Zoolficar Khan—*watchfully*," replied the other in a pointed manner; "and hourly now I may expect a cossid with a firmaun from Cabul."

"The Hazarees are in arms in your rear, and, ere your cossid comes, there may be a chupao in the night, and the fort may be looted."

"By them, or your people?"

"Nay, I said not mine, aga."

"But you thought it," was the blunt response.

"Who, save Allah, may pretend to know what another man thinks?"

"Well, we are prepared alike to protect ourselves and to keep or slay; yea—for it may come to that—to slay, root and branch, those Kaffir hostages. I would not betray my trust, were you Kedar Khan with all his wealth!" continued Saleh Mohammed, flushing red, and speaking as earnestly as if he really felt all he said, while referring to that ancient king of Toorkistan, whose fabled riches were so great, that when on the march he had always before him seven hundred horsemen, with battle-axes of silver, and the same number behind, with battle-axes of gold.

So far as slaughter was concerned, if that sequel were necessary, Zoolficar Khan felt sure that Saleh Mohammed would keep his word; and he was about to retire partially baffled, with his mind full of visions for securing the plunder by a midnight attack on the Dooranees, either while in the fort or when on the march; and he was casting a furtive glance to where he had last seen Mabel, combining it with a low salaam to his host, when, ere he could take his leave, a strange figure on a foam-covered yaboo rode furiously into the fort and dismounted before them. He was almost nude; his lean body, reduced to bone and brawn, was powdered with sandal-wood ashes; his hair hung in vast volume over his back and shoulders; his only garment was a pair of goat-skin breeches; a gourd for water hung by a strap over his shoulder, and this, together with a long Afghan knife, a large wooden rosary of ninety-nine beads, and a knotted staff, completed his equipment.

"Lah-allah-mahmoud-resoul-Allah!" he yelled, flourishing the staff as he sprang from his shaggy yaboo.

"We know that well enough, Osman Abdallah,"

said the Dooranee chief, impatiently, to the Arab
Hadji, for it was he who came thus suddenly, like a
flash of lightning; " but from whence come you?"

" Cabul; or the mountains near it, rather."

" To me?"

" Yes, Khan, with a message from the Sirdir,"
replied this fierce, wild, ubiquitous being, whose
skin bore yet the scarcely healed marks of Waller's
sword-thrust, as he drew from his girdle a sorely
soiled scrap of paper, and bowed his head reve-
rentially over it; for the bearer of a letter from such
a personage as the Prince Ackbar must treat the
document with as much respect as if he himself
were present.

" And what of the Sirdir?" asked Saleh, starting
forward.

" Allah kerim; he has been defeated by the
Kaffir's dogs at Tizeen—routed by Pollock Sahib—
totally!"

" Silence, fool!" cried the Dooranee, with a swift,
fierce glance at the Toorkoman, as he snatched from
the hands of the Hadji, and without a word of
greeting or thanks, the little scroll, and then opened
it deliberately and slowly, as if the disposal of a
flock of sheep were the matter in hand, and not
the lives or deaths, the captivity or liberty, of so
many helpless human beings. The missive contained but three words, and the seal of Ackbar—

" *March to Kooloom.*"

And Zoolficar Khan, who peeped over his shoulder without ceremony, had read it too. The beetle brows of Saleh Mohammed were close over his fiery eyes, as he said, haughtily—

"Where is this place? I may ask, as you have read the name."

"Kooloom—it is a steep, rugged, and perilous journey, Khan."

" And what am I to do when I get there? " asked Saleh Mohammed, ponderingly, of himself, and not of his companion.

" But you are not yet there," said the latter, in a low voice.

" How—what do you mean ? "

" The way may be beset. Have I not said that it is perilous? "

" Well, perhaps we shall not go," replied the other, with an unfathomable smile; and with low salaams they separated, each quite ready for and prepared to outwit the other.

One fact they had both learned: Ackbar Khan was defeated, and *not* victorious!

CHAPTER XIX

"THEN you have seen the fighting against the Kaffirs, I suppose?" asked Saleh Mohammed, grimly.

"Seen! Nay, Khan, I fought against them in person; at Jugdulluck, the defence of the village was entrusted to me——"

"And lost by a Hadji," said the Khan, with a sneer.

"Yes, even as the heights of Tizeen were lost by a Khan," retorted the other.

"A Khan—who?"

"Amen Oolah—who was killed there."

"Was the slaughter great?"

"Of the Faithful, mean you?"

"Yes: I ask not of the Kaffirs—may their white faces be confounded!"

"The slaughter might remind Azrael, and the angels who looked on us, of the Prophet when he fought at Bedr. It was not so great, of course, as that of the Feringhees when they left Cabul; for

Ackbar's orders were then, that but *one* should be left alive, if even that; but the white smoke, as it rolled on the wind, along the green sides of the hills, and ascended skyward out of the deep, dark Passes, was like that which shall precede the last day, and for two moons fill all space, from the east to the west, from the rising to the setting of the sun."

"Silence!" grumbled Saleh Mohammed, who was full of earnest thought, and in no mood for religious canting just then, as the orders of Ackbar and the collateral news of his defeat perplexed, while the hints and covert threats of the Governor of Bameean alarmed and irritated him. "So this is all you know, Hadji Osman?"

"All, save that I have a letter for Pottinger Sahib."

"From whom?" asked the chief, sharply.

"Shireen Khan, of the Kuzzilbashes."

"Fool! why not speak of this before? Yet perhaps it is as well that yonder Toorkoman dog is gone," exclaimed Saleh Mohammed, as he impetuously tore the missive from the hand of the cunning Hadji, who probably knew its contents; for a most singular leer came into his repulsive face, as he watched the dark visage of the Dooranee, seeming all the darker in the twilight now; for the golden flush was dying in the west, and its fading light fell faintly on the rock-hewn edifices and wondrous colossi that towered on the hill-slope above the fort, one half of which was sunk in shadow.

The Arab Hadji, as his creed inculcated, loathed the infidels, but this loathing did not extend to their loot and treasures; he was not indifferent to their wines and other good things (in secret, of course), and he loved their golden English guineas and shining rupees—their shekels and talents of silver—quite as much as any of "the cloth" (not that he indulged in that commodity), the reverend faquirs, doctors, and dervishes of enlightened Feringhistan; so, for "a consideration," he had actually brought a message to a "Kaffir," concerning the redemption of his companions. The letter briefly detailed the victory of General Pollock at Tizeen, placing beyond a doubt the rout of Ackbar, and his flight to Kohistan, and suggested that the Major, in his own name and those of five other British officers, who were prisoners with him, should offer to Saleh Mohammed the sum of twenty thousand rupees as a ransom for all—especially the ladies and children—the sum to be paid down on their release; and a glow of triumph, satisfaction, and avarice filled the keen eyes and face of the old Dooranee as he read over the words carefully thrice; and then stroking his mighty beard, as if making a promise to himself, and seeming already to feel the rupees loading his girdle, he exclaimed—

" Shabash ! Allah keerim ! (Very good ! God is merciful !) The Major Sahib will act like a sensible man, and trust to my generosity. The game of Ackbar—whose dog is *he* now ?—is about played out at Cabul ; he is checkmated—has not a move on the board. So Saleh Mohammed may as well act mercifully, and treat with the Feringhee Major for the ransom of his people."

The night was passed as usual, after prayers were over, in stupor or the wonted listlessness of despair, by the captives, who were crowded all together in the mud hovels of the fort, their Dooranee guards lying outside in their chogahs, poshteens, and horse-cloths ; but in the morning they saw with surprise that a new flag—a scarlet one—had replaced the sacred green, which had floated on the outer wall at sunset.

And each asked of the other what might this portend ? It was the signal that Saleh Mohammed had revolted from the cause of Ackbar Khan ; but of what his own movements or measures were to be they knew nothing yet. This new feature in affairs bewildered and baffled the ulterior views of Zoolficar Khan, who was still more surprised when, soon after dawn, the old Dooranee, with a detachment of his people, sallied from the fort, attacked and captured —not, however, without resistance, some sharp firing, and use of the sabre—a whole convoy of provisions

which passed *en route* for Bokhara—an act of daring
for which he found it difficult to account, as it would
be sure to rouse the terrible Emir of that kingdom
again these intruders in Toorkistan; but doubtless,
thought Zoolficar, the Afghan must know his own
plans and power best.

Loth, however, not to pick up something in the
broils or forays that were so likely to ensue, he
began gradually to muster his Toorkoman followers,
desiring them to draw to a head in a wood near the
Bameean river, about nightfall, to watch the Dooranees in the fort, and to gall or attack them either
in advancing or retiring therefrom; but, ere dark-
came, there occurred what was to him a fresh source
of surprise, and to Saleh Mohammed of serious
alarm, while it chilled with a new-born fear the
hearts of the prisoners, to whom Major Pottinger
had now communicated his letter, his promises and
plans, with all the tidings of the Hadji, thereby for
a time exciting their wildest and most joyous anticipations (at a moment when hope had sunk to its
lowest ebb) of freedom and restoration to the
world: so friends were rushing to congratulate
friends, and weeping with happiness, mothers were
wildly clasping their children to their breast, and
all were giving thanks to God.

Affecting ignorance of any change that had taken
place in the mind of the Dooranee, towards evening

Zoolficar Khan in all his bravery, but alone, rode to the gate of the fort, when, greatly to his wrath, he was denied admittance by Saleh Mohammed in person.

"Take care lest you are the dupe of your own fortune," said he haughtily.

"Covet not the goods of another, aga," responded Saleh, who had now resumed his Oriental amplitude of costume.

"Are we to understand that you have abandoned the cause of Ackbar?"

"Fate has done so—wallah billah—why should not I?"

"How now about Khedar Khan and his riches, O Saleh Mohammed the Incorruptible?" laughed the Toorkoman.

"Dare you mock me?" asked the Dooranee, scowling, with his hand on a pistol.

"No; but what means all this change since yesterday?"

"It means that what is good for me may be bad for you? Who can read the book of destiny? The same flower which gives a sweet to the bee gives poison to reptiles?"

"Does all this mean that you will neither sell nor barter?" asked Zoolficar, shaking haughtily his huge turban and white heron's plume.

"Exactly.—that I will do neither," replied the Dooranee, with a mocking laugh.

"Then, by the hand of the Prophet, there perhaps come those who may deprive you of all you possess!" exclaimed the young Toorkoman, with fierce triumph, as he pointed suddenly along the road that led towards the Akrobat Pass.

The sun, now in the west, was shedding a lovely golden light along the brilliantly green slopes of the mighty mountains, whose snow-capped peaks stood up sharply defined, cold and white, against the deep, pure blue of the sky. The barren and desolate Akrobat Pass, overhung by rocks of slate and limestone, yawned like a dark fissure between the masses of the impending hills, and out of it a cloud of white dust was now seen to roll, spreading like mist, and increasing in magnitude like the vapour released by the fisherman in the Arabian story from the vase of yellow copper on the sea-shore.

On and on it came—onward and downward into the plain where the Bameean river winds, and where the silent city of the Colossi towers upon its rock-hewn hill.

Bright points began to flash and gleam ever and and anon out of this coming cloud of dust—points that could not be mistaken by a soldier's eye,—and speedily the whole advancing mass assumed the

undoubted aspect of a great body of armed horsemen, whose tall spears shone like stars, as they
came on at full speed from the mountains!

"Hazarees—wild Hazarees or Eimauks—by Allah!" exclaimed the Toorkoman, gathering his reins
in his hands; "a chupao—an attack on you, Saleh
Mohammed! Now look to your damsels and spoil,
for you will be looted of every kusira!"*

With a shout of exultation and defiance, he wheeled
round his horse, and galloped away towards the
wood and river.

The Arab Hadji, Osman, declared these new-
comers to be some Usbec cavalry, whom he had seen
but yesterday encamped by the side of the river
Balkh.

"Kosh gelding! Usbecs, Toorkomans, or Hazarees,—let them come and welcome; they shall
not find us unprepared!" exclaimed Saleh Mohammed through his clenched teeth, while his
black eyes shot fire, and he rushed away for his
weapons, and, by all the horrible din that his
Hindostanee drummers and buglers could make,
summoned his quaint-looking followers to arms;
for, in that lawless land, he knew not whose swords
might be uplifted against them now, as the downfall
of Ackbar would encourage all to make spoil of his

* An Afghan coin, worth about ·083 of a penny, English.

adherents. Even in the kingdom of Afghanistan there were bitter quarrels, and the tribes were all divided against each other now.

In a moment the fort became a scene of the most unwonted bustle. The Dooranees are one of the bravest of the Afghan clans, and this party of them prepared to make a resolute defence, and, if necessary, to sell their lives as dearly as possible. Muskets, matchlocks, and jingalls were loaded on every hand. The gate' of the fort was hastily closed and barricaded behind with earth, and an old brass 9-pounder gun, covered with Indian characters—a perilous and too probably honey-combed piece of ordnance, which was found in the place—was propped on a heap of stones, just inside the entrance, where it was loaded with bottles, nails, and other missiles, to sweep a storming party.

Meanwhile all the European male prisoners, under Major Pottinger, were now armed to make common cause with their late guards; and among them many a pale cheek flushed, and many a hollow eye lighted up once more, at the prospect of a conflict, though the weapons with which our poor fellows were armed were only quaint matchlocks, rusty tulwars, and old notched Afghan sabres.

And now in front of the column of advancing horse, two cavaliers came galloping on at head-long speed, far before all their comrades, whose ranks were loose and confused, and all unlike Europeans; so Saleh Mohammed, his face darkened by a scowl, his eyes glistening like those of a rattlesnake, and his white beard floating on the wind, crouched behind the old and mouldering wall, adjusting with his own hands a clumsy jingall, or swivel wall-piece, with the iron one-pound shot of which he was prepared to empty the saddle of one of those two adventurous riders—he cared not a jot which.

Thus far we have followed Anglo-Indian history; and now to resume more particularly our own narrative.

CHAPTER XX.

TOO LATE!

WHEN Doctor C——, though the anxious and watchful eyes of Rose Trecarrel were bent upon him, had shaken his head so despondingly, and thereby gratified · the professional spleen of the long-bearded Abu Malec, he had done so involuntarily, and from sincere medical misgivings that his aid had been summoned when too late; and with tears in her eyes, did Rose needlessly assure him that, until she had seen him enter the sick room, she knew not of his existence, or that he had been permitted to survive.

To this he replied by taking both her hands kindly within his own, for he was a warm-hearted Scottish Highlander, and in turn assuring her that, " until brought to the fort of Shireen Khan by the Hakeem, he also had been ignorant of the vicinity of her and her companion; but without proper medicines," he added, " little could be done—now especially."

Yet she hoped much. He gave her valuable

advice, and the Khanum, too, and promised to return without delay, and with certain prescriptions, made up from his little store kept in Cabul for the few wounded soldiers who were hostages there. He rode off, and Rose's blessings and gratitude went with him. No curiosity as to the relations of the nurse and patient—peculiar though their circumstances—prompted a question from the doctor. That Rose should attend the sick officer seemed only humane and natural. Who other so suitable was nigh? And to find one more European —a friend especially—surviving, was source of pleasure enough!

The doctor retired; but, instead of hours, days went by, and he returned no more; for on the very evening of his visit he was seized and despatched, with all the rest, under Saleh Mohammed, to Toorkistan. In another place the doctor was thus enabled to be of much value to Mabel Trecarrel, and *en route* towards the desert did much to alleviate her sufferings, and restore her health; but the assurance he gave her that he had seen her sister and Denzil Devereaux too, and that they were safe—perfectly safe—in the powerful protection of Shireen Khan, did more to this end than all his prescriptions.

But his advice ultimately availed but little the patient he left behind, for Denzil grew worse—sank

more and more daily; he had but the superstition
and follies or quackery of Abu Malec to interpose
between him and eternity.

Terribly was Rose sensible of all this, as she sat
and watched by the young man's bedside in that
desolate room of the fort; for it was intensely
desolate and comfortless, an Afghan noble's ideas
of luxury and splendour being inferior to those
possessed by an English groom. Save the bed on
which he lay, two European chairs and a trunk
brought from the plunder of the cantonments, it was
as destitute of furniture as the cell of a prison; and,
as if in such a cell, daily the square outline of the
window was seen to fall with the yellow sunshine on
the same part of the wall, and thence pass upward
obliquely as the sun went round, till it faded away
at the corner, and then next day it appeared again,
without change.

And there sat the once-gay, bright, and heedless Rose Trecarrel, the belle of the ball, of the
hunting-meet, of the race-course, and the garrison, with a choking sensation in her throat, and
a clamorous fear in her heart, Denzil's hot,
throbbing hand often clasped in one of hers, while
the other strayed caressingly over his once-thick
hair, or what remained of it, for by order of Doctor
C——, she had shorn it short—shorter even than
the regimental pattern; and so would she sit,

watching the winning young fellow, who loved her
so well—he, whose figure might have served a
sculptor for an Antinous in its perfection of
form, wasting away before her, with a terrible
certainty that God's hand could alone stay the
event; and whom she had but lately seen in all
the full roundness of youth and health, with a
face animated by a very different expression from
that now shown by the hollow, wan, and hectic-like
mask which lay listlessly on the pillow—listlessly
save when his eyes met hers, and then they filled
or grew moist with tenderness and gratitude,
emotions that were not unmixed by a fear that
the pest, if such it was, that preyed on him might
fasten next on her. Then *who* should watch over
Rose, as she had watched over him, like a sister or
a mother?

His head, in consequence of the blow he had
received from the pistol-butt of the fallen Afghan—
the wretch he had sought to succour in the Khyber
Pass—was doubtless the seat of some secret injury;
for not unfrequently he placed his hand thereon and
sighed heavily, while a dimness would overspread
his sight, and there came over him a faintness from
which Rose, by the use of a fan and some cooling
essences—the Khanum had plenty of them—would
seek to revive him, and again his loving eyes would
look into hers.

"Ah, you know me again," she would say, in a low soft voice, and with a smile of affected cheerfulness; "you are to be spared to me, after all, Denzil—we shall live and die together."

".Nay—not die together, Rose: don't say die together, darling."

"Why?"

"That would be too early—for you, at least."

"You deem me less prepared than yourself, Denzil. Perhaps I am; yet what have I to live for now?"

"Do not talk so, Rose."

"God will take pity on us, Denzil, and will make you well and whole yet," she would reply, and kiss the aching head that rested on her kind and tender bosom; and with all the young girl's love, something of the emotion almost of maternal care and protection stole into her heart, as she watched him thus; he clung to her so, and was so gentle and so helpless.

"If—if—after this" (he did not say, "after I am gone," lest he should pain her even by words)—"if, Rose, after all this, you should ever meet my sister —my dear little Sybil—you will tell her of me—talk to her about me, talk of all I endured, and be a sister to her, for my sake—won't you, Rose?"

"I will, Denzil—I *shall*, please God."

"Oh yes—yes; one who has been so good to me,

could not fail to be good to her, and to love her for her own sake—for mine perhaps."

And then Denzil would look half vacantly, half wildly up to the ceiling, and marvel hopefully yet apprehensively in his heart where was now that homeless sister, so loved and petted at Porthellick, and whom we last saw crouching by the old cottage door near the stone avenue, on that morning when her mother died, and when the cold grey mist was rolling from the purple moorland along the green slopes of the Row Tor and Bron Welli.

Alas! her story Denzil knew not, and might never, never, know it.

But he was beginning now to know and to *feel* that "the God who was but a dim and awful abstraction before" seemed very close and nigh. No fear was in his heart, however: he was very calm and courageous, save when he thought of Rose's future, and how lonely and lost she should be when he was gone. This reflection alone brought tears from him; it wrung his heart, and made him the more keenly desire to live.

No Bible or Book of Common Prayer had Rose wherewith to console either the sufferer or herself; all such had gone at the plunder of the cantonments and the baggage, and had likely figured as cartridge paper at Jugdulluck and Tizeen; but no printed or hackneyed formulæ could equal in depth or earnestness the silent yet heartfelt prayers she put up for Denzil and herself.

"My poor Denzil—poor boy! I never deserved that you should love me so much : I have thought so a thousand times!" Rose would whisper fervently, and, heedless of any danger from fever, and perhaps courting it, place his brow caressingly in her neck, and kiss his temples, as if he were a child, telling him to "take courage, and have no fear."

"Fear! why should I fear death, Rose?" he would respond, speaking quickly, yet with difficulty— speaking thus perhaps to accustom himself to the topic, or to accustom her, we know not which; " why should I fear death, since I know not what it is? Why fear that which no human being can avert or avoid, and which so many better, braver, and nobler than I have so lately proved and tested in yonder Passes?—aye, Rose, my mother too, at home—my father on the sea—Sybil perhaps— all!"

Then his utterance became incoherent, his voice broken, and Rose felt as if her heart were broken too; for when he spoke thus, there spread over his young face a wondrous brightness, a great calm ; and the girl held her breath, in fear, if not awe, for she read there an expression of peace that denoted the end was near.

All was very still in the great square Afghan fort and in the Khan's garden without.

The summer sun shone brightly, and the birds, but chiefly the melodious pagoda-thrush—the king of the Indian feathered choristers—was there; and the flowers, the wondrous roses of Cabul, were exhaling their sweetest perfume. There the world, nature at least, looked gay and bright and beautiful; but here, a young life, that no human skill, prayer, or affection could detain, was ebbing away so surely as the sea ebbs from its shore, but not like the sea to return.

If Denzil died, what had she to live for? So thought the heedless belle, the half coquette, the whole flirt, of a few months past; but such were "the uses" or the results of adversity. Was not the end of all things nigh? Without Denzil Devereaux and his love, so tender, passionate, and true, what would the world be? and her world, of late, had been so small and sad! This love had been all in all to her; and now all seemed nearly over, and nothing could be left to her but forlorn exile and the gloom of despair.

As there is in memory "a species of mental long-sightedness, which, though blind to the object close beside you, can reach the blue mountains and the starry skies which lie full many a league away," so it was with Denzil; and now far from that bare and desolate vaulted room in the Afghan fort, from the mountains of black rock that overshadowed it, and all their harassing associations, even from the presence of the bright-haired and pale-faced girl who so lovingly watched and soothed his pillow, the mind of the young officer flashed back, as if touched by an electric wire, to his once-happy home. Again his manly father's smile approved of some task or feat of skill performed by bridle, gun, or rod; again his mother's dark eyes seemed to look softly into his; the willowed valley (that opened between steep and ruin-crowned cliffs towards the billowy Cornish sea), the little world of all his childhood's cares and joys, was with him now, and with that world he was mingling over again in fancy, though death and distress had been there as elsewhere; the hearth was desolate, or strangers sat around it; their household gods were scattered, and home was home no longer, save in the heart, the memory, of the dying exile.

And so, for a time, his thoughts were far away even from Rose and the present scene. Far from the images that were full of the warlike and perilous present, he was revelling in the past, and talked fluently, confidently, and smilingly with the absent, the lost, and the dead. Often he said—

"Lift my head, dearest mother; place your kind arm round my neck and kiss me once again."

And Rose obeyed him, and he seemed to smile upward into her face ; and yet he knew her not, or saw *another* there.

Then he talked deliriously of his father's rights, of his mother's wrongs, and of his cousin, Audley Trevelyan, till his voice sank into whispers and anon ceased.

This was what Shakspeare describes as the

"Vanity of sickness ! fierce extremes,
  In their continuance, will not feel themselves.
Death having preyed upon the outward parts,
Leaves them invisible ; and his siege is now
Against the mind, which he pricks and wounds
With many legions of strange fantasies,
Which, in their throng and press to that last hold,
Confound themselves."

He fell asleep ; and, without prolonging our description further, suffice it that poor Denzil never woke again, but passed peacefully away. . . .

Rose sat for a time in a stupor, like one in a dream. Summoned by her first wild cry, the Khanum was by her side now.

Denzil, so long her care, her soul, her all, lay there, it would seem, as usual—lay there as she had seen him for many days ; yet why was it that his presence, and that rigid angularity and stillness of outline, so appalled her now ?

As the crisis so evidently had drawn near, strongly and wildly in the girl's heart came the crave for medical, for religious, for any Christian aid or advice; but there none could be had, any more than if she had stood by the savage shores of the Albert Nyanza; and now the dread crisis was past!

So, from time to time the pale girl found herself gazing on the paler face of the dead—of him who had so loved her—gazing with that mingled emotion of incredulity, wonder, and terror, awe and sorrow, which passeth all experience or description.

There was no change in the air; there was no change in the light: one was still and calm, and laden with perfume; the other as bright and clear as ever: and the blaze of yellow sunshine poured into the room precisely as it did an hour ago; but now it fell on the face of the dead!

And the clear voice of the pagoda-thrush sang on; but how monotonously now!

Rose was stunned, and sat crouching on the floor, with her face covered by her hands, her head between her knees, and her bright dishevelled hair falling forward in silky volume well nigh to her feet. Ignorant of what to say, or how to soothe grief so passionate, the Khanum, unveiled, hung over her in kindness of heart, but with one prevailing idea—that the death of an idolater must be very terrible; that already the fiends must be contesting for the possession of his soul; that the prescribed portion of the Koran had not been read to him; and even if

it had been, what would it avail now, till that day
when the solid mountains and the soft white clouds
should be rolled away together by the blast of the
trumpet of Azrael?

So his last thoughts had been of his dead mother,
as Rose remembered, and not of *her*. Her father
was dead; Mabel was gone to Toorkistan, too surely
beyond ransom or redemption: oh, why was *she*
left to live?

If the *sense of exile* is so strong in the heart of
the Anglo-Indian, even amid all the luxuries and
splendours of Calcutta, the city of palaces—amid
the gaieties and frivolities of Chowringhee,—what
must that sense have been to the heart of this
lonely English girl, far away beyond Peshawur, the
gate of Western India, beyond the Indus, fifteen
hundred English miles, as the crow flies, "up-
country," from the mouth of the Hooghley and the
shore of Bengal—where the railway whistle will
long be unheard, and where Murray, Cook, and
Bradshaw may never yet be known!

Notwithstanding all that Rose had undergone of
late, and all that she had schooled herself to anticipate as but too probable, she was still unable fully
to realise the actual extent of the misfortunes that
threatened her. Much of that deep misery which
Sybil had endured elsewhere, when crouching in the
damp and mist outside her mother's door, came

over Rose's spirit now. Henceforward, she felt that life must be objectless; that safety or pursuit, freedom or captivity, sea or land, must be all alike to her; and for a time her poor brain, so long oppressed by successive sorrows and excitements, became almost unconscious of external impressions, and she sat as one in a dream, hearing only the buzz of the summer flies and the voice of the pagoda-thrush.

Suddenly another sound seemed to mingle with the notes of the birds; it came on the air from a great distance. She started and looked wildly up— her once-clear hazel eyes all bloodshot and tearless now.

What was it? what *is* it? for the sound was there, and she seemed to hear it still, and the Khanum heard it too!

Nearer it came, and nearer.

It was the sound of drums—drums beaten in regular marching cadence, coming on the wind of evening down from the rocky pass in the hills of Siah Sung.

Oh, there could be no mistake in the measure— British troops were coming on; and how welcome once would that sound have been to the young soldier who lay on his pallet there, and whose ear could hear the English drum no more!

She started to the window, and looked forth to the

black mountains, which, though distant from it,
towered high above the Kuzzilbashes' fort. The
dark Pass lay there, its shadows seeming blue rather
than any other tint, as the receding rays of the
setting sun left it behind; but her eyes were dim
with weeping and with watching now, so Rose,
with all her pulseless eagerness, failed to see the
serried bayonets, the shot-riven colours tossing in
the breeze, or the moving ranks in scarlet, that
showed where the victorious brigades of Pollock,
Sale, and Nott were once more defiling down into
the plain that led to humbled Cabul.

Welcome though their sound, they had come, alas,
too late!

The drums were still ringing in her ears; and this
familiar sound, like the voices of old friends, caused
her now to weep plentifully. Once again she turned
to the bed where Denzil lay so pale and still, his
sharpened features acutely defined in the last light
of the sun; and she felt in her heart as she pressed
her interlaced hands on her lips, seeking to crush
down emotion—

> "So the dream it is fled, and the day it is done,
> And my lips still murmur the name of one
> Who will never come back to me!"

CHAPTER XXI.

THE PURSUIT.

THE same evening of this event saw the Union Jack floating on the summit of the Bala Hissar, and our troops in or around Cabul, in the narrow and once-crowded thoroughfares of which—even in the spacious and once-brilliant bazaar—the most desolate silence prevailed. The houses of Sir Alexander Burnes, of Sir William Macnaghten, and all other British residents were now mere heaps of ashes, and their once-beautiful gardens were waste. Human bones lay in some; whose they were none knew, but they remained among the parterres of flowers as terrible mementos of the past.

Having, among many other trophies, the magnificent and ancient gates of Hindoo Somnath with them, the victorious troops of General Nott were encamped around the stately marble tomb of the Emperor Baber, where the British were watering their horses at the Holy Well, quietly cooking their rations of fat-tailed dhoombás or of beef, newly shot, flayed, and cut up, after a long route; and the natives were gravely boiling their rice and otta; while the staff officers, Generals Pollock, Sale, Nott, Macaskill, and others, some on foot and some on horseback, were in deep conference about a map of Western India, and Bokhara, and as to where the hostages were, and what was to be done for their relief, if they still lived.

Waller, who in his energy and anxiety had come on with the advanced guard of cavalry, looked around him with peculiar sadness. Save Doctor Brydone and one or two others, he alone seemed to survive of all the original Cabul force; and every feature of the place before him was full of melancholy memories and suggestions of those he could never see again, and of the past that could come no more.

To Sir Richmond Shakespere, his new friend, he could not resist the temptation of speaking affectionately and regretfully of the dead, and the places associated with them. He found a relief to his mind in doing so.

"A time may come," said he, as they sat in their saddles twisting up cigarettes, and passing a flask of Cabul wine between them, while the syces gave each of their unbitted nags a tobrah of fresh corn, "when these Passes of the Khyber Mountains may be as familiar to the English tourist as those of Glencoe and Killycrankie are now—for there was a day when even the land beyond *them* was a *terra incognita* to us; and a time may come when the lines of railway shall extend from Lahore even to Peshawar—ay, and further—perhaps to the gates of Herat—though it may not be our luck to see it; but I can scarcely realise that in our age of the world, an age usually so prosaic and deemed matter-of-fact, men should see and undergo all that *we* have undergone and seen, and in a space of time so short too!"

Would a quiet home, a peaceful life, after a happy marriage, ever be the lot of him and Mabel? Loving her fondly and tenderly, with all the strength that separation, dread, and doubt and sorrow, could add to the secret tie between them, he had almost ceased to have visions of her associated with admonitions and prayer from a lawn-sleeved ecclesiastic; a merry marriage-breakfast; a bride in her white bonnet and delicate laces, and smiling bridesmaids in tulle. Such day-dreams had been his at one time; but amid rapine and slaughter, battle and suffering, they had become dim and indistinct, if not forgotten!

"Yes, Waller," replied his companion, after a pause, "a British army—we have actually seen a British army, with all its accessories and appurtenances, exterminated at one fell swoop!"

"All this place is full of peculiarly sad memories to me, Sir Richmond."

"Doubtless; and, like me, you won't be sorry when we all turn our backs on it for ever, as we shall do soon."

"True. See! yonder lie our cantonments, ruined walls and blackened ashes now; beyond them are the hills where, with my company—not one man of which is now surviving, myself excepted—I scoured the fanatical Ghazees from rock to rock, and far over the Cabul river, so victoriously! Here, by that old tomb and ruined musjid, we once had a jolly picnic: half the fellows in the garrison, and all the ladies were there—the band of the poor 44th too. By Jove! I can still see the scattered fragments of broken bottles and chicken bones lying among the grass."

"I have felt something of this regret when coming on the remembered scene of an old pig-sticking party or bivouac," replied Sir Richmond, with a half-smile at the unwonted earnestness of Waller, who had seemed to him always a remarkably cool and self-possessed man of the world; but he knew not the deeper cause he had for feeling in these matters. "You may say, as an old poem has it—

'Now the long tubes no longer wisdom quaff,
Or jolly soldiers raise the jocund laugh;
The scene is changed, but scattered fragments tell
Where Bacchanalian joys were wont to dwell.'

Is it not so, Waller?"

"By this road I smoked a last cigar with Jack Polwhele, of ours, and Harry Burgoyne, of the 37th," resumed Waller. He remembered, but he did not care to add, how broadly they had bantered him about Mabel Trecarrel on the evening in question. "And all round here," he resumed, pursuing his own thoughts aloud, "are the scenes of many a pleasant ride and happy drive. Here I betted and lost a box of gloves with the Trecarrels."

"You seem to have always been betting on something with those ladies, and with a gentleman's privilege of losing."

"It was on the Envoy's blood mare against Jack Polwhele's bay filly, in the race when Daly, of the 4th Dragoons, won the sword given by Shah Sujah," said Waller, colouring a little. "There, by those cypresses, I once met the sisters half fainting, one day, with heat, their palanquin placed in the shade by the gasping dhooley-wallahs; so, at the risk of a brain fever, I galloped to the Char-chowk for a flask of Persian rose-water, fans, and so forth."

"The Trecarrels again! By the way, it seems to me," said the other, "that of all the friends you have lost, those two young ladies—one especi-ally——"

What the military secretary of General Pollock was about to say, with a somewhat meaning smile, we

know not, save that he was heightening the colour
of Waller's face by his pause; but a change was
given to the conversation by the opportune arrival
of Shireen Khan, of the Kuzzilbashes, mounted, as
usual, on his tall camel, and accompanied by a few
well-appointed horsemen. He had ascertained that
" Shakespere Sahib " was the *katib*, or secretary, to
the victorious Feringhee general, and had come to
tender, through him, his services to the family of
the fallen Shah, to the conquerors, to the Queen
they served, and, generally, to the powers that were
uppermost.

Many of the Afghan chiefs, who, with their
people, had acted most savagely against us,
were now extremely anxious to make their peace
with General Pollock; and though it can scarcely
be said that towards the end (after his own
jealousy of Ackbar's influence, fear of his growing
power that curbed all private ambition, caused
a coolness in the Sirdir's cause) Shireen and his
Kuzzilbashes had been our most bitter enemies,
yet he and they were among the first now to
meet and welcome the conquerors of Ackbar,
against whom they had turned, not as we have
seen Saleh Mohammed meanly do, in the time
of his undoubted humiliation and defeat, but when
in the zenith of his power; and now this wary old
fellow, who played the game of life as carefully and

coolly as ever he played that of chess, knew that the
protection he had afforded to Rose Trecarrel and to
Denzil—the supposed Nawab—must prove his best
moves on the board—his trump cards, in fact; and
as a conclusive offer of friendship, he now offered
six hundred chosen Kuzzilbash horsemen to follow
on the track of Saleh Mohammed, and rescue the
whole of the prisoners, a duty on which Shakespere
and Waller at once joyfully volunteered to accompany them.

" Shabash ! " he exclaimed, stroking his beard in
token of faith and promise, " puṅah-be-Kodah !—it
is as good as done; and the head of the Dooranee
dog shall replace that of the Envoy in the Char-
chowk ! "

Waller soon divined that the lady now residing in
Shireen's fort must be no other than the younger
daughter of " the Sirdir Trecarrel," who was spirited
away on the retreat through the Passes, on that
night when the Shah's 6th Regiment deserted; but
of *who* " the Nawab " could be he had not the
faintest idea, until he and Shakespere galloped
there, saw the living and the dead, and heard all
their sad story unravelled.

With her head, sick and aching, nestling on the
broad shoulder of Bob Waller, as if he was her
only and dearest brother, Rose told all her story
without reserve, and it moved Waller and his com-

panion deeply, to see a handsome and once-bright English girl so crushed and reduced by grief and long-suffering; yet her case was only one of many in the history of that disastrous war. She ended by imploring them to lose no time in following the track of those who had borne off her sister and the other hostages.

No words or entreaties of hers were necessary to urge either Waller or Shakespere on this exciting path; and instant action became all the more imperative when Shireen announced that he had sure tidings from Taj Mohammed Khan, and also from Nouradeen Lal, the farmer, who had been purchasing horses on the frontier, that all the lawless Hazarees were in arms to cut off the entire convoy; and that if a junction were once effected between them and the Toorkomans of Zoolficar Khan, all hope of rescue would be at an end.

The permission of the general was, of course, at once asked and accorded, and it was arranged, that, immediately upon their departure, a body of cavalry and light infantry should follow with all speed to second and support them.

Kind-hearted Bob Waller waited only to attend the obsequies of his young comrade (while the Kuzzilbashes were preparing); and over these we shall hasten, though of all the Cabul army he was, perhaps, the only one interred with the honours of war; the battle-smoke had been the pall, the wolf and the raven the sextons, of all the rest!

The spot chosen was a little way outside the Kuzzilbashes' fort, on the sunny and green grassy slope of a hill, where a grove of wild cherry-trees rendered the place pleasant to the eye. From her window Rose could alike see and hear the rapid ceremony; for by the stern pressure of circumstances it was both brief and rapid. No prayer was said; no service performed; no solemn dropping of dust upon dust; no requiem was there, but the drums as they beat the "Point of War," after the last notes of the Dead March had died away.

The quick, formal commands of the officer came distinctly to her overstrained ear, as the hurriedly constructed coffin of unblackened deal, covered by the colour of the 44th Regiment, was being lowered, as she knew, for ever, into its narrow bed; the steel ramrods rang in the distance like silver bells, and flashed in the sunshine; then a volley rang sharply in the air, finding a terrible echo in her heart, while the thin blue smoke eddied upward in the sunshine; another and another succeeded, and Rose—the widowed in spirit—as she crouched on her knees, knew *then* that all was over, and the smoke of the last farewell volley would be curling amid the damp mould that was now to cover her lost one.

Anon the drums beat merrily as the firing party, after closing their ranks, wheeled off by sections, with bayonets fixed, and Denzil Devereaux was left alone in his solitary and unmarked grave, just as the sun set in all his evening beauty ; and a double gloom sank over the soul of Rose Trecarrel.

CHAPTER XXII.

THE HOSTAGES.

SWIFTLY rode Shakespere, Waller, and their six hundred Kuzzilbashes on their errand of mercy, and midnight saw them far from the mountains that look down 'on Cabul. Of all his five thousand horse, old Shireen had certainly chosen the flower. All these men rode their own chargers, and all were armed with lance and sword, matchlock and pistols; all had their persons bristling with the usual number of daggers, knives, powder-flasks, and bullet-bags, in which the Afghan warrior delights to invest himself; and all wore the peculiar cap from which they take their name—a low squat busby, of black lambs'-wool, not unlike those now worn by our Hussars, and having, like them, a bag of scarlet cloth hanging from the crown thereof.

To avoid all suspicion or attention *en route*, Waller and Shakespere had cast their uniforms aside, and rode at their head *à la Kussilbashe*, dressed in poshteen and chogah, and armed with lance and sabre.

The discovery of Rose Trecarrel—an event so unexpected and unlooked for after all that had occurred—seemed to Waller as an omen of future good fortune, and his naturally buoyant spirits rose as he rode on. The expedition was full of excitement, especially for a time: it was an act of courage, mercy, and chivalry, that all Britain should eventually hear of; and Mabel was at the bourne, for which they were all bound. Even poor Denzil, so recently interred, was partially forgotten: soldiers cannot brood long over the casualties of war, especially while amid them; and Denzil's death was only one item in a strife that had now seen nearly fifty thousand perish on both sides.

However, let it not for a moment be thought that Waller was careless of his friend's untimely end, his memory, or his strange story; for, ere he left Rose, he had promised that as soon as he could write, or get "down country" again, one of his first acts should be to seek out and succour "this only sister" of whom poor Devereaux had always spoken so much and so affectionately.

When he parted from Rose, leaving her in the safe and more congenial protection afforded by the European camp, she had not been without one predominant fear. As friends had come too late to save or succour Denzil, they might now, perhaps, be too late to rescue Mabel and her companions from this new conjunction of enemies against them, even in Toorkistan. Besides, Ackbar the Terrible, with the ruins of his infuriated army, was to fall back on the deserts by the way of Bameean, and thus, to avoid him, the two British officers, with their Kuzzil-bashes, at one time made a judicious detour among the hills.

At Killi-Hadji, they found traces of the first halt made by the caravan outside the old fort, where a shepherd had, as he told them, seen the captives; thence by the mountain pass and the fair valley of Maidan, where a Hadji bound afoot for the shrine of Ahmed Shah at Candahar, the scene of many a pilgrimage, told them that the risk they ran was great, as the Hazarees were undoubtedly drawing to a head in the Balkh; and this was far from reas-suring, as they were conscious of having far out-ridden their promised supports.

"Let us push on, for God's sake!" was ever Waller's impatient exclamation at every halt, however brief; and even Sir Richmond Shakespere, with all his activity and energy, was at times amused by the restlessness of one who seemed by nature to be a rather quiet and easy-going Englishman.

"These are tough rations, certainly," said he, as they halted for the last time near the Kaloo Moun-tain, and masticated a piece of kid broiled on a ramrod at a hasty fire (broiled ere the flesh of the shot animal had time to cool), and washed it down by a draught from the nearest stream.

"Tough, certainly; but we get all that is good for us."

"If not more," added Shakespere, pithily; "for this is feeding like savages—or Toorkomans, who drink the blood of their horses."

"At a halt, when marching up country, I always used, if possible, like a knowing bachelor, to tiff with a married man."

"Why?"

"You will be sure to find that he has some daintily made sandwiches, cold fowl, or so forth, in his haversack: the women, God bless them, always look after these little things. But that is all over now; we are no longer in Hindostan. A little time must solve all this—the safety of our friends——" added Waller, looking thoughtfully to the distant landscape; and as if repenting of a momentary lightness of heart, "I would give all I have in the world——"

"Say all you owe," suggested Shakespere, smiling.

"Well, Sir Richmond, that *would* be a round sum perhaps—to see them all within musket shot of us. As for ransom, I have but my sword at their service. I can't do even a bill on a Hindoo schroff, or raise money on a whisker, as John de Castro did at Goa;

but I can polish off a few of those savages, as they deserve to be."

The dawn of a second day saw them descending the mighty ridges of the Indian Caucasus, and a picturesque body they were, with their bright parti-coloured garments floating backward on the wind; their black fur caps with scarlet bags, their dark, keen visages and sable beards, their polished weapons and tall tasselled lances flashing in the uprisen sun, as they galloped, without much order certainly, at an easy but swinging pace, over green waste and grey rocky plateau, up one hill-side and down another, now splashing merrily, and more than girth deep, through the clear, sparkling current of some brawling mountain nullah whose waters had been unbridged since Time was born—their horses light in body, with high withers, fine and muscular limbs, square foreheads, small ears, and brilliant eyes, and to all appearance full of speed, spirit, and a strength that seemed never to flag.

And sooth to say, the gallant Kuzzilbashes took every care to preserve those qualities so desirable alike for pursuit or flight.

At every brief halt, they were carefully unbitted, unsaddled, groomed, and lightly fed, and picketed in the old Indian fashion, with the V-ended heel-rope fastened round both hind fetlocks and secured to a single pin; near cuts over the hills were taken, but rivers were never forded or swum, unless the horses were perfectly cool; once or twice, pieces of goat's flesh were rolled round their bridle-bits; and hence by all this care, the cattle of the whole troop, unblown and ungalled, were in excellent order, when, on the fourth day—for their progress had been swifter than that of Saleh Mohammed, as they were unincumbered by women, children, camels, and ponies—they left the Kaloo Mountain behind, and ere long, without seeing aught of Hazarees or Toorkomans, though always prepared for them, they came in sight of Bameean, towering on its green mountain, its elaborate but silent temples and great solemn giants of stone reddened by the bright flood of light shed far across the plain by the sun, which was setting amid a sea of clouds that were all of crimson flame.

In deepest purple the shadows fell far eastward; the gleam of arms appeared on the walls of the old fort in the foreground, when Waller and Sir Richmond Shakespere darted forward, by a vigorous use of the spur, far outstripping their less enthusiastic followers. After they had carefully reconnoitred the fort through their field-glasses, Shakespere began to rein in his horse, and check its pace.

"Waller," said he, "a red flag has replaced Ackbar's invariable green one on the fort. We had better parley."

"But we have neither trumpet nor drum."

"Nor would those fellows understand the sound of either, if we had; but look out—pull up, or, by Heaven, we shall be fired upon! You are rash, Waller, and in action seem quite to lose your head."

"But my hand is ever steady—ay, as if this sword were but a cricket bat," retorted Waller, whose blue eyes were sparkling with light.

"True, my dear fellow; but to be potted now, when within arm's length of those we have risked so much to save, would be a sad mistake."

"Egad, yes ; and that old devil with his jingall—for a jingall it is—may speedily send one of us into that place so vaguely known as the next world," responded Waller, as he tied a white handkerchief to the point of his sword, and then Saleh Moham-med Khan was seen to unwind and wave the cloth of his turban in response.

By this action they knew that all idea of resist-ance was at an end, and that they should be received as friends. The gates of the fort were unbarricaded and thrown open, and many of the ladies now began to appear, timidly but curiously and expectantly, thronging forward to meet those whom they had been told were come "to meet and to save them."

Waller, who had manifested an air of blunt and

soldierly resolution and energy up to this period,
now felt his emotions somewhat overpowering, or
perhaps he wished to see and hear something of
Mabel, before making himself known; so checking
his horse, he permitted Sir Richmond Shakespere,
as his leader, to ride forward.

Lifting his Kuzzilbash cap, his frank English
face, though sunburned and lined, beaming with
pleasure and joy the while,

"Rejoice," he cried, enthusiastically, "rejoice,
ladies! Your delivery is accomplished. Dear ladies
and comrades, all your fears and your sufferings are
at an end!"

There was no loud or noisy response; the emotions of all were too deep and heartfelt for such utter-
ances; and, with feelings which no description can
convey to the imagination, Waller and Shakespere
found themselves surrounded by the captives, male
and female, exactly one hundred and six in number,
of all ranks—captives whom by their energy, activity, and rapid expedition they had saved from a
fate that might never have been known; for the
news of their arrival caused Hazarees and Toorkomans alike to disperse, and even Zoolficar Khan
abandoned all idea of attempting to carry them off.

The happiest moments of existence are perhaps
the most difficult to delineate on paper; but Bob
Waller, as he folded Mabel Trecarrel sobbing

hysterically to his breast, laughing and weeping at
the same moment, despite and heedless of all the
eyes that looked thereon—he a thorough-bred
Englishman, and as such innately abhorrent of " a
scene"—forgot the crowd, the Kuzzilbashes, the
Dooranees, the grinning grooms and dhooley-
wallahs—he forgot all in the joy of the moment, or
by a chain of thought remembered only a passage of
" Othello," when, in garrison theatricals, he had
once figured as the Moor, with Harry Burgoyne for
a Desdemona—

> " If it were now to die,
> 'Twere now to be most happy ; for I fear
> My soul hath her content so absolute
> That not another comfort like to this
> Succeeds in unknown fate."

And Sir Richmond Shakespere, as he stood smiling
by the centre and blissful-looking group (now beginning clamorously to pour questions upon him), ladies
and officers, hollow-eyed, haggard, and pale, began
to perceive what had made Captain Robert Waller,
of the Cornish Light Infantry, take so deep an interest in the Trecarrels, and why he had been the
most active, energetic, and, so far as danger went,
the most reckless staff officer during our perilous
advance up the Passes and in the subsequent
pursuit.

Waller did not find Mabel quite so much changed

as he had feared she might be; yet she was the
wreck of what she had been in happier times—the
tall, full-bosomed, and statuesque-looking English
girl, with clear, calm, bright, and confident eyes.
The latter were still bright, but their lustre was
unnatural; their expression was a wild and hunted
one; her colour was gone, and her cheeks were
deathly pale. But all in the group of hostages were
alike in those respects. For many months, had they
not been daily, sometimes hourly, face to face with
death?

But Waller, as she hung on his breast and looked
with eyes upturned upon him, had never seemed
so handsome in her sight: his form and face were
to her as the beau-ideal of Saxon manliness and
beauty; but his complexion, once nearly as fair
as her own, was burned red now, by the exposure
consequent to the two last campaigns; his forehead
clear and open, his nose straight, his mouth large
perhaps, but well-shaped and laughing; and then he
had in greater luxuriance than ever his long, fair,
fly-away whiskers; and, save his Afghan dress, he
looked every inch the jolly, frank, and burly Bob
Waller of other times, especially when, as if he
thought "the scene" had lasted long enough, he
drew Mabel's arm through his, led her a little way
apart, and proceeded leisurely to prepare a cigar for
smoking.

"So Bob, dear, dear Bob, my presentiment has come true after all," she exclaimed; "and this horrid Bameean has seen the end of all our sorrows!"

"But it was *not* such an end as *this* your foreboding heart had anticipated, Mabel," replied Waller, caressing her hand in his, and pressing it against his heart.

Major Pottinger, who had now the command, ordered that all must prepare at once to quit Bameean, and avoid further risks by falling back on their supports, lest Ackbar Khan might come on them after all.

To lessen the chance of that, however, the wily Saleh Mohammed, who knew by sure intelligence from his scouts that Ackbar was to proceed, with the relics of his army, through the Akrobat Pass into the Balkh, advised that all should take a circuitous route towards Cabul; and this suggestion was at once adopted by the now-happy hostages and the escort.

Two days afterwards, as they were traversing the summit of a little mountain pass, their long and winding train of horse and foot guarded by Kuzzil-bash Lancers and the wilder-looking Dooranees, they came suddenly in sight of those whom General Pollock had sent to meet and, if necessary, to succour them.

These were Her Majesty's 3rd Light Dragoons, the 1st Bengal Cavalry, and Captain Backhouse's train of mountain guns, all led by Sir Robert Sale in person; and who might describe the joy of that meeting, when the rescued hostages cast their eager eyes and hands towards them in joy, and when they saw the old familiar uniforms covering all the green slope, while the cavalry came galloping and the infantry rushing tumultuously towards them!

The dragoons sprang from their horses, the infantry broke their ranks, and the men of the 13th Light Infantry crowded round the wife of their colonel and the other rescued ladies, holding out their hard brown hands in welcome; eyes were glistening, lips quivering, and many a hurrah was, for a time, half choked by emotion and sympathy, while officers and soldiers again and again shook hands like brothers that had been long parted.

Friends now met friends from whom they had been so long and painfully separated; wives threw themselves exultingly and passionately into the arms of their husbands; daughters leaned upon their fathers' breasts and wept. Many there were whose widowed hearts had none to meet them there; and many an orphan child stretched forth its little hands to the ranks wherein its father marched no more, though some might give a kiss or a caress to " Tom Brown's little 'un—Tom that was killed at Ghuznee," or to the

" little lass of Corporal Smith—poor Jack that was killed with his missus at Khoord Cabul ; " but these sad episodes were soon forgotten amid the general joy.

Wheeled round on the mountain slope, the artillery thundered forth a royal salute ; muskets and swords were brandished in the sunshine ; caps tossed up, to be caught and tossed up again ; reiterated English cheers woke the echoes of the hills of Jubeaiz, which seemed to repeat the sounds of joy to the winds again and again.

CHAPTER XXIII.

THE DURBAR.

" COINCIDENCE," saith Ouida, "is a god that greatly influences human affairs;" and the sequel to our story will prove the truth of this trite aphorism, when we now change the scene from Cabul to our cantonment, in the territory between the Sutledge and the Jumna—to the Court Sanatorium of Bengal —the country mansion of the Governor-General at Simla, a beautiful little town of some five hundred houses, built on the slope of the mighty Himalayas, where, amid a veritable forest of oak, evergreens, and rhododendron, and the loveliest flora a temperate zone can produce, surrounded by that wondrous assemblage of snow-covered peaks that rise in every imaginable shape (a portion of those bulwarks of the world, that slope from the left bank of the Indus away to the steppes of Tartary and the marshes of Siberia), the representative of the Queen retires periodically to refresh exhausted nature, and mature the plans of government in those cool and pleasant recesses, where the punkah is no longer requisite;

where one may sleep without dread of mosquitos and green bugs, nor welcome cold tea at noon as preferable to iced champagne.

By the time that Audley Trevelyan had reached this occasional seat of government—the Balmoral of India—Lord Auckland, whose vacillation and mismanagement of the Cabul campaign gave great umbrage, had returned to Britain, and another Governor-General had arrived—one who boldly stigmatised the Afghan project of his predecessor (now created an earl) " as a folly, and that it yet remained to be seen whether it might not prove a crime ; and so Audley presented, of necessity, the reports and Jelalabad despatches of Sir Robert Sale to this new Viceroy, whose firmness of character and past promise as a statesman gave a guerdon that we should yet retrieve all that we had lost of prestige beyond the Indus; to which end he took the executive power from the weak hands of those secretaries to whom it had been previously committed, and resolved to wield it himself, though he found in India a treasury well-nigh empty, an army exasperated, and the hearts of men depressed by fears for the future.

But tidings of the storming of Ghuznee by General Nott, of the advance upon Cabul, the recapture of it after our victory at Tizeen, and the rescue of the hostages, followed so quickly upon each other to Simla, that soon after the arrival of Audley, he was informed that as there would be no necessity for his return to Jelalabad, he was to remain provisionally attached to the staff, either till he could rejoin his regiment, or our troops re-entered the Punjaub—a little slice of India, having a population equal to all that of England. So by this arrangement he found himself a mere idler, a dangler attached to the Viceregal court, where now the glorious war that Napier was to inaugurate against the treacherous Ameers of Scinde was schemed out, and where a series of reviews, dinners, balls, and a durbar, or assembly of the native princes, was proposed to welcome Pollock's troops when they came down country, and were once again, as the Viceroy expressed it, in " our native territories ; " and the programme of all those gayeties was to be fully arranged when his lady and other ladies of the mimic court arrived, after the rainy season, which continues there from June till the middle of September, was nearly over.

On the first day of October, when her ladyship and the suite were to arrive, the durbar of native princes was to be held, and the final proclamation of the Governor-General concerning the affairs of Afghanistan was to be read aloud and issued. As this was but an instance of Anglo-Indian pageantry, though Audley Trevelyan rode amid the brilliant staff of his Excellency, and it all led to something of more interest, we shall only notice it briefly.

The durbar was, indeed, a magnificent spectacle! On a great plateau of brilliant green, smooth as English turf, that lies near the ridge which is crowned by the white plastered mansions of Simla, dotted here and there and finally bordered by dark clumps of heavily foliaged oaks, towering rhododendrons, and over all by mighty, spire-like Himalayan pines; it took place under a clear and lovely sky, and the locality was indeed picturesque and impressive; for in the distance, as a background, towered that wonderful sea of snow-clad peaks, covered with eternal whiteness—peaks between which lie the deep paths and passes that lead to Chinese Tartary, the wilderness of Lop, and the deserts of Gobi. Here and there amid the green clumps and gardens full of rare trees and lovely flowers, a white marble dome, or a tall and needle-like minaret, each stone thereof a miracle of carving, broke the line of the clear blue cloudless sky.

On this auspicious occasion all the Rajahs, Maharajahs, chiefs, Maliks, Sirdirs, and other men of rank, from the protected Sikh territory that lies between the Sutledge and the Jumna, and even from beyond it, were present with their trains of followers, in all the gorgeous richness of oriental costume, bright with plumage, silks, and satins, brilliant with arms and the jewels of a land where sapphires and diamonds, rubies and opals, seem to be plentiful as pebbles are by the wayside in Europe.

At the extreme end of the plateau stood the lofty, parti-coloured tent of the Viceroy, with its cords of silk and cotton; within it was placed a dais that was spread with cloth of gold, and covered by a crimson canopy. On each side of his throne, ranged in the form of an ellipse, were divans or seats for six hundred Indians of the highest rank, while all the officers of the garrison, the guards, and the staff, in their full uniform, with all their medals and orders, added to the splendour of the spectacle, when chief after chief was introduced, duly presented, and marshalled to his seat in succession, amid the sound of many trumpets.

Opposite this ellipse were ranged their followers, on foot or horseback; and immediately in the centre of all, were drawn up in line more than fifty elephants, stolid, and well-nigh motionless, trapped in velvet and gold from the saddle to their huge, un-wieldy feet, bearing lofty and gilded howdahs, some like castles of silver, wherein were the wives and families of some of the princes present. All around glittered spears and arms; scores of dancing-girls were there too, richly dressed, singing the soft monotonous airs of the land in Persic or Hindoo-Persic; and a mighty throng of copper-coloured natives, turbaned and scantily clad in a cummerbund or the dhottie at most, made up minor accessories of the general picture.

Over all this, Audley, on foot and leaning on his sword, was looking, glass in eye, with somewhat of the listlessness of the *blasé* Englishman; for he had been amid scenes so stirring of late, that mere pageantry failed alike to impress or interest him. Neither cared he, assuredly, for the address of the Governor-General, who was announcing in the Oordoo language that, the disasters in Afghanistan having been fully avenged, the army of the Queen would be withdrawn for ever to the eastern bank of the Sutledge; then his glances began to wander over the bright group of English ladies, so brilliantly dressed, so exquisitely fair, to the eye accustomed so long to Indian dusk, and who now attended the recently arrived wife of the representative of British royalty.

Among them was one whose face and figure woke a strong interest in his heart. Her dress was very plain, even to simplicity—too much so for such a place; her ornaments were very few, all of jet, and rather meagre. All this his practised eye could take in at a glance; but there was something about her that fascinated and riveted his attention.

Not much over nineteen, apparently, and rather petite in stature, she looked consequently younger—

more girlish than her years; but her figure was
graceful, her air indescribably high-bred, and having
in it a hauteur that, being quite unconscious, was becoming. Her eyes were dark, her lashes long and
black, her complexion colourless and pure, and her
thick hair was in waves and masses, dressed Audley
scarcely knew in what fashion, but in a somewhat
negligent mode that was sorely bewitching.

Her face was always half turned away from where
he stood; for she, utterly oblivious of the Oordoo
harangue of his Excellency, was toying with her fan
or the white silk tassels of her gloves, while chatting
gaily, confidently, and with a downcast smile to
a young officer of the Anglo-Indian Staff, and clad
in the gorgeous uniform of the Bengal Irregular
Cavalry.

That she was a beautiful girl, a little proud, perhaps, of the *sang-azure* in her veins, was pretty evident; that she might be impulsive, too, and quick to
ire, was also evident, from the little impatient glances
she gave about her, by a quivering of the white eye-
lid, and an occasional short respiration; that she
might be a little passionate too, if thwarted, was suggested by the curve of her lips and chin. For the
critical eye of Master Audley Trevelyan saw all this;
but his spirit was seriously perplexed: he had certainly seen this attractive little fair one before—but
where?

He was about to turn and ask some one near concerning her, when a hand was laid on his shoulder,
and a young officer, whose new scarlet coat, untar-
nished epaulettes, and fair ruddy face announced
him fresh from Europe, said smilingly,

"Ah, Trevelyan, how d'ye do?—remember me,
don't you?"

"I think so: surely we met at Maidstone, when I
first joined."

"Maidstone! why, you griff, I should think so.
Don't you remember leaving us at Allahabad, after
Jack Delamere died?"

"By Jove, Stapylton—Stapylton, of the 14th!
How are you, old fellow?"

"The same;" and they shook hands, as he now
recognised a brother subaltern of his old Hussar
corps.

"And you are here on the staff?" said
Stapylton.

"Like yourself; but *pro tem.* till sent off to
head-quarters. You came up country with her ladyship?"

"Ah—yes."

"Who is that lovely girl near her?"

"Which?"

"She in the white silk, and lace trimmed with
black—a kind of second mourning I take it
to be."

"Oh, you needn't ask with any interested views. A proud, reserved minx is that little party; but she has been going the pace with that fellow of the Irregular Horse, to whom she is talking and smiling now, and did so all the way out overland. It was an awful case of spoon in the Red Sea, just where Pharaoh was swallowed up; and the Viceroy's wife is very anxious to make a match of it, as a plea for an extra ball."

"But who is she?"

"Oh, some interesting orphan."

"But her name?"

"A Miss Devereaux—Sybil Devereaux. I made an acrostic on it off the Point de Galle," added the ex-Hussar, as the object of their mutual interest turned at that moment casually towards them, and for the first time looked fully in their direction; and then Audley, while he almost held his breath, recognised the dark eyes, the minute little face, the firm lips, and even now could hear the once-familiar voice of Sybil; but she was talking smilingly to another; and as the words of the heedless Stapylton began to rankle in his heart, something of anger, jealousy, and pique mingled with his astonishment.

Another was now playing with Sybil the very part that he had done at Cabul with Rose, to the exasperation of poor Denzil, whom, for months before

he really died, Sybil had schooled herself to number
as among the slain in Afghanistàn; hence her little
jet ornaments and black trimmings, the only tribute
she could pay his memory now.

CHAPTER XXIV.

THE LAMP OF LOVE.

AND this fellow of the Irregular Horse—this fellow who was so insufferably good-looking, and seemed to know it too—this interloper, for so Audley Trevelyan chose to consider him—what manner of advances had he already made, and how had she received them, on that overland route, so perilous from the propinquity and the hourly chances it affords of acquaintance ripening into friendship, and of friendship into love?

Was he only to meet her unexpectedly, and, by that strange influence of coincidence already referred to, to find himself supplemented, it might be, and on the verge of losing, if he had not already—deservedly as he felt—lost her?

Did it never occur to the Honourable Mr. Audley Trevelyan that, separating as they did, there were a thousand chances to one against their ever meeting again in this world, and, more than all, the world of India?

He watched long and anxiously; there was no

sign of her seeing or recognising him, and, placed where they were, apart, he had neither excuse nor opportunity for drawing nearer her. The durbar closed at last; a banquet, solemn and magnificent, followed; then, on lumbering elephants and beautiful horses, the various dignitaries withdrew, each followed by his noisy and half-nude *suwarri*. A small but select evening party of Europeans was invited that night to the house of the Viceroy; thither went Audley; and there, as he had quite anticipated, they met, not in the suite of rooms, however, but in the magnificent gardens, where there was a display of those wonderful rockets, stars, wooden shells that burst in mid air, displaying a thousand prismatic hues, and many others of those pyrotechnic efforts, in which the Indians so peculiarly excel.

In a walk of the garden, while actually seeking for her, he met Sybil face to face, but leaning on the arm of the same brilliantly dressed officer; for no uniform is more gorgeous or lavish than that of the Irregular Horse, for fancy, vanity, and the army-tailor "run riot" together. He was carrying his cap under his other arm, and seemed entirely satisfied with himself and his companion, in whose pretty ear he was whispering, while smiling, with all the provoking air of a privileged man.

"Ah, Miss Devereaux—you surely remember

me?" said Audley, bowing low, with a flush on his brow, and, despite all his efforts, an unmistakable sickly smile in his face.

Sybil grew a trifle paler, as she presented her hand, with a far from startled expression; for she had been quite aware that he was somewhere about the Viceregal Court, and therefore, to her, the meeting was not quite so unexpected.

"You do not seem surprised?" said he.

"Why should I, Mr. Trevelyan, when I knew that you were here?" she replied with perfect candour; "but I am so—so delighted—indeed I am, Audley;" then perceiving that there was an undoubted awkwardness in all this, she coloured, while her eyes sparkled with vexation, and she introduced the two gentlemen rather nervously by name, and then added, in an explanatory tone, to the cavalry officer, "He is quite an old friend, believe me—the same who saved my life. Surely I told you?"

"I am not aware—oh yes—perhaps," drawled the other: "at Cairo, was it not?"

"No, no—in Cornwall."

"But it was in Cairo you told me, when we visited the citadel by moonlight——"

"And we are, as I said, such old friends," she added hastily.

"That, doubtless, you will have much to say to

each other. Permit me; for I am perhaps *de trop*,"
interrupted the other, twirling a moustache, and
looking somewhat cloudy; "but I shall hope to see
you ere the trumpets announce supper;" and with
a smiling bow he resigned Sybil to Audley's
proffered arm, and retired with a good grace to join
another group.

"Sybil," said Audley, after a half-minute's pause,
during which he had been surveying her with fond
and loving eyes, "by what singular incidence of the
stars are we blessed by meeting thus?"

"You may well ask, if such you feel it to be," she
replied calmly, and her voice made his heart vibrate
as she spoke; "yet it is simple and prosaic
enough. I am here solely by the influence of
misfortune."

"Misfortune?"

"Yes."

"Oh, explain."

"When poor mamma died, what was left for me
but to eat the bread of dependence?—and I am a
dependent now."

"Sybil!"

"I came to India as that which you find me."

"And that is——"

"The humble friend—the companion, for it is
nothing more in plain English—of the Governor-
General's lady. Mamma gone—Denzil, too, in

Afghanistan—was I not fortunate in finding such a home ?"

"My poor Sybil," exclaimed Audley, gnawing his moustache and pressing her soft hand and arm against his side. Then he became silent, as the past and present, for a little, held his soul in thrall; and far from the brilliant fête of the Anglo-Indian Court his mind flashed back to other days, and he saw again only Sybil Devereaux and the purple moorland, the solemn rock-pillar, the lonely tarn, with its osier isles, the long-legged heron and the blue kingfisher amid its green reedy sedges, and in the soft sunlight the grey granite carns cast their shadows on the lee, as when he had seen her on that day when first they met; and much of shame for himself and for his father mingled with the memory and his emotion.

But there was a change here !

The poor, pale girl, who had so anxiously and wearily sought to sell her pencilled sketches and water-coloured drawings in the shops of the little market town, who so often with an aching heart took them back, through the mist and the rain and the wind, to the humble cottage where her mother lay dying, was now in a very different sphere, richly though modestly dressed, easy in air and bearing, perfectly self-possessed, surrounded by wealth and rank, yet with all the secret pride of her little heart, meek, gentle, and happy in aspect.

She, too, was silent for a time, during which she glanced at him covertly and timidly.

"Here again was Audley," was the thought of her heart; "did he love her still? Had he truly loved her, even *then?*" was the next thought, and her heart half answered, "Yes—he had loved her, but only as the wordly love;" and this fear, this half-conviction, dashed her present joy. Yet no woman wishes to believe, or cares to admit even to herself, that the power she once exerted over a man's heart can, under any circumstances, pass altogether away.

"Sybil," said he, "you, any more than I, cannot have forgotten all our past, and the scenes where we met—the wild shore, the precipices, the grey granite rocks of our own Cornwall; and that awful hour in the Pixies' Cave, too—can you have forgotten that?"

"Far from it, Audley,—I have forgotten *nothing*; and now I must remember the difference of rank that places us so far—so very far apart," she added with a strange flash in her eye and a quiver in her short upper lip.

"Come this way, dear Sybil. I have much to say—to talk with you about—but we must be alone;" and he led her down a less frequented

walk, apart from the company, the strains of the
military music, the coloured lights and lanterns
that hung in garlands and festoons from tree to
tree, and the soaring fireworks that ever and anon
filled the soft dewy air with the splendour of many-
hued brilliance.

"Will this not seem marked?" asked Sybil
nervously and almost haughtily.

"How?"

"I must beware of attracting notice now—here
especially; and you are no longer the mere Audley
Trevelyan of other times."

"Then, dearest, who the deuce am I?" asked he,
laughing.

Sybil had seen the Hindoo maidens—slender,
graceful, and dark-eyed girls—launching their love-
lamps from the ghauts upon the sacred waters of
the Ganges—watching them with thrills of alternate
joy and fear, as they floated away under the glorious
silver radiance of the Indian moon. She had heard
their wails of sorrow if the flame flickered out and
died; or their merry shouts and songs of glee
if they floated steadily and burned truly and
bravely. Audley's affection had been to her as
a light in her path that had vanished; but now
her love-lamp seemed to be lit again; for Audley,
with admirable tact, conversed with her as if on
their old and former footing, expressing only what

he felt—the purest and deepest joy at thus suddenly meeting her again, and he had too much good taste to make the slightest reference to the gossip of his friend Stapylton, the ex-Hussar, though certainly he had neither forgotten it, nor the unpleasantly off-hand mode in which it had been communicated to him.

"But how strange—to come to India, my dear girl, of all places in the world! What led you to think of it?" he asked.

"Have I not already told you? I did not think of it: chance threw the offer in my way; and I had two sufficient reasons, at least, for accepting of it."

"And these—bless them, say I!—these were——"

"That my brother, dear Denzil, was here—here then, at least."

"And I—too?"

"I do not say so—least of all must I say so *now;* and then Lady——'s offers were most advantageous to a penniless girl like me. You and, more than all, your father, deemed me no suitable match for you, when we were in England—when I was an inmate of my parent's house at Porthellick. You see, I speak quite plainly, Audley, and as one who is quite alone in the world; now, when by death and—and misfortune, I am reduced to eat the bread of dependence, the matter is worse than ever."

"But you love me still, Sybil—do you not?"

She was silent and trembling now.

"Speak," he urged; "you do love me still?"

"Yes, Audley."

"And will marry me, Sybil?"

"No."

"You love another then—another in secret?"

"No—one may not, cannot, love two."

But Audley thought of Stapylton and that devilish Irregular Horseman, and struck the heel of his glazed boot viciously into the gravel of the path.

CHAPTER XXV.

CONCLUSION.

AFTER a pause he resumed—

"There is something in your tone, Sybil, that I do not understand. Doubtless your heart has much to accuse me of; but I have been the victim of circumstances, of my father's odd whimsical views—his selfishness, in fact; but here I can cast all such at defiance," he added, gathering courage as he perceived that she still wore on her hand—and what a pretty plump little hand it was!—his diamond betrothal ring—the diamond that whilom had figured as an eye of Vishnu, till Sergeant Treherne poked it out with his bayonet at Agra. "Listen, dearest Sybil; we are far away from England with all its insular and provincial prejudices—away from those local influences which my family exercised over me—my father's hostility, my mother's sneers, and so forth. I am secure of staff appointments—better these than casual loot or batta, I can tell you. I am independent of home allowances; and, to talk solidly and plainly, can think now in earnest of matrimony. Listen to me, Sybil;" and glancing hastily about, he tried to slip an arm round her, but she nimbly eluded him, and said—

"Then you have not heard the news we brought up country with us?"

"News!"

"Yes—my poor Audley."

"About what?"

"Your change of circumstances."

"Mine!—dearest Sybil, what can you mean?"

"Your succession to the title."

"Circumstances—title!—explain, in Heaven's name, Sybil."

She then told him that his father had died suddenly—died, as the *Morning Post* announced, in the same library at Rhoscadzhel, and somewhat in the same manner, as his late uncle, when he was in the act of composing a long and elaborate paper legally reviewing the merits of the Afghan war; another grave had been opened and closed in the family tomb; another escutcheon hung on the porte-cochère of the princely old manor-house; and that he, Audley Trevelyan, was now Lord Lamorna, as the Governor-General would doubtless announce to him on the morrow.

And in his lonely tomb beside the Kuzzilbash fort lay one who could never dispute the family honours with him, and whose sorrows and repinings were past for evermore.

Audley was overwhelmed for a few minutes by this unexpected intelligence. There had been no great love, no strong tie, no fine yet unseen ligament, between father and son; yet the dead man *was* his father, and he knew had ever been proud of him. He was shocked, but not deeply grieved; and "some natural tears he shed:" no more.

His father, however, prudential and unscrupulous in his children's interests, had always been cold, prosaic, undemonstrative, and unloveable to them and to all. Hence he passed away, having so little individuality that the blank made by his absence left no craving, and required no filling up; but, nevertheless, for a time, his cold, pale eyes and equally cold, glittering spectacle-glasses came vividly back to his son's memory.

Audley was, however, to say the least of it, so much disconcerted by the news Sybil had given him, that he lacked sufficient energy to retain her when she was swept from his side by the officer of the Irregulars, on a theatrical flourish of the vice-regal trumpets announcing that the supper-rooms were open.

The course of balls and other entertainments that followed the durbar and the news from Cabul were attended by neither Sybil nor Audley, now recognised and congratulated by all the European society at Simla as Lord Lamorna, and by the Viceroy, who offered him all the leave he might require to settle his affairs at home. Sybil had her brother's recent death to plead; and she looked forward with intense interest to seeing Waller, and to the returning army, though Denzil was no longer in its ranks.

They heard at Simla, how General Pollock had dismounted or destroyed every cannon in the Balla Hissar and in the city, and given to the flames the Mosque of the Feringhees, an edifice built by the vanity of Ackbar to consecrate and commemorate the sanguinary destruction of Elphinstone's army; the great bazaar also, once the emporium of the Eastern world; and how all the castles and forts of the khans and chiefs had likewise been given to the flames; how the sky was reddened for days and nights, and that the fiery gleam of the burning city was still visible on the close of the fourth day, when our rear guard was defiling through the mountains of Bhootkak on their homeward route to the Sutledge. Thus was the massacre of Khoord Cabul finally avenged; but, as Sybil thought in her heart, " would it restore the dead ? "

Their graves, unmarked and unconsecrated, and the ruined city alone remained to tell of the strife that had been. A touching address, signed by all the ladies whom his energy and activity had done so much to rescue, was delivered to Sir Richmond Shakespere; and with Taj Mohammed Khan, the discarded Wuzeer of Cabul, a beggared fugitive and exile, as the sole friend who accompanied them, our troops came down on their homeward way, laden with spoil, and among it the great gates of Somnath, an object of adoration to the Hindoos; and thus ended the fatal war in Afghanistan.

Audley had been duly informed by letters, that his brother-officer, Waller, and the Trecarrels were also coming down country, and should ere long be at Ferozpore or Simla; and Sybil, who had now heard all the story of Rose and Denzil, longed, with a longing that no words can describe, to see her.

There is no emotion in this world more delightful, and nothing perhaps more beautiful, than a young girl's first dream of love; for a young man's first affair of the heart is even different in some respects. It is so full of innocence, of simplicity and truth, if the girl is pure and ingenuous; it is so full, also, of a new-born mystery, a charm, and a world of thought, of chance and risk, where there may be triumph or defeat, victory or failure, sorrow perhaps, and joy perhaps—but still she hopes, above all, a delight and happiness hitherto unknown. Hence it becomes absorbing; and such had been Sybil's love for Audley at home when she had the shelter of her mother's breast, and such for a time it had been after they were to all appearance so hopelessly separated; and now, after a lull, or being for a space, as it were, suppressed and crushed well-nigh out, by change, by distance, time, and travel,—now the love-lamp shone again.

And Audley, ere he had heard of his succession to that title which should have been Denzil's, had fated Denzil lived, had made her an abrupt but formal proposal of his hand. Would he renew it now?

She was not left long in doubt; for under the cognizance and with the express approbation of the wife of the Viceroy, who deemed herself in the place of mother and protectress to Sybil, he renewed his offer, and then the lady judiciously left the cousins —for such he had told her they were—to settle the matter between them.

"Ah, Audley," said Sybil, "too well do you know how I am situated; what or whom have I to cling to in this world—but you, perhaps?" she added, with a low voice, while her breast heaved, and her half-averted face was full of passionate tenderness. "Now that my poor Denzil is gone, nor kith, nor kin, nor inheritance — what can I offer you in return?"

"Yourself, darling; what more do I ask in this world?" he said, in a low and earnest voice, as he gradually drew her nearer him; and as her hand went caressingly on his neck, it seemed to him a dearer collar than either the Bath or Garter could be, for " what is all the glory of the world compared with the joy of thus meeting—thus having those we love ? "

" Now, Sybil," said he, " you find how difficult it is to forget that one has loved——"

" And been beloved," murmured the girl.

" More than all by such a pure-souled heart as yours. You remember our first meeting by the tarn ? "

" Could I ever forget it ? "

" And our learned disquisition on flirtation, too. How odd it seems now, darling."

" And dear old Rajah—you have not our rough, shaggy *introducteur* with you," said Sybil, smiling.

" Poor dog, no. I left him at home in Rhos-cadzhel, and, somehow, he is dead ; that is all I know about it—so Gartha told me in a letter."

" All who love me die—even the poor dog. Surely they would be kind to your pet, for your sake."

" They—well, I don't know—doubtless."

Audley cared not to say that, by his lady-mother's orders, the dog had been destroyed as a nuisance—the last legacy of his comrade, poor Delamere, who died in the jungle.

"Ah, if my dear Denzil had lived to see this day!" said the happy girl, after a pause that was full of thought.

"Sybil, God knows how for your sake, even at the time when I never, never, hoped to see you more, I sought to protect and love your brother; but he repelled, avoided, and seemed to loathe me. Yet he saved my life in the [Khyber Pass. It was through sorrow for his mother—and—and, perhaps, love for Rose Trecarrel; for he would be jealous of me, among other things, poor lad!"

"And she—she?"

"Rose was very heedless, Sybil; but, after all Bob Waller has written, let us not talk of the past now. You will learn to love her well, I know."

"I hope so: I must—I shall, for Denzil's sake."

"My sweet little love!—my Sybil, so tender and so true!" exclaimed Audley, pressing her with ardour to his breast.

But a short time ago, Sybil had been hoping that she would forget him; hoping, while journeying towards the land where he was—the land of the Sun—she who long since should have been his wife. She had striven for forgetfulness, hopelessly, yet with something of earnestness in the desire; and now that she had heard his voice again, the old spell was upon her—the spell of past hours, of remembered days—the spell of her lover's presence; and to be with him, the girl acknowledged in her heart, was to be in heaven again!

But now, we fear that we have intruded upon them quite long enough.

And so, till the time came when they should be joined by Waller and the Trecarrels (for companionship, it had been arranged that they should all take the journey by dawk and river-steamer, and then the overland route home together), the days passed pleasantly and swiftly at delightful Simla, in rides and drives among its wonderful scenery; where the netted bramble, the great strawberry, and giant fern covered all the rocks; the soft peach, the dark plum, the rosy apple, and the golden pear grew wild; and the dark-green pines, vast in proportion as the stupendous Himalayas, from whence they sprang, cast a solemn shadow over all, making deep and leafy recesses where the monkey swung by his tail, the buffalo browsed at noon, the leopard and the wild hog lurked for their food; by mountain villages that clustered near the fortified dwelling of the chieftain whose tower was built like the cone of an English glass house; by hill and vale, rock and stream, where flocks were grazing, watched by shepherds, quaint and savage-looking as their rural god, the son of

Mercury, and by Thibet mastiffs, that reminded Sybil of her lover's four-footed friend, the Rajah of past days; and ever and anon, as they drove, or rode, or rambled, they talked, as lovers will do, of their future home in Cornwall, with all its associations so dear to them, and now so far away, and so they would marvel

> " What feet trod paths that now no more
>   Their feet together tread ?
> How in the twilight looked the shore ?
>   Was still the sea outspread
> Beneath the sky, a silent plain,
> Of silver lamps that wax and wane ?
> What ships went sailing by the strand
> Of that fair consecrated land ?"

Waller arrived at Simla to find himself gazetted in the *Bengal Hurkaru* as major, and to get, like Audley, his glittering Order of the Dooranee Empire from the hands of the Viceroy; therefore he hung it round the white neck of Mabel, while Rose fell heiress to that which should, had he survived, have been her father's decoration.

So the schemes, the plotting with the wretched solicitor, Sharkley, and all the avarice of Downie Trevelyan availed him nothing in one sense; for now the daughter of that Constance Devereaux he had so cruelly wronged was coming home to Rhoscadzhel as the bride of his son, and in her own hereditary place as the Lady of Lamorna.

It is but. justice to his memory, however, to record, that having some premonition or presentiment that death was near, or might come on him as it came on his older kinsman, something of the spirit of the Christian and the gentleman got the better of the more cold-blooded and sordid training of the lawyer ; and Downie wrote out, sealed up, and left a confession concerning the two papers he had obtained and destroyed ; and this document was found tied up with his will, in the library of Rhoscadzhel, by Messrs. Gorbelly and Culverhole, his astounded solicitors. Not that any act of roguery surprised them, but only the folly of any man ever committing the admission thereof to ink and paper.

Audley and Sybil were but one couple out of several especially among the rescuers and the rescued, who were seized with matrimonial fancies to make Simla gay, after the retreat from Cabul—the result of propinquity, perhaps, and the system of chances. We may briefly state that they were married by the chaplain of the Governor-General, who gave the bride away ; and not long after, Waller gave Mabel's marriage-ring a guard, wherein was set a jewel, the envy of all the ladies there—the sapphire which he had plucked from the steel cap of Amen Oolah Khan at the Battle of Tizeen.

At Simla Rose was thus twice a bridesmaid, and a lovely one she looked.

But was Rose ever married in the end? some may ask; for such a girl could not be without offers, especially in India. We have only to add, that the once-gay and heedless Rose Trecarrel is unwedded still.

On many a grey carn and lofty and rugged head-land in Cornwall were fires, lighted by the miners and peasantry but chiefly about Rhoscadzhel—bea-cons so bright in honour of the new lord and lady, that they shone far over land and sea, and in such numbers that the Guebres and fire-worshippers of old, could they have seen them, might have deemed that the adoration of the Fire-god was again in its glory, as when the Scilly Isles were consecrated to the sun; and Derrick Braddon, who, on the strength of recent changes, had installed himself as a species of deputy-governor or major-domo at Rhoscadzhel, had a deep carouse, in which he was fully assisted by Messrs. Jasper Funnel, old Boxer, and others of the plush-breeched and aiguilletted fraternity.

Meanwhile, those whose fortunes we have followed throughout the campaign of Western India and the retreat from Cabul were speeding homeward, and when from the coast of Orissa they saw the steamer awaiting them in the rough and dangerous roadstead of Balasore, where usually the Calcutta pilots leave the home-bound ships, they hailed the bright blue world of waters as an old friend; for, to our island-born, "the sea, the sea," is what it was to the returning Greeks of old Xenophon!

"Now, Mabel," said Waller, as with a lorgnette in her pretty hand, she surveyed the roadstead— the plain gold hoop on that hand being in Bob Waller's eyes the most charming trinket there, "a few weeks more, and all these foreign seas and shores will be left far behind; we shall be home at our little place that looks from Cornwall on the apple-bowers of Devon. Ha! Trevelyan, you and I shall then each sit down under his own vine and fig-tree in peace, and enjoy a quiet weed, like the patriarch of old—if the said patriarch ever possessed one. What say you, my Lady Lamorna?" he added, as he assisted Sybil's light figure to spring from the hand-some and well-hung carriage in which they had travelled from Calcutta.

Sybil only smiled, and looked joyously at the sea, as she threw up the white lace veil of her bridal bonnet; and Audley, too, was gazing on the sea.

"Waller, we have undergone much," said he— "days of danger, and nights of anguish, yet we have survived them all, and been true to the end, and in the past have fully realised the force of the maxim that—

'Come what come may,
Time and the Hour runs through the roughest day.'"

THE END.

BRADBURY, EVANS, AND CO., PRINTERS, WHITEFRIARS.

ANTHONY TROLLOPE'S WORKS

NEW AND CHEAPER EDITION.

Price 2s. each, Picture Boards; 2s. 6d. Cloth.

LOTTA SCHMIDT.	MARY GRESLEY.
DOCTOR THORNE.	RACHEL RAY.
THE MACDERMOTS.	TALES OF ALL COUNTRIES
CASTLE RICHMOND.	MISS MACKENZIE.
THE KELLYS.	THE BERTRAMS.
BELTON ESTATE.	WEST INDIES.

Price 4s. Cloth (Double Vols.), price 3s. Picture Boards.

ORLEY FARM.	CAN YOU FORGIVE HER?
PHINEAS FINN.	HE KNEW HE WAS RIGHT.

"In one respect Mr. Trollope deserves praise that even Dickens and Thackeray do not deserve. Many of his stories are more true throughout to that unity of design, that harmony of tone and colour, which are essential to works of art. In one of his Irish stories, 'The Kellys and the O'Kellys,' the whole is steeped in Irish atmosphere ; the key-note is admirably kept throughout ; there is nothing irrelevant, nothing that takes the reader out of the charmed circle of the involved and slowly unwound bead-roll of incidents. We say nothing as to the other merits of the story—its truth to life, the excellence of the dialogue, the naturalness of the characters—for Mr. Trollope has these merits nearly always at his command. He has a true artist's idea of tone, of colour, of harmony ; his pictures are one ; are seldom out of drawing ; he never strains after effect ; is fidelity itself in expressing English life ; is never guilty of caricature. . . . . We remember the many hours that have passed smoothly by, as, with feet on the fender, we have followed heroine after heroine of his from the dawn of her love to its happy or disastrous close, and one is astounded at one's own ingratitude in writing a word against a succession of tales that 'give delight and hurt not.'"—*Fortnightly Review.*

Lightning Source UK Ltd.
Milton Keynes UK
UKHW011353050119
334855UK00007B/983/P